"You're going to tell him the truth today and now—here at the park—or I will," Jonah said in a voice of steel.

"I don't want to be cheated of knowing my son one more day."

She nodded. "All right, Jonah. I guess you have that right."

"Damn straight I do. What have you told him about me—about us?" Jonah asked. "Did you tell him we're divorced?"

"Yes. I told him that the army was important to you, and you were gone most of the time, so we decided it would be best to part. I told him you wanted out of the marriage."

"Kate, that's a damned lie," Jonah said, standing again and pacing away from her, fury making him shake once more. He whipped around. "You're the one who walked."

Dear Reader,

Welcome to another month of excitingly romantic reading from Silhouette Intimate Moments. Ruth Langan starts things off with a bang in *Vendetta,* the third of her four DEVIL'S COVE titles. Blair Colby came back to town looking for a quiet summer. Instead he found danger, mystery—and love.

Fans of Sara Orwig's STALLION PASS miniseries will be glad to see it continued in *Bring On The Night,* part of STALLION PASS: TEXAS KNIGHTS, also a fixture in Silhouette Desire. Mix one tough agent, the ex-wife he's never forgotten and the son he never knew existed, and you have a recipe for high emotion. Whether you experienced our FAMILY SECRETS continuity or are new to it now, you won't want to miss our six FAMILY SECRETS: THE NEXT GENERATION titles, starting with Jenna Mills' *A Cry In The Dark.* Ana Leigh's *Face of Deception* is the first of her BISHOP'S HEROES stories, and your heart will beat faster with every step of Mike Bishop's mission to rescue Ann Hamilton and her adopted son from danger. Are you a fan of the paranormal? Don't miss *One Eye Open,* popular author Karen Whiddon's first book for the line, which features a shape-shifting heroine and a hero who's all man. Finally, go *To The Limit* with new author Virginia Kelly, who really knows how to write heart-pounding romantic adventure.

And come back next month, for more of the best and most exciting romance reading around, right here in Silhouette Intimate Moments.

Yours,

Leslie J. Wainger
Executive Editor

Please address questions and book requests to:
Silhouette Reader Service
U.S.: 3010 Walden Ave., P.O. Box 1325, Buffalo, NY 14269
Canadian: P.O. Box 609, Fort Erie, Ont. L2A 5X3

Bring on
the Night
SARA ORWIG

Silhouette®

INTIMATE MOMENTS™
Published by Silhouette Books
America's Publisher of Contemporary Romance

SILHOUETTE BOOKS

ISBN 0-373-27368-1

BRING ON THE NIGHT

This edition published by arrangement with Harlequin Books S.A.

® and TM are trademarks of Harlequin Books S.A., used under license.
Trademarks indicated with ® are registered in the United States Patent
and Trademark Office, the Canadian Trade Marks Office and in other
countries.

Visit Silhouette Books at www.eHarlequin.com

Printed in U.S.A.

Books by Sara Orwig

Silhouette Intimate Moments

Hide in Plain Sight #679
Galahad in Blue Jeans #971
*One Tough Cowboy #1192
†*Bring on the Night* #1298

Silhouette Desire

Falcon's Lair #938
The Bride's Choice #1019
A Baby for Mommy #1060
Babes in Arms #1094
Her Torrid Temporary Marriage #1125
The Consummate Cowboy #1164
The Cowboy's Seductive Proposal #1192
World's Most Eligible Texan #1346
Cowboy's Secret Child #1368
The Playboy Meets His Match #1438
Cowboy's Special Woman #1449
*Do You Take This Enemy? #1476
*The Rancher, the Baby & the Nanny #1486
Entangled with a Texan #1547
†*Shut Up and Kiss Me* #1581

*Stallion Pass
†Stallion Pass: Texas Knights

SARA ORWIG

lives in Oklahoma. She has a patient husband who will
take her on research trips anywhere from big cities to old
forts. She is an avid collector of Western history books.
With a master's degree in English, Sara has written his-
torical romance, mainstream fiction and contemporary
romance. Books are beloved treasures that take Sara
to magical worlds, and she loves both reading and writ-
ing them.

Prologue

"Revenge is better than money," the man said quietly. Raking his blond hair away from his face, he stood in the hallway of San Antonio's busy airport and glanced again at the listing that showed Flight 10 from Amarillo, Texas, was on time.

Through the windows the man could see bright sunshine outside, no bad weather to interfere with incoming flights. Inside the lobby people hurried to and fro, pilots strode past on their way to departure gates, lines grew longer at the security checks.

The man waited patiently, his gaze searching the crowd. He wanted to make certain that the flight had arrived and the special passenger was on it. His blue eyes scanned each dark-haired man, pausing briefly on first one and then another. Then his gaze was arrested.

A tall, black-haired man in a charcoal knit sport shirt and jeans crossed the airport lobby and headed toward a rental car desk, where he set his flight bag on the floor and spoke to a smiling attendant.

The man watched him smile even as his fingers curled and his fists knotted. ''You're hurrying to get your inheritance, aren't you, Colonel Whitewolf? You think you're so tough, with your Special Forces training. None of it will do you any good. You'll see. You'll go down. You'll be first, then the others. It's already started. While you get your car, I'll go out to the ranch and have it ready for you. A real *warm* welcome.'' He laughed softly.

He walked outside and hurried to a black, two-door sports car he had stolen only an hour earlier. The tags had been changed and he knew no one would bother him.

He started the engine and pulled out of the parking space, glancing in the rearview mirror at the terminal, thinking about Colonel Jonah Whitewolf, who was probably still inside at the rental desk.

''When I get through with you, you'll regret you ever accepted your inheritance. You're trained to deal with an enemy you can see. Now you'll have to deal with an enemy you won't see. Welcome to Texas, Colonel. Welcome to hell.''

Chapter 1

A bullet could change a man's life in the blink of an eye, Jonah Whitewolf knew, but he'd never expected to have his life transformed while sitting quietly in an office.

As he stood at the car rental desk in San Antonio the memory of that moment in April still haunted him.

He recalled how he had listened in stunned disbelief as the lawyer quietly read from John Frates's will, listing the inheritance: "To Jonah Whitewolf, to whom I am profoundly indebted, I bequeath the Long Bar Ranch, which is the Frateses' working cattle ranch. This ranch, the livestock, the house, the land, the mineral and water rights and everything included in the ranch, shall go to Jonah Whitewolf to do with as he deems proper. In addition to the Long Bar Ranch, one and a third million dollars is hereby bequeathed to Jonah Whitewolf to do with as he sees fit.''

In shock, Jonah had stared at the lawyer. Her announcement was a moment cast in his memory forever. He could still remember how his surroundings had become unforgettable—the beautiful blond lawyer's oak desk, her gold pen and pencil set, her slender hands holding papers as she read, the tall clock quietly ticking, the faint scent of roses in a crystal vase on a polished wooden table. Every sight, sound and smell had been etched in memory in that instant when his world changed entirely....

While the attorney had continued reading, Jonah had glanced at Michael Remington and Boone Devlin, two of his closest buddies from past days in Special Forces. Five years ago, the three of them, along with another Special Forces friend, Colin Garrick, deceased, had rescued John Frates when he had been held hostage in Colombia. Because of that rescue the three survivors of the mission were now inheriting fortunes. Mike Remington looked as shocked as Jonah felt, but then Mike's inheritance had been an incredible surprise: John Frates's town house in Stallion Pass, Texas, a million and a third dollars—and John's baby daughter.

Boone had seemed equally shocked by his bequest of a nationally famous quarter horse ranch. Jonah had been faintly relieved that he hadn't received a baby, although he had been plenty shocked to be willed a cattle ranch plus the money. He recalled thinking how ironic at this point in his life to inherit such a thing. Had the inheritance come six or seven years ago, he would have been able to save his marriage.

Unbidden, memories of his ex-wife, Kate, had crept into his thoughts. He had loved her then, and her loss still hurt today. Kate's image floated into his consciousness: silky chestnut hair, enormous hazel eyes, thick dark lashes. An ache in his chest brought him back to reality, and he forced the memories away.

His job in Special Forces had caused the divorce. If he had had a ranch and a fortune, how different life might have been! He closed his mind to that course of thinking. What-ifs could ruin your life.

A cattle ranch and over a million dollars... His family

would be ecstatic for him. Jonah thought about his present job—working around the world, putting out oil well fires. A ranch would give him an opportunity to settle in one place. On the other hand, he would be more isolated than ever.

The amount of money was staggering. He was well paid in his job, but this was wealth beyond anything he had ever dreamed of.

The minute the lawyer, Savannah Clay, finished reading the will, she looked at them with her big blue eyes. "You each will receive a copy of the document. Do any of you have questions?"

Silence was heavy in the room and the attorney had arched her brows. "No questions?"

"I'm not sure I believe this is happening," Jonah stated quietly.

"It's already happened," Savannah replied in a well-modulated, no-nonsense voice. "John Frates felt strongly about what he wanted to do with his fortune."

Again the silence was broken only by the ticking of the tall clock in her office. Once more she asked, "None of you has a question?"

"Yes," Jonah said. "If I choose not to keep the ranch, can I sell it?"

"There are papers to sign, but yes, once this inheritance is legally yours, you are free to do with it as you choose."

Jonah nodded. "If we sell, we get the money, plus the million and a third that each of us inherited?"

"That's correct," she replied firmly. "That's only a portion of the Frates fortune. For the rest of their lives, his in-laws, Dina Frates's parents who are in rehab, will be provided for. There is a foundation, trusts, other bequests to charities. But the three of you got his personal things and part of the Frateses' estate. He intended Colin Garrick to have a share as well, but upon Colin's demise, he changed the will and that money was divided, which is why each of you got a million and a third. He rounded up the total to make it equal.''

''How soon do we have to see about all this?'' Jonah asked. ''I'm supposed to leave for Russia next Sunday.''

''There's no hurry. The ranch has an excellent foreman and manager. John Frates was just there part of the time and had nothing to do with running the place.''

''So we're free to sell these inheritances?'' Boone repeated.

''Yes,'' Savannah Clay answered. While she talked to him, Jonah looked at Mike, who was silent and white as snow. His friend kept raking his fingers through his wavy black hair, an uncustomary gesture.

Jonah had seen Mike shot and he had seen Mike in critical, life-threatening situations. Remington was a cool, quick thinker, able to move and act swiftly, tough as well as brave, but at the reading of the will he had seemed on the verge of fainting.

''Are you all right?'' Jonah whispered as the others talked.

Mike swiveled his head and gave Jonah a glassy-eyed stare. ''Yes,'' he murmured, but Jonah wasn't convinced. Mike was not his usual take-charge self. Yet Jonah knew that inheriting a baby would be a shock far greater than inheriting ranches, as he and Boone had.

''Any questions, Colonel Remington?'' the attorney asked.

''Yes, but I'll wait until the others are through so I don't take up their time,'' Mike replied.

Even though they protested, Mike did wait, and finally Jonah and Boone signed papers, got their copies of the will and left the lawyer's office.

''What a day this has been,'' Boone remarked as they stepped into the sunshine. ''When I flew in here, I thought the three of us would have a reunion and that would be it.''

''Yeah. Life takes strange turns,'' Jonah replied. ''Nobody knows that any better than the three of us do. I wish Colin were here to claim his inheritance.'' Both men were silent until they reached black cars parked side by side. Then they stopped and faced each other. Boone had his hands on his hips, his tan sport coat pushed open. ''See you back at the hotel. I'm going to swim, and then let's have happy hour and celebrate our inheritance,'' he said with a grin.

''Sounds fine with me. I'm still in shock,'' Jonah replied as he shed his navy suit coat and pulled off his navy tie.

''I think all three of us are in shock, but Mike's been hit the hardest. And I don't blame him. Thank goodness he's the one with the baby,'' Boone said, unlocking his car door and tossing his sport coat on the seat.

''Yeah, I guess.'' Jonah felt an aching twist deep inside.

''Man, you're still hung up about your ex? Get over her,'' Boone said, turning back to frown at Jonah. ''You can marry again and have a passel of kids.''

''Boone, have you ever been in love, even once? I mean really in love?'' Jonah asked, mildly annoyed by his friend's remarks.

''Hell, no, not like you were. And I'm not going to be, either. No marriage chains for me. Lighten up.'' With a flash of white teeth, Boone Devlin grinned. ''The world has lots of beautiful, exciting women. You need to get out and about and forget her.''

''Sure,'' Jonah answered dismissively, remembering what a playboy Boone was.

''And don't bury yourself on a ranch, although there's small danger of that. You'll sell your inheritance as fast as I intend to sell mine.''

''Maybe not. I'm going to think about it and look the place over.''

''What do you know about cattle ranching?''

''I told you that my grandfather had a ranch, and I spent

every summer there when I was growing up," Jonah replied.

"You move to a ranch and you'll be a hermit," Boon warned, jiggling his car keys in his hand.

"As if I socialize a lot out in the oil field."

Boone laughed and opened the door of his car. "See you at the hotel." Each climbed into his rental car and drove out of the lot.

Jonah shoved those April memories aside and smiled at the clerk behind the rental counter. Moments later, he strode out of the San Antonio airport into bright sunshine on a cool, early June morning. After quitting his job and selling the home he owned in Midland, Texas, he was back in San Antonio to look at his inheritance for the second time.

He wanted to work the ranch, and from the time he'd made his decision, his eagerness to make the move had grown.

In the space of time between his first trip to San Antonio and this one, another shock had transpired. Savannah Clay, the lawyer who had read John Frates's will to them, had married Mike Remington—a marriage of convenience to give Frates's baby girl a mother and father. Jonah was surprised, and wondered how happy Mike was with the arrangement.

As Jonah neared the gates to the ranch, however, he forgot about Mike Remington. Green fields spread endlessly to the horizon. Stands of oaks gave shade to the hills, which were bright with patches of wildflowers. All land he owned... Then Jonah spotted two spirals of gray smoke rising against the deep blue sky, and he wondered what was burning.

As he drove along, watching the plumes of smoke darken and expand, Jonah had a gut feeling that something was wrong. The ranch hands could be burning off a field, but he didn't think so.

Clamping his teeth together, he pressed the accelerator, speeding along until he reached the turn to the ranch house, then bouncing over the cattle guard. The ominous black smoke increased and he gunned the engine, skidding on gravel along the drive.

In the distance he heard sirens that only confirmed his suspicions. Another few seconds of driving and he saw bright orange tongues of flame spiraling in the sky. He caught up with a pickup truck speeding ahead of him.

Then, at another turn, the ranch house, barn and out-buildings came into view. Trees burned in two areas while flames shot up one wall of the barn, Jonah saw, but the roof hadn't yet caught and men were pouring water on the blaze. Men fought the three blazes.

Other men carried equipment out of the barn. The wail of sirens grew louder as Jonah ran to help save the barn.

He approached the gang pouring water on the barn fire. Jonah took a hose from one of the men to relieve him, and directed ranch hands where to turn other hoses. He yelled for someone to get a ladder, and in seconds he'd braced the ladder against the barn wall. He climbed to the roof, tugging the heavy hose up with him and then motioning to a man on the ground to turn the water on again.

Flames danced in front of Jonah's face, but he knew if they could keep the roof from going up they could contain the fire.

Two pumper trucks had arrived and started to spray big streams of water on the blaze. They could easily reach the roof, so Jonah tossed down his hose and climbed back down the ladder.

When he reached the ground, he took the hose and ran around to the entranceway, planning to go into the burning barn.

"Mr. Whitewolf! Don't go in there!" Scott Adamson, the barrel-chested foreman, yelled at him.

Jonah shook his head and charged into the barn, where he spotted flames in a far corner. Dragging the hose, he ran forward and turned the hose on the conflagration.

A cowboy arrived to help him, and Jonah motioned to the loft. "I'm going up," he yelled above the roar of the fire.

"That blaze could consume the loft in minutes," the man warned, but Jonah was already climbing. "Pass the hose to me," he called.

The man climbed behind Jonah, then handed him the nozzle. Jonah tugged on the hose and turned it on the flames.

Sweat poured off him and he could hear men yelling outside, but within minutes the blaze inside seemed under control.

When he climbed down from the loft, there were four other men in the barn, fighting the dying fire. He looked at the charred structure and knew the corner would have to be rebuilt, but the flames would be doused in minutes and the barn had been saved. The other fires had been brought under control.

He handed the hose to one of the cowboys. "I want to look around in here," he said, skirting smoldering embers. "Keep the water flowing, because this could all burst back into flame."

It took him only five minutes to find where he thought the fire had started. He straightened up and strode outside, past firemen who kept hoses trained on the charred and blackened wood. Cowboys had turned off the spigots to the ranch's well water, no longer needed now.

Scott Adamson walked up to Jonah and shook his hand. "Thanks for your help, but you shouldn't have put yourself at risk by going into the building."

"It was safe enough," Jonah said, brushing aside his

foreman's concern. "I need to talk to one of the officials about the fire. It was deliberately set."

"Aw, hell!"

"You don't sound surprised or shocked," Jonah said, his eyes narrowing.

Adamson took his hat off to wipe sweat from his brow and rake his red hair back from his face. "We've had bad things happen lately. Some sick cattle—someone put poison in a water tank—some smashed fences. I thought it was kids doing pranks that got out of hand, but now I don't know. This happened in broad daylight. Plus it was three separate fires. Someone set them. Fortunately, one of the men spotted the fires when they had just started and we had men close at hand to fight the flames."

"It doesn't look like the work of kids."

"C'mon. I'll introduce you to Tank Grayson. He's the man you need to talk to. He knows fires, but then I guess you do, too."

Jonah spent the next thirty minutes with the thin, blond fireman, who went inside the barn with him and confirmed Jonah's suspicions.

"We'll have an official analysis, but you're right. This was started with kerosene and rags. So was the one in the trees. Anyone opposed to you moving here?"

"Not that I know of," Jonah answered, perplexed. "Scott Adamson said that other things have been happening around here—poison in a stock tank. That kind of thing."

The fireman shook his head. "This could have been a hell of a lot worse. We'll let you know what we find out."

Jonah shook hands with him and went outside to thank all the others for their help. As he shook his foreman's hand and thanked him, Scott nodded.

"Anytime there's a fire, everyone pitches in. We're fortunate to have a good supply of well water, and Mr. Frates put in a fine system of water mains and spigots. Otherwise this barn would have been gone.''

''Well, I'm grateful for everyone's help. We can rebuild that corner and it'll be like new again. I'll see if I can't arrange a bonus for everyone with the next paycheck.''

''That would make a lot of guys happy, although they didn't do this for a bonus.''

''I know that, but they took some risks fighting that fire.''

''Not like the ones you took.'' Scott eyed Jonah. ''I guess you're going to live up to your reputation.''

''How so?''

The older man shrugged as he looked at the barn. ''All that Special Forces stuff… Damn, I don't know why anyone would do this.''

''I don't, either. Well, I'm going to go get cleaned up.''

He glanced down the road at houses of people who worked on the ranch. If the fire had gotten out of control it could have spread to the bunkhouse, office and other outbuildings. They had been lucky. Jonah headed to the sprawling ranch house. Entering through the back door, he walked quietly through spacious rooms where sunlight spilled across polished hardwood floors and over classic furniture. Even though he was moving his things in tomorrow, it was still difficult to realize this was all his.

The house was rustic, yet with state-of-the-art appliances and conveniences, and a collector's elegance to its antique furniture. Jonah didn't know much about antiques, but Kate had been into collecting and had taught him a little about styles she liked.

He was spending tonight at the ranch, but he wanted to return to town and buy a pair of boots. He also planned to get pictures developed from a disposable camera he'd picked up on the way, to send to his folks.

When Jonah drove back to San Antonio, he was certain he had made the right choice about his future. He had had the past two months to think about it, and he wanted to keep the Long Bar Ranch, welcomed the changes it would bring to his life.

After purchasing boots, he put the package in the car and stood on the sidewalk in the hot sunshine. Tomorrow morning, before he left for Midland, he was to have breakfast with Mike and Savannah. Right now it was two o'clock in the afternoon, and he wanted to develop the pictures he had taken of the ranch so he could show them to his family back home. He smiled to himself. The ranch seemed to be in excellent shape, with enough land and stock to make it one of Texas's largest and most successful cattle ranches.

As soon as he had made his decision, he'd felt restless, impatient to get moved in. Would he be buried out on the ranch and become a hermit, as Boone Devlin had predicted? At the moment Jonah didn't care. The Long Bar would give him a stable life, a purpose, and the work would be something he liked to do—a lot more interesting than struggling with a burning oil well.

Climbing into the rental car, he drove into the parking lot of a drugstore and went inside. After leaving his film to be developed, he roamed the aisles, picking up a magazine to read at the ranch tonight, getting a couple of candy bars and another disposable camera. Then he headed back to the front of the store with his purchases.

Walking up the aisle, Jonah could see the cash register where customers paid on their way out. There was a short line, and he glanced at the people waiting there. Suddenly he froze in shock.

A tall woman stood there. Her back was turned to him, but he knew her at once. Her thick mane of unruly chestnut hair was as unmistakable as her long legs and tiny waist. It was his ex-wife, Kate Valentini Whitewolf.

For a moment, time seemed to fall away, as he remembered hours he'd spent lying in bed with her, holding her in his arms. Kate, warm and soft, laughing up at him, and then the laughter changing as her eyes darkened with passion and she wrapped her slender arms around his neck, pulling him down to kiss him…

Jonah groaned and ran his hand across his eyes, bringing himself back to the present with a jolt. Kate was there— only yards away. She wore a denim skirt, a red cotton blouse, with sandals on her feet and bracelets on her arm.

His first impulse was to grab her elbow and turn her to face him. ''Kate,'' he whispered, aching all over. How he had loved her! Then he remembered the pain of her leaving him, and he knew he should look away, let her walk out of the store. Speaking to her wouldn't do anything except stir up old hurts.

Why was she in San Antonio? Jonah wondered. It had been five years since he had last seen her.

Other memories flashed in his head. They had met when he'd been stationed at Fort Bragg, North Carolina, and she had lived in Fayetteville. It had been a hot July afternoon when she had swerved to avoid hitting a squirrel, and instead had run into his car.

Since they were in a residential area, neither of them had been going fast, and it had been a mere fender bender. But Jonah recalled her embarrassment and his amusement. The moment he had stepped out of his car and looked at her, his pulse had started galloping.

She had been wearing cutoffs, with her hair in a ponytail, and his first thought was that she was a kid. But then she'd gotten out of the car, revealing her long legs and tiny waist, her lush breasts, and he always wondered later if he had fallen in love right there during that first glance. While they exchanged insurance information, he'd made a date to take her out to dinner that night.

He had met her family and learned she was an only child and had few relatives, but the few she had all lived in Fayetteville. She'd had a successful job in advertising. Three months later, they were married.

It took only seconds for those memories to flash in Jonah's mind as he stared at her. Then he noticed movement at her side. A small child was tugging on her hand, and she looked down and spoke to him.

Pain sliced into Jonah as if someone had stabbed him.

He had known that Kate would remarry. She was too beautiful, too appealing, too sexy to stay single for long. But the child was proof of her union, and it hurt to face the reality. The boy looked about four or five years old. He had straight black hair and skin darker than Kate's, as if he had already been out in the sun a lot this spring.

Their divorce had taken place five years ago. She hadn't wasted any time in finding someone else, Jonah thought bitterly.

As if drawn by a will stronger than his own, Jonah's attention returned to Kate's face. While he moved toward her, he argued with himself whether or not to say hello, mentally telling himself to walk on past, stay out of her way and keep her out of his. She was a married woman now, with her own life, just as Jonah had his. Why open old wounds?

A few more steps and he was beside her, and she turned and looked into his face.

The impact of gazing into her thickly lashed hazel eyes was another blow to his middle, one that stole his breath and made his pulse jump erratically. Those seductive green-gold eyes could change hue with passion, vary with different colors of clothing, sparkle with humor and melt with love. Big eyes, a wide mouth, prominent cheekbones... She was always more vivid and striking than anyone around her. Today gold-and-red earrings dangled from her ears, giving her a gypsy look that went with her wild cascade of hair.

"Hello, Kate," he said quietly. It hurt, remembering the terrible pain of breaking up the marriage.

As she looked at him, her eyes widened, her jaw dropped and all color drained from her face.

He frowned and reached out to steady her, because she looked as if she might faint. She caught the counter edge and held it in a white-knuckled grip. He was amazed at her reaction. Could she be *that* unhappy to see him, in a chance encounter in a public place?

"Kate?"

"Hello, Jonah," she whispered, and he could see her make an effort to pull herself together. She blinked, licked her lips and stared at him. If he had drawn a gun on her, he didn't think she could have looked more terrified.

"Are you all right?" he asked, feeling upset by her reaction.

"Yes," she answered. "I'm surprised to see you." She was mumbling, barely loud enough to be heard. "We—we need to go," she stammered.

When she started to turn away, Jonah knew she would walk out of his life again, which was what she wanted. And he had to let her go because long ago their lives had separated.

"Mommy," the little boy said, tugging on her arm.

Jonah had forgotten the child, but looked down at him now. When their gazes met, Jonah felt as if he had smashed into a brick wall. His breath left his lungs and his pulse roared in his ears. The shock he had experienced inheriting a ranch and fortune was nothing compared to what he felt now.

He blinked and stared, looking into brown eyes as dark as an inky night. The hint of prominent cheekbones to come, the childish nose that already had a slightly hawkish shape…this was a face Jonah knew well, from his own childhood pictures.

There was a stunned silence while Jonah's brain registered what he was seeing. He stared dumbly, his mind piecing together the truth.

Then his knees weakened, and he started to shake as he stared in disbelief, knowing he was looking at his own son.

Chapter 2

When Jonah looked at Kate, he saw the truth in her eyes and realized why she had been so stunned to see him. Throughout those years, he'd had a son, and she had kept that fact from him.

The truth and all its implications, plus his first reaction of riveting shock, began to transform his emotions.

A slow, burning fury started in the pit of his stomach and spread until he had to clench his fists and struggle to contain his rage. Never in his life had he yelled at a woman or touched one in any manner to cause hurt, but he wanted to shout at Kate now and he wanted to shake her. Instead, not trusting himself to speak, he held his temper and inhaled deeply.

Someone jostled him, and he realized they were partially blocking the aisle. He caught Kate's arm, careful to not grip her tightly, knowing he had to keep a check on the anger boiling within him.

"Let's get out of here," he said through clenched teeth,

turning toward the door and leaving the camera, candy and magazine behind.

She took the child's hand and all three of them went outside into the hot sunshine. Jonah moved to the shade of a tree, away from the drugstore entrance. He dropped her arm and looked again at the child and then back to Kate.

"How old is he?"

"He's four. In a few months, he'll be five," she replied, and Jonah flinched as if hit. Five years ago was when Kate had walked out.

"You knew when you left me," he said, thinking about the divorce and the battles they'd had. "You knew, Kate! Dammit, how could you!"

"Please," she whispered, "not here."

He wanted to shout that they would talk here and now, but he had to think about his child. "We have to talk," Jonah declared.

"I know that," she answered, and glanced at their son. Jonah realized she didn't want the little boy to overhear the conversation. "But not here and not now. This is my son, Henry," she said. "Henry, meet…" Her voice trailed away. When words failed her and she looked stricken, Jonah realized she had been unprepared to ever cross paths with him.

"It's Jonah," he said to the boy, extending his hand.

Jonah took the small hand offered to him, wanting to pull the child into his arms and hug him. But he knew he couldn't. It took great effort to keep from staring at Henry. Jonah scanned every inch of the little boy, memorizing forever the child's straight black hair, slender frame and wide, thickly lashed eyes. His slightly full lips and that hawkish nose that had been passed down to nearly every male in Jonah's family, and more than a few of the females.

"Hello, sir," the boy said politely.

Jonah tried to smile as he released the child's hand, but failed.

"I'm staying at a motel. I can give you my phone number—" Kate began, but Jonah shook his head. He wasn't giving her a chance to disappear again.

"No, Kate," he interrupted. "Let's go to a park and talk right now. Henry can play while we talk. C'mon. I have a car."

Wide-eyed, she stared at him and slowly nodded. "We have to get Henry's booster seat from my car. I'd drive, but with the car packed with our belongings, there's no room." He linked her arm in his, trying to ignore the jump in his pulse when he touched her. She took Henry's hand, and they got the booster seat and then walked to Jonah's rental car, where Jonah held the door while she climbed inside. As soon as Jonah secured the booster seat, Henry got into the back and buckled himself in.

They drove in silence to the park, and Jonah wondered whether Henry was an extremely quiet, shy child or if he had picked up on his mother's anxiety.

After they parked in the shade of an elm, the three of them walked to a wooden park bench that was close to swings and playground equipment. As Henry ran off to climb on a wooden structure, Jonah and Kate sat on the bench, leaving a wide space between them. As soon as they were settled, he turned to her.

Gazing at her profile, he realized she had changed. She was far thinner now, her skin drawn tightly over those prominent cheekbones. His gaze drifted down to her long, shapely legs, which stirred his desire even when he didn't want them to.

"Are you married?" he asked bluntly, and she shook her head.

"No, I'm not."

"Why didn't you tell me about my son?" he demanded, still trying to control the fury that burned in him.

She turned to look at him, gazing steadily, with a lift of her chin. "It wouldn't have mattered if I had told you. You wouldn't have left Special Forces just because your wife was pregnant.''

"I had a right to know," he said, each word clipped with suppressed anger that he struggled every second to control.

She flinched as if he had struck her. "I know you did," she said, looking away and watching Henry. "But it would have made it harder to separate, and I wanted out of the marriage. And you had your life, the life you wanted more than anything else.''

"Don't say that I wouldn't have cared about my son," he said tightly, clenching his fists again.

"I know you would have cared," she stated quickly, "but it wouldn't have changed anything." She shook her head and sunlight caused golden glints in her thick brown hair.

"It might have, Kate."

"You know it wouldn't have!" she snapped, then bit her lip and looked away. Henry had climbed into a large sand-box and was digging in the sand, and both his parents stared at him.

"How could you keep silent? How could you keep my son from me?" Jonah asked, pulling on his earlobe.

"I know I shouldn't have," she replied in a tight voice.

"Damn straight you shouldn't have!" he snapped. "It's not just me you cheated, but his grandparents, aunts, uncles and cousins, and Henry himself! Dammit, Kate!''

She turned, fire flashing in her eyes and color spilling into her cheeks. "We divorced! Even if you had known, I would have tried to get full custody, and since you were out of the country most of the time, I probably would have succeeded.''

"You don't know that. Would you have kept him from his grandparents?" Jonah asked, thinking about how much his mother and dad loved their grandchildren.

Kate closed her eyes and rubbed her forehead.

"You cheated me out of knowing my son as a baby and

a toddler. Not even a picture, Kate. No knowledge of his existence, and you never planned to tell me! Damnation!'' Jonah swore in a deadly quiet voice. He was furious, hurt, close to rage, yet even so, he wanted to reach out and touch her. She still dazzled him, and that angered him even more.

''You didn't want us!'' she snapped, looking him in the eye defiantly. ''Your military life was the most important thing to you!''

Jonah took a couple of deep breaths. His pulse was pounding and he felt hot. Standing, he jammed his fists into his pockets and walked a few steps, feeling a pent-up need to move while he tried to calm himself.

He knew he needed to think before he spoke, because every word between them was loaded and could explode into a fiery fight or disaster. He was angry with Kate, angry with himself for still finding her incredibly attractive. How could he want to kiss her when she had done such a terrible thing? Yet when he looked at her lips, all he could do was remember—even through a haze of fury.

''I'm out of the military now, and I want to know my son,'' Jonah declared.

She caught her lip with her teeth, looking at Henry and frowning. ''You're going to hurt him.''

''Never,'' Jonah replied emphatically. ''Do you think knowing his father is going to hurt him?''

''No,'' she admitted with a sigh. ''I know you would never deliberately hurt any child, much less your own son.''

''What are you doing in San Antonio?'' Jonah asked.

''I just got a job here,'' she replied.

''Where are you staying?''

When she named a motel that was part of a low-priced chain, he looked more closely at her. Her purse was frayed, her sandals scuffed and worn. She wore a dime-store watch. He wondered what had happened, because when they had been married she had had an excellent job as an account executive with an advertising agency.

"Why did you leave North Carolina? Are your folks still there?"

She looked away and shook her head. "No. Both of my parents died—Dad died in January and Mom in April."

"I'm sorry, Kate. Their deaths were close together and that's rough. What happened to them?"

"They were terminally ill, both with heart trouble. After their deaths, I closed things up and found a job here, and we just arrived in town. I have to find a place to live and a day care for Henry." She looked at Jonah. "So where do we go from here? Do you live here, too?"

"Yes. And I intend to get to know my son." He glanced at Henry and then back at her, thinking of the future. "I'll take you to court over this if I have to, Kate."

She looked away, but not before he saw tears fill her eyes. Her tears didn't diminish his anger, however.

"Don't run away, either," he added tersely. "I'll find you. I can promise you that."

"I won't run. I suppose we'll have to work out times and all that…. Have *you* remarried?" she asked, turning to study him.

"No, I haven't."

She shook her head and looked away again. Wind blew her long hair, and he could remember its softness when he'd wrapped his fingers in it.

"When do you start this new job?" he asked.

"Monday morning."

Surprised, he arched his brows. "That leaves you just this weekend to find a place to live and a day care. That's cutting it close."

"I needed to start work as soon as possible."

Jonah sat down again on the end of the bench and rested his elbows on his knees, watching Henry in the sandbox. The little boy was digging, carefully building a structure. Jonah's thoughts seethed, and he tried to think calmly what to do next.

"Jonah, I should go," Kate said, locking her fingers together tightly in her lap. "I can give you my phone number and the number of the place where I'll be working, but right now, this afternoon, I should be looking for a place to stay. That's what we've been doing all day today."

She opened her purse and fumbled for a pen and paper. Jonah's hand closed over hers and her gaze flew up to meet his.

"I'll take you to dinner tonight and we can plan what we'll do."

"I don't have any time before this job starts. Can we wait until I've had a week or two?"

"You're going to tell him the truth today, right now—here at the park. Or else I will," Jonah said in a voice of steel, a tone she had never heard before and knew she couldn't argue with. "I don't want to be cheated out of knowing my son one more minute."

She rubbed her forehead again. "Please wait. I can't deal with all this at once."

"I've waited five damn years!" Jonah snapped. "I'm not waiting another moment."

She nodded. "All right, Jonah. I guess you have that right."

"Damn straight, I do. What have you told him about me—about us?" Jonah asked. "Did you tell him that we're divorced?"

"Yes. I told him that the army was important to you and you were gone most of the time, and we decided it would be best to part. I told him you wanted out of the marriage."

"Kate, that's a damn lie!" Jonah said, standing again and pacing away from her, fury making him shake once more. He whipped around. "You're the one who walked."

"I know, but I was afraid he would keep hoping you would come back," she explained.

The anger Jonah was keeping in check tore at him. He

clenched and unclenched his fists and took deep breaths, knowing he needed to calm down.

"Children accept life as it comes to them," Kate continued in a subdued voice, her words running together as she spoke quickly. "My parents were around the first couple of years. Dad wasn't well the past three years, nor was Mom for the last two, but for a while Henry had a father substitute." She turned to face Jonah squarely.

"It hasn't been easy this past year. Mom and Dad were very ill, and I had to quit my job to take care of them. Since I couldn't give a lot of attention to Henry, he's learned to entertain himself, but he's also a little shut off. He's a solemn child and sensitive, and I think he picks up on what is going on around him. Don't intimidate him."

"I don't intend to intimidate him, Kate. I want to love him," Jonah said in a clipped tone while he looked at the little boy playing in the sand by himself. Other children ran around the playground together, but Henry kept to himself, and Jonah wondered how solitary the child's life had been.

"You named him for your dad, didn't you?" he asked.

"Yes. Henry Neighbor Whitewolf."

"So you let him keep my name?" Jonah remarked in surprise. "And his middle name is my dad's? Why did you do that, when you intended for Henry to never know his grandfather?"

"I thought someday I would take him to meet your folks, but then time began to pass and my parents got sick. I had a baby to care for and I just didn't do anything about it. I never had a quarrel with your folks, Jonah."

He gritted his teeth and shook his head, not trusting himself to speak. After a long silence, he said, "It was pretty shabby treatment, Kate, to keep the knowledge of their grandchild from them."

She locked her fingers together. "I suppose you're right, but if I had gone to see them or called or let them know

in any way, you would have showed up and I was afraid
of a custody battle.''

"Well, we need to talk about that one.''

She glanced at her watch. "I won't run away. As of
Monday morning, I'll be an advertising executive for Beck-
man and Holloway, a San Antonio ad agency, and I'm really looking forward to it.''

"Sounds like a great job,'' he said.

"I think it will be. It'll pay more than the one I left.''
She looked at Henry. "Right now, we haven't had lunch,
and I know Henry should eat. I need to try to find an apartment today, and I have an appointment this afternoon with
a day care. Can we talk next week?''

"No. You're not putting me off now. I'll take you both
to lunch.''

"You don't need to do that,'' she argued quietly. "I have
a lunch packed in a cooler in my car. Jonah, be reasonable—we can talk tomorrow.''

Jonah shook his head. "Let's go to lunch and talk. You
can look at apartments later. Right now, I want to go tell
him I'm his father. I've been out of his life for too long
already.''

They stared at each other, and he could feel the muscles
clenching in his jaw. He hurt as if every bone in his body
were broken, ached with longing for the years he hadn't
known his child. Hot anger still consumed him, and to his
chagrin, he still found his pulse racing every time he looked
at Kate. He didn't want her to have that power over him,
but she did. He just hoped he never let his need for her
show. When he thought what she had done, keeping Henry
from him, he decided it would be better to keep his basic
male reaction hidden from her.

He was astounded that she would try to keep his son a
secret. That was a side of her he had never known.

"I'm going to tell him,'' Jonah said, finally breaking the
silence.

"No!" She gripped his arm and he inhaled, hating the hot tremor that sizzled through him from the touch of her fingers. She yanked her hand away as if she had touched burning metal. "I'll go tell him right now," she said, looking at Jonah intently, her gaze searching his features. "You've changed, Jonah. You're a hard man."

"You've changed, too, Kate. And what you did was—" He bit back the word he was about to say. It was over, and from this hour on, he would know his son and his son would know him. And in that moment, Jonah knew what he could do for the future.

"I'll go tell him, but this is going to be sudden," she repeated.

"I'm not the one who caused it to be that way. Go tell him."

She clamped her lips shut, but nodded and turned away. He watched the slight sway of her hips and drew a deep breath. "Damn," he whispered to himself. She was still beautiful and she could still stir him with a look or even the slightest physical contact. To him, she was the most beautiful woman he had ever known. He couldn't see her any other way. Not even now, when he was so angry with her.

For too many reasons he ached as he watched her sit down in the grass near the sandbox and talk to Henry. Their son. Jonah couldn't get over the knowledge. He had a son! Henry Neighbour, named for his dad and her father.

Jonah thought of his parents. His father would stoically say nothing about not being told about Henry all these years, but would simply pick up with the present. His mother would cry buckets over the lost years and pour out her love on this grandson, if Kate would let her.

Children's laughter floated in the air, along with the whistles of birds. A faint breeze blew, and shadows shifted over him as Jonah sat waiting in the shade of a tall cottonwood tree. While he watched his ex-wife with their son, he thought of his future and the plans he had already made, and now what lay ahead and what he should do.

While Kate talked to Henry, the boy turned and stared at Jonah, who gazed back, aching inside. He wanted to go put his arms around his son and hug him. He longed to hold Henry. Five years and he had never yet held his child.

"Oh, dammit, Kate," he whispered, and started walking toward them.

Henry got up and brushed off the sand, and Kate took his hand as they approached Jonah. The boy was slender, too quiet and withdrawn, yet there was absolutely no mistaking that Henry was his son, Jonah thought.

As he walked up to them, Kate and Henry stopped. Jonah kept his eyes on the boy, who watched him when he hunkered down in front of him. "I'm your dad, Henry."

"Yes, sir," Henry said quietly, frowning at him.

"I'm glad to see you and I want to get to know you."

Nodding solemnly, Henry stared in silence at Jonah, who had held on to control long enough. He succumbed to impulse, reaching out to pick up Henry, standing and hugging the child, trying to hide the tears that stung his eyes.

"Henry," he whispered.

The little boy's arms wrapped around his neck, and Jonah gritted his teeth and squinted, fighting the knot in his throat and the hot tears that threatened to spill. He hadn't cried since he was too young to remember, but it was all he could do now to hang on to his emotions. At the same time, he didn't want to let go of Henry. He held his son in his arms, marveling at the miracle that had been given to him. A son. He had a son!

"I love you," he whispered.

Reluctantly, he set Henry on his feet, knowing he might have been too emotional for the child. When all this was so new to Henry, Jonah had hoped to keep a lid on his feelings and slowly get acquainted with his son.

He glanced at Kate and she turned away quickly, but not

before he glimpsed tears in her own eyes. "Come on, Henry. We have to eat lunch," she said.

"Yes, ma'am," he replied, falling into step beside her.

"I'm taking you to lunch, Henry," Jonah said. "Where do you like to eat?"

The boy looked up questioningly at his mom. "If you insist, Jonah, let's go to a cafeteria so he can eat some vegetables," she said.

"Sure," Jonah agreed. "Did you go to preschool, Henry?"

"No, sir," he replied.

"He starts kindergarten this year," Kate said.

Wondering about his son's life, Jonah continued asking questions and getting yes or no for an answer. He held the car doors for Kate and Henry, noticing his ex-wife's long, shapely legs when she slid into the vehicle.

At the cafeteria Henry stood in the line between them. Fighting the temptation to constantly touch him, as if to reassure himself that Henry was real, Jonah watched him, taking in everything he did, marveling at the child.

As they started through the line, Jonah leaned down to Henry's level. "You get whatever you want to eat. Anything."

Wide-eyed, Henry looked up at Kate, and she nodded, giving Jonah a searching look.

"I want that," Henry replied, pointing to a bowl of bright blue cubes of gelatin.

Jonah couldn't resist brushing Henry's head lightly. When the boy turned to look up at him, Jonah smiled. Henry smiled in return and then his attention went back to the food spread before him. In minutes he had a tray filled with fried chicken, the gelatin, mashed potatoes and gravy. When he pointed to some corn, Kate spoke up.

"Henry, you have enough. You'll never eat all of what you've taken."

"Let him get it, Kate," Jonah said quietly, and then he

turned to Henry. "I told him to get whatever he wants and I don't mind. If it's all right with your mother, go ahead, Henry. Get the corn and whatever else you want."

Kate looked at Jonah and then nodded to Henry, who took the dish of corn. Next, he wanted a fluffy white roll, and then chocolate cake.

They sat at a table by a window, where they could see across a grassy expanse to cars moving on the busy thoroughfare.

Henry cleaned up the bowl of gelatin first and then started on his fried chicken and mashed potatoes. While he ate, Jonah turned to Kate. "We need to work something out."

She nodded and gave him a worried glance. "We'll work out a schedule, but please understand, Jonah, I have to get settled and get him into a day care facility."

"When are you moving your things from North Carolina?"

"There wasn't much to move. I sold nearly everything before I left, and we're sort of starting over now."

Surprised, Jonah remembered the house he had shared with Kate, a comfortable three-bedroom home in a booming neighborhood. Kate's parents' house had been a desirable two-story in a pleasant, older suburb. In the divorce he had let Kate have the house and one car.

She kept her eyes down as she ate, and he studied her again, sure her clothing and jewelry were inexpensive.

"You sold both houses and you didn't keep any furniture—not what we had or any of your folks' things?" he asked, giving her close scrutiny.

"I kept a few little things, which I have in the car with me," she replied, shaking her head.

"Kate, what happened?" he asked, puzzled by her answer. "Even if our possessions gave you bad memories, you loved your parents' things. I can't believe you let them go. What did you do with them?"

"I sold them," she said, busily cutting a thick slice of roast beef. "This is a delicious lunch, Jonah."

"So you don't have furniture? Are you going to rent a furnished apartment?" he asked, surprised again, and realizing things must have gone really badly for her to sell both houses and all the furniture. Yet where had the money gone?

"Yes," she admitted with obvious reluctance.

"Why, Kate? You had a rewarding job and your dad had his own business."

"I'm sure you remember that Mom and Dad had the roller rink."

"Sure, I remember. It was a thriving operation," he replied.

"It was up until the time that we married, but it started slipping then. By the time we divorced, the neighborhood had changed and a bigger, newer rink was built in a better part of town. Instead of getting out, Dad held on. During that time he lost their health insurance because he couldn't keep up the premiums. Finally he lost the business."

"Sorry, Kate," Jonah said tightly, still consumed by anger over Henry, and trying to listen as well as think ahead and make some plans. "What happened then?"

"Dad got a job selling furniture, but it wasn't an adequate salary and he didn't have benefits. Then he had a stroke."

"Sorry," Jonah repeated, remembering Kate's father, with his bushy brown hair and his booming voice. The man had seemed so jovial and strong.

"Mom had a part-time job," Kate continued. Jonah gazed into her wide, hazel eyes, his gaze lowering to her full, red lips. He didn't want to look at her mouth or recall her kisses, but he did remember vividly, far too clearly. He caught the faint scent of her perfume. Memories from the past mixed with anger from the present, and he had to struggle to focus on what she was telling him.

"...but she had to quit to take care of Dad, and then suddenly I was taking care of both of them. They sold their house and moved in with me."

"So why don't you have *your* things? Surely you didn't sell them, too."

She nodded. "Yes, I did. I had to, because of their heart troubles. Without insurance, the medical bills were astronomical, and I had to quit my job to take care of them."

"You have an aunt and uncle and cousins. Didn't any of them help?"

"No, they didn't," she replied, shaking her head. "They have their own families to take care of. But I managed and didn't have to go into debt, and I have some money saved for us to start out on. Also, I think I have a promising job lined up. This was a temporary setback, and we survived it."

He gazed into her luminous eyes and knew if anyone could cope with tough times, it would be Kate. There was a practicality to her, enabling her to get to the essentials. He had always admired her for her ability to handle the tough moments, until the tough moment had been her decision to leave him. But then, that survivor instinct of hers might have been what caused her to walk out on him.

"I'm sorry about your folks," he said, truly meaning it because he had liked her parents.

She nodded. "They were relatively young to have that all happen, although Dad was thirteen years older than Mom."

"How'd you find the job here?" Jonah asked.

"Through the Internet."

She wiped her mouth daintily, and he looked at her lips again for a moment, then tore his gaze away. He didn't want to remember sexy nights and hot kisses and a myriad other seductive moments with Kate.

He watched Henry, who was steadily eating every bite of food in front of him. So was Kate, and Jonah wondered if they had been going hungry. Again he noticed how thin both of them were. Kate's blouse looked a size too large.

If she had had a hard time, he was sorry, but it angered him to think that his son had been in dire straits. If she had only let Jonah know, Kate could have so easily avoided any hardships. As swiftly as he thought that about her, Jonah realized that Kate was independent enough to shoulder her own burdens and not expect help from others, much less from an ex-husband who didn't know about their child.

"Who are your friends, Henry?" he asked, turning his attention to his son.

"Matthew and Billy," the child answered.

While Jonah talked to Henry about his playmates back in North Carolina, Kate savored her potatoes and spinach. For the past few days, during the long drive to Texas from North Carolina, they had lived on peanut butter sandwiches and cold cuts and whatever else she could buy cheaply and pack in the car.

While he talked to Henry, she studied Jonah. He looked even more handsome than when they had been married. Tall, black-haired, with those midnight brown eyes that Henry had inherited, Jonah had an air of self-assurance and command that he hadn't had before. Eyeing his navy knit sport shirt surreptitiously, she could tell he had filled out with solid muscle.

During their initial encounter in the drugstore, she had thought she would faint. Never had she expected to see Jonah in this part of Texas. She had always known she should tell him about his son, but it was easy to put off contacting him, and at first, anger at him got in the way. By the time they had parted, she had been furious with him for sticking to his wild lifestyle and staying in Special Forces, which trained him for dangerous assignments.

When she had walked out on him, she hadn't known she was pregnant. She'd discovered that the first week she was on her own, but in her anger, she hadn't wanted to tell Jonah or go back.

She had intended to tell him about his son eventually, but it got easier and easier to put it off. When she went through childbirth, Jonah was out of the country on an assignment, and by the time he was back home, she didn't want to tell him at all.

Finally, enough time passed that she didn't want to face his wrath or the complications he would cause. When their paths didn't cross for a year, she'd begun to believe they might never cross again. When her parents both became terminally ill, she couldn't think about anything except their care and looking after Henry. With her excellent job gone, times had been harsh and lean, because every penny went into caring for the three people dependent on her.

With a rush of warmth, she looked at Henry. He was a lovable little boy, an easy child to raise. She knew he was solemn and didn't have the preschooling he should have had at this age, but he was bright and affectionate, and she loved him with all her heart.

Her gaze shifted to Jonah, noting that imperial nose, his prominent cheekbones and thickly lashed eyes. As her gaze drifted down to his mouth, she remembered too clearly moments of passion and how Jonah's kisses could turn her to mush.

She was surprised he hadn't remarried, but then, his career was his life, and it stood in the way of other commitments. Still, he was breathtakingly handsome, and a lot of women were drawn to men like Jonah. He had an old-world courtesy about him that females liked. Kate had been fully aware of the fury he had controlled today when he had learned about Henry.

Jonah had never lost his temper with her—not in their bickering about his career, not even in the last bitter argument when she had walked out on him. He had always kept his voice down, always kept his wits about him. But she had once seen him wade into a fight to save a slender guy who was being beaten by a gang of men, and Jonah had been wild and fierce and frightening. And he had ended the battle in seconds.

At the first sight of him today, she had hated how her pulse jumped. When he'd taken her arm to help her into the car, she had felt the contact to her toes. After all this time and even when she didn't want to, she still responded instantly and totally to him.

She wondered if he was stationed in San Antonio now. Wondered if there was a regular woman in his life. She glanced at him again, to find his dark gaze on her, and as she looked quickly away, she tingled all over.

She was self-conscious about her clothes, which were old and worn, and she hated that she had had to reveal all her problems to him. If they were going to have this chance encounter, she wished it had been a month from now, after she had found a place to live and gotten her first paycheck from what promised to be an exciting job.

"Want some more water, Kate?" Jonah asked.

"Yes, please," she answered politely, knowing they were both being courteous for Henry's sake, and that every time Jonah looked at her, his dark eyes still blazed with anger.

She watched as he picked up the large pitcher with ease and filled her glass. She had always loved the shape of his strong hands, his blunt fingers with nails clipped short.

"Thanks," she said, remembering his touch, knowing how his hands could take her to ecstasy. She looked away and tried to stop thinking about him, to stop memory piling on top of memory. But today had been a shock, one she'd been totally unprepared for.

"Would you like more milk, Henry?" Jonah asked.

"He's fine—" she began, but when Henry nodded, Jonah got up to cross the room to the cafeteria line. Kate watched his long-legged stride. He was so broad-shouldered, his back tapering to a waist still as narrow as when they had married. He wore jeans and loafers, but she could remember Jonah naked, his warrior's body fit and virile and breathtaking.

Stop thinking about him, she ordered herself. She looked away before he glanced back and caught her watching him.

He returned, opening the carton and pouring chocolate milk for Henry, who smiled up at him.

Guilt swamped her. It hurt to watch the two of them together, because she had not only cheated Jonah, she knew she had cheated her son. Henry deserved to know his father, whose only crime was to like his dangerous lifestyle and feel it was his mission to save people and help the world, even at his family's expense.

She looked at her watch and then at Jonah, gazing into his eyes, which snapped with fury.

"I have an appointment in thirty minutes to view an apartment," she reminded him.

"I've been thinking about that," Jonah said. "I want to be able to see Henry."

"We'll work something out," she assured him, rubbing her forehead. "This isn't the time or place to do so," she added, glancing at the child. She didn't want to talk about visitation rights or custody battles in front of Henry, who, now that he had a full tummy, was beginning to turn his attention completely to Jonah. Henry's big eyes were fixed on his newfound father, studying every inch of him, from the watch on his wrist to the loafers on his feet. Henry scanned Jonah's features slowly, as if memorizing them.

"If we're finished here, we can talk as we walk to the car," Jonah suggested, standing and coming around to hold her chair.

She nodded, wanting to get rid of him before he saw her years-old vehicle, piled high with the only belongings they owned.

Stepping outside into the sunshine, they headed for Jonah's car.

"If you'll just take us back to the drugstore, my car is parked there," she said. "You can give me your phone number. I don't have one yet, but you know where I'll work, and I can give you that number."

"Kate," Jonah said, taking her arm while Henry hopped on one foot ahead of them. "I think I have a temporary solution for you that would save you money and enable me to get to know my son."

Feeling weak in the knees at his touch, she turned to face him. Even though she was five feet nine inches tall, she had to look up at him, because he was six-two.

"What are you referring to?" she asked.

"I just inherited a ranch. That's why I'm here in San Antonio."

"You're going to live on a ranch?" she asked in disbelief. "You're not in Special Forces?"

"No, I'm not," he answered. "I got out of the military, and yes, I'm going to live on the ranch."

"You won't last six months," Kate remarked swiftly, without thinking, "unless you're raising and riding wild bulls. You like life on the wild side too much, Jonah."

A muscle worked in his jaw, and she knew she had deepened his anger, but she had blurted the truth.

He watched Henry while he took deep breaths in an obvious struggle to get his temper under control. "I have a lot of room. Move into the ranch house with me. You can commute to work and I can get to know Henry."

Stunned, she stared at him, caught unaware by an offer she had never dreamed of getting.

Chapter 3

"That's crazy, Jonah! I'm not moving in with you!" she whispered, wanting to avoid Henry overhearing them. So far he seemed wrapped in his own world. She didn't know if Jonah was propositioning her, or what he had in mind, but it was impossible.

"It's a large ranch house," Jonah said calmly, as if he were explaining the situation to Henry. "If we don't want to, we don't have to see each other. Living on my ranch would save you paying rent until you get your feet on the ground."

"Jonah, I can't imagine—" she began, but he interrupted her.

"Wouldn't it help you to live rent-free for the next six or eight months?"

She thought of what that would be like—a gift, heaven-sent. An enormous break. At the same time, it would mean living with Jonah.

If she did, she might risk falling in love with him and being hurt all over again. She knew that because she was responding to him now. Yet, undoubtedly Jonah was in her life and would be until Henry was grown.

"Yes, it would help," she murmured, possibilities spinning in her mind.

"If you'd like, I can take you out to look at the place. It's furnished, and you and Henry can move in today. I'm staying out there tonight, and tomorrow I'm going home to get my things."

"This is so sudden," she said, rubbing her forehead. She wished she could choose a different course, but this was such a godsend for her.

"It'll solve some of your problems," he said, as if the matter was settled. "Cancel your appointment to look at that apartment, and let's go to the ranch." Jonah held out his cellular phone.

She looked up to meet his gaze. What was she doing? she wondered. Did he know what he was asking? The past hour had been strained, and Jonah was steeped in anger that she knew was going to last a long time. And this volatile chemistry between them—did he feel it, too, or was she the only one who would have to fight that magnetic attraction, as strong as it had been when they first met?

"Kate, you could save the money to get a better place," he reminded her. "During the day I can keep Henry with me, and if we need to, I'll hire a nanny. Henry is my son, and I want to do things for him."

She was weak in the knees again. After all the responsibilities she had shouldered alone for the past five years, to have such an offer of help was overwhelming.

"I know you'll be a great dad to him and a role model," she said, convinced there was only one answer to give. Yet she felt an enormous reluctance. She didn't want to rely on Jonah any more than she wanted to find herself loving him again. If she had ever been completely over him…

Kate didn't want to think too much about that, either.

Bright sunshine spilled over him, highlighting his black

hair. Looking relaxed, with his hands splayed on his narrow hips, he stood close enough that she could catch a faint scent of his woodsy aftershave. His jaw was clean-shaven. He was still dangerous to her heart, and she was sure that, ranch or no ranch, he was still as wild and impulsive as ever.

"Are you going to let Henry do risky things?"

Jonah looked at the boy, who was squatting down and watching a bug crawl along the edge of the sidewalk.

"Kate, you don't have a right to ask me what I'm going to do. I can go to court and take him away from you for what you've done."

She gasped, pain shooting through her because his words terrified her. At the same time, guilt swamped her, because to a degree, she knew he was right.

"And you think, under the circumstances, that we can stay under the same roof? I don't think so, Jonah."

"We won't see much of each other at all. It's a big house, as I said, and we can arrange it so we aren't together." He looked at Henry again. "And to answer your question, I won't let him do anything beyond the ordinary kid stuff. He can climb a tree, dabble in the creek, learn to ride."

"Horses?"

"Right, Kate. I'll find a gentle one for him. I don't want him hurt, either. Let's go look at the place."

Standing on the sidewalk, she stared into his brown eyes and debated with herself. Her life had just changed, but how big would the changes be? She wanted to tell Jonah no and walk away, as she had five years before, but this time she couldn't. Because of Henry, her life was tied to Jonah's now.

She sighed and nodded. "It would help a lot if I didn't have to pay rent for a while."

"All right. Let's go."

"Let me cancel my appointment," she said, doing so

quickly. As soon as she returned his phone, she said, "I can follow you in my car."

Jonah shook his head. "Come with me, and we'll stay there tonight," he said, and in spite of the circumstances, his words made her tingle. "I'll send someone into town to get your car."

"Fine," she said reluctantly, yet seeing little choice. Free rent would give her and Henry a wonderful financial boost.

"Henry," Jonah said, raising his voice to normal level, "let's go look at where you might live for a time. You and your mom might move into my house. It's out in the country."

Henry brightened and walked beside Jonah, and Kate moved to Henry's other side so he was between them.

Jonah held the car doors for both of them again, and then she watched him walk around to the driver's side. She didn't want to live under the same roof with him. When they'd divorced, it had taken her forever to stop crying over him, but this seemed the only solution right now.

Jonah slid behind the wheel and in minutes they were driving along a freeway in San Antonio, while Henry asked questions about the ranch and Jonah answered.

"How did you inherit a ranch in the Hill Country?" she asked. "I thought all your family was up in the Panhandle."

"I didn't inherit from a relative," Jonah replied. "It was a man whose life I helped save when he was a hostage—remember? The one in Colombia?"

She took a deep breath, because that assignment had been the last straw. That particular mission had sounded suicidal. At the time, she'd known that Jonah told her very little about what he had to do. Just enough for her to never expect to see him alive again when she kissed him goodbye. And that was when she had given him an ultimatum to choose between her or Special Forces. He had said he couldn't quit the military.

"Although I'm glad you got something rewarding out of that," she said, remembering too clearly, "I'm surprised you're moving here."

"I'll see how I like ranching. I always liked it when I was a kid."

"That's different, Jonah. You didn't have full responsibility."

"Nope, but this ranch looks like a promising place for me to be."

As they sped out of the city, heading north to the ranch, they rode in silence. For the first half hour, all Kate could do was think about the gift of no rent for the coming months, and what a wonderful help that would be to her finances. Her spirits lifted, and she tried to avoid contemplating living under the same roof with Jonah, or his fury, or the future. She wanted to bask in relief over the problems his offer solved for her.

The land was green from spring rains, and wildflowers still dotted the hillsides. At one point they reached barbed wire fencing that stretched into the distance. "This is the south boundary of my ranch," Jonah said.

As she continued looking out at endless pastureland, she realized they were passing a lot of acres.

At last Jonah turned the car off the state highway onto a hard-packed dirt road, between tall stone posts. On one of the posts a sign held the Long Bar brand. Kate glanced back to see Henry sitting up, straining against his seat belt to see out the window when they bounced across a cattle guard.

She looked at the rolling hills and saw cattle grazing in the distance. She had imagined something on a much smaller scale, and when they topped a rise and she saw a sprawling ranch house and other buildings, her surprise grew. "Jonah, this operation is enormous. You inherited all of it?"

"Yes. It's mine now, lock, stock and barrel."

"What about the other guys in on the rescue? You didn't go get the hostage single-handedly."

"Nope. There were four of us back then. We lost Colin Garrick in the line of duty. Boone Devlin inherited a quarter-horse ranch, and Mike Remington inherited the house in town and the man's baby daughter."

"A baby? There weren't any relatives?"

"Only John Frates's in-laws. They were unfit for parenthood and are in a rehabilitation center now. Dina Frates's father had been in prison, and both are alcoholics. They couldn't take the baby."

"Who cares for them?" Kate asked.

"They have a lifetime trust established for them by John. Savannah Remington is the attorney for it."

"How sad about the grandparents," Kate remarked. She was curious about the man they had rescued. "No wonder someone held him hostage, if he had this kind of money. What happened to Colin?" she asked, remembering a handsome guy full of life.

"He was killed on a mission," Jonah answered, bringing back to her the seriousness of what he'd been involved in and what he had chosen over their marriage.

"Wasn't Colin married?" she asked, thinking back and remembering the same woman with him each time she had seen him.

"Nope, engaged. They were planning on marrying. I heard she's married someone else now."

"I'm sorry. That's sad. I don't know how you got used to so much needless death, Jonah."

"I don't know that anyone ever does get used to it."

"Oh, yes. You did, or you would have been too horrified to go back into that life. And you have all this now," she said, still amazed.

"That's right. I can keep it or I can sell it. I've thought it over and decided to keep it for a time and see how I like it. It's a successful cattle ranch."

Her head whipped around. "You won't stay here long, because this will be much too quiet for you, too placid. I can't imagine you doing this for more than six months or so."

"We'll see," he said tightly. "Kate, my job was to do some good in the world, not to live dangerously. But that's old territory, and there's no need to go there now."

"No, there's not. How long have you been out?"

"Almost a year."

"So what have you been doing?"

"Working for an oil company," he replied, a muscle working in his jaw.

"Doing what for an oil company?" she persisted, wondering how much he had changed over the years, if at all.

"Fighting well fires," he replied, and she shook her head. He hadn't changed in the least. He had merely gone from one high-risk job to another. She looked again at the lush land surrounding them and the fantastic ranch house looming closer. She couldn't imagine him staying out here, herding cattle and mending fences and keeping books. In a few months, he would be gone.

"Look, Mom, there are cows!"

"Yes, there are, Henry," she replied as they neared a pasture where more Herefords grazed.

"There are horses, too, Henry. I'll let you ride one this evening," Jonah said.

"You will?"

Henry's voice was filled with so much eagerness and anticipation that Kate looked back at him again. His eyes were wide and sparkling. "I get to ride a horse," he said to her in awe, and she was saddened. Had she cheated Henry badly by keeping his father from him?

She had never thought about Jonah as being a super father, because she'd never thought about him being present enough to be any kind of a dad to a child. He had seemed so wrapped up in his military life that she had never expected him to be deeply interested in a family. Had she been wrong? And had she denied not only Jonah, but Henry as well?

"Look, there's a barn!" Henry exclaimed.

Jonah took out a cell phone and called someone, and in seconds she realized he was talking to one of his ranch hands, telling him that he would be staying the night on the ranch and he had brought guests.

She listened as Henry bounced in the seat with excitement, and Jonah made arrangements for a gentle horse to be brought up to the corral.

She ran her hand across her head. This was a bonanza for her and for Henry in so many ways, yet at the same time she was putting her heart and her future in jeopardy. She looked at Jonah and drew a deep breath. Handsome, commanding, he was too many appealing things. If he turned out to be a loving, attentive father for Henry, she knew he would be just that much more irresistible to her. And she knew full well that he was still the same risk-taker he had always been, the same man who lived life on the edge and didn't mind wading into a fight to help someone even when doing so put him in jeopardy.

When Jonah led them into a house large enough to be a mansion, Henry's eyes were wide. He became quiet, and she was certain that he was awed by the enormous new home where they would live. She was a little awed herself.

"Wow! Mom, are we going to stay here?" he asked in his childish voice.

"Yes, you are," Jonah answered before she could.

Her astonishment grew when they strolled into a large kitchen with a living area at one end of the room. Elegant glass-fronted oak cabinets, above a limestone floor and state-of-the-art, built-in appliances, looked wonderful to her. An adjoining eating area held a rectangular oak table and ten ladder-back chairs. A china vase filled with silk flowers was centered on the table. The house reflected the wealth of the previous owner, and she could hardly believe that it now belonged to Jonah.

"This is huge," she exclaimed. "You'll need a maid to keep it."

"Actually, one comes with the place," Jonah replied quietly.

"Jonah, this is fabulous! What an enormous inheritance."

"Yeah, I was shocked, too, Kate. All we did was accomplish our mission."

"You saved the man's life."

"That's what I was supposed to do. All three of us have been in shock over our inheritance."

Henry had gone to the window to look outside, so was out of earshot when Kate turned to Jonah. "You're handsome and now you're wealthy, Jonah. Women are going to be interested in you. Won't we be in your way here?"

"Nope. If we need to make adjustments or other arrangements, we can," he said, gazing steadily back at her. When he did, she could feel the air ignite between them.

In spite of all the arguments, their opposing views, his fury today and her determination to remain detached, the sparks were still there, as volatile and hot as ever. Her own gaze was locked onto his dark, enigmatic eyes. She couldn't catch her breath or look away, and although she hated it, she had to admit that part of her wanted to throw her arms around him and kiss him endlessly.

At the same time, another part wanted to resist with every ounce of her being. She didn't want to look at Jonah and be set ablaze with desire, or touch him and ignite a firestorm of longing. Yet there was no mistaking what she was caught up in and unable to stop any more than she could stop breathing.

It was obvious that he was feeling sparks, too, and fighting his emotions as much as she was, because a muscle worked in his jaw and his fists were clenched again. Breaking eye contact, he turned abruptly, and she let out her breath.

"How can we live under one roof?" she asked softly.

"Damn easily," he snapped, turning back, and this time his eyes flashed with a different fire. She knew instinctively that anger was his protection from the sparks that danced between them, just as shock had been her barrier the first hour with him. Swiftly, her shock at seeing him was wearing off, now that he knew the truth concerning Henry, and she had no shield except logic and determination, which was a weak buffer against the appeal that Jonah held for her.

"All I have to do is look at my son and I know I want you here," Jonah said. "You're part of Henry. It would hurt him to be taken from you, Kate. If it didn't hurt him, I wouldn't hesitate."

Jonah's words cut into her like a knife, yet she knew she deserved them, and she could understand his hurt and anger. She closed her eyes and took a deep breath.

Henry walked around the room, looking at everything and then returning to Kate's side. "This is a big house."

"Yes, it is."

"C'mon, Henry," Jonah said, hoisting Henry to his shoulders, "I'll show you around."

Henry clung tightly to Jonah, and for an instant Kate wondered if he was frightened. But then she saw his grin and realized he liked being on Jonah's shoulders. When he had been a toddler, her father had carried him that way. By the time Henry was three years old, her father hadn't been able to do so, and Henry probably didn't even remember that he ever had.

She saw that Henry was going to take to Jonah completely. Her son had missed having a father, and now not only was Jonah concerned about him, he could also enrich his life as well as become a role model for him.

She trailed after Jonah and Henry as they entered an

opulent family room with rough, hand-hewn beams across the sixteen-foot-high ceiling. The furniture was dark wood, with the chairs and sofas covered in brown leather. The plank floor gleamed with polish, and a massive slate fireplace filled one end of the room. The pavilion-style space had a great view of a swimming pool and surrounding terrace.

"Oh, my!" Kate exclaimed, looking at the beautiful, sparkling water behind a black, wrought-iron grill. "I'm glad there's a fence around the pool," she said. "Henry doesn't swim."

"Don't worry, Kate. He'll be all right and the fence is sturdy," Jonah said.

She turned her attention to the family room. "The house looks old, but they must have done it over in recent years," she observed, gazing at a built-in entertainment center and a bar at one end of the room.

"It looks that way," Jonah replied. "None of us knew John Frates very well, and our total knowledge of him involved his being a hostage."

She crossed the room to a credenza. "Someone liked elegant antique furniture," she said. "This period piece is beautiful."

"The lawyer told me they had a decorator do the house. You can pick a bedroom, Kate, and select one for Henry. There are twelve bedrooms and eight bathrooms in this place—one bedroom downstairs and the rest upstairs. I've already decided to take the master bedroom."

"That's fine, Jonah. It doesn't matter," she replied. Only it did matter. She needed a bedroom a mile away from him.

He swung Henry to the floor and she watched the flex of taut muscles in his arms and back as his shirt stretched tightly across his shoulders.

"We're going to live here, Mommy?" Henry asked in a subdued voice, and she wondered if he was overwhelmed by the house.

"Yes, we are for a while."

He looked at the window. "There's a swimming pool," he said quietly, casting a worried glance at Jonah.

"Yes, and you'll get to go in it sometime, when one of us is with you," she said. "Right now, let's look around the house so we'll know where things are."

He stayed close by her side as they went through a formal living room, and Jonah watched him, thinking he was too quiet for a little boy and wondering if his shyness was because of his new father's presence.

The moment Kate stepped inside the living room, she gasped. "Look at this, Jonah! That looks like a marble Chippendale chimney piece. My word, I wonder where he got this and what it cost!" she exclaimed, crossing the room to look at the ornate mantel.

"You'd know more about that than I do," Jonah remarked dryly, watching her hips sway, desire still burning in him in spite of all his efforts to fight it.

"What a magnificent armoire!" she exclaimed. She moved around the room, gushing over the furniture, while Jonah smoldered and watched her, his emotions warring. Anger and desire were tearing him apart. He didn't want to feel either one, but he was consumed by both. Thinner, more pale, Kate still was the most beautiful woman he had ever known.

"Dammit," he said softly under his breath. "Let's look at the rest, Kate."

She entered the dining room, which she found to be even more spectacular than the kitchen and family room. It was an immense space with another beamed ceiling, and fancy iron chandeliers that hung above a gleaming, dark wood table that could easily seat two dozen people.

Another mammoth stone fireplace filled one wall and crystal pieces sparkled in a tall breakfront on a credenza.

"That man didn't have any relatives?" she asked, turning and catching Jonah looking at her in a manner that set her pulse fluttering again. Instantly, he walked away from her.

"His wife had a family, but her parents are in rehabilitation and not fit guardians. They are taken care of financially for their lifetimes. The property and the baby went to the three of us," Jonah replied solemnly.

He motioned to her. "Down this way," he said, "is a media room, a music room, a games room, a sunroom, a library. A portico connects the house to a cabana. In the cabana is a workout room."

"Jonah, this house is going to take a fortune to maintain!" she exclaimed. "We ought to pay you to live here."

"There's no need to, Kate. I can manage it," he said. "This is a highly profitable ranch."

"You're so fortunate and—" When she bit off her words, he turned to look at her, his brows arched in curiosity.

"And what?"

"You deserved to get this for risking your life to save his. It's ironic that you saved him and then he came home and something happened to him."

"John and Dina drowned off the coast of Scotland in a boating accident. It was their first trip on their own after their daughter's birth and she was too small. The nanny looked after her."

"They left the baby behind? That's awful," Kate exclaimed, and then caught Jonah staring at her with such anger that she bit her lip and turned away. He was probably thinking that it wasn't as awful as what she had done, because they'd been killed accidentally, while she had kept Henry from him deliberately.

They looked at the house, selected bedrooms, and then Jonah told Henry he would take him to look at the barn and livestock. Before they left her, Jonah turned to Kate.

"Give me your car keys and I'll have someone fetch your vehicle."

"It's in the drugstore parking lot, one with North Carolina plates," she said, giving him a description of her eleven-year-old car while she dug in her purse and pulled out keys, handing them to Jonah. When she did, their hands brushed—a slight contact, yet the touch was electric. He looked up into her eyes, and in that moment raw desire burned between them.

As she jerked her hand away, he turned abruptly. "Let's go, Henry," he said. Jonah glanced back at Kate. "I'll put some steaks out to thaw. The kitchen and pantry looked fully stocked."

"Fine," she answered breathlessly, stunned by the intense reaction she was having after all these years, when she'd thought she had gotten over being responsive to him. "We had a big lunch and a late one," she added. "Neither Henry nor I will be hungry for a while."

"When I go home tomorrow to get my things, I want you and Henry to come with me so my folks and Henry can meet each other. I'll get the plane tickets and then we'll drive back here."

She nodded, knowing she should let them meet, but her first thought was the long drive meant hours in the car with Jonah. She saw in her future that they would be thrown together constantly, and it was going to be a rocky time, if not impossible.

As father and son left the house, she watched them. It was an incredible turn of events in their lives, and she was still dazed by the sudden upheaval in her plans.

She turned back to the bedroom she had hastily chosen because it was next to a child's room, one done in primary colors. She was thankful it wasn't all in pink, since Jonah had told her the Frateses' baby was a girl.

Anywhere under the same roof would be impossible to be far enough away from Jonah's room to insulate her heart. As it was, his room was next to hers. He had a huge master bedroom that ran the length of the house on the side overlooking the pool and terrace. Each bedroom had its own balcony.

She looked at the skylighted room she had chosen and realized it was larger than any bedroom she had had before. It held a double bed that had a massive carved headboard she guessed was antique. A dresser and chest of drawers matched the bed, and a tall armoire stood on one side of the room. The green-and-white decor was cheerful in the afternoon sunlight spilling through wide windows. She was surrounded with luxury that she would have relished and enjoyed tremendously if it hadn't included living with Jonah. Life with him would keep her constantly on edge.

Two hours later Henry returned, chattering, dusty and with sparkling eyes. Her car had been brought to the ranch and her things carried in by men who now worked for Jonah. She'd met them as they brought her suitcases up the stairs, then helped Jonah take a crib out of the nursery and put in a bed for Henry.

While the men worked, Kate ran a bath for her son and soon had him bathed and changed into his blue pajamas. She had found the pantry was fully stocked, as Jonah had promised, and she'd fixed an early supper for Henry, knowing he would be exhausted from the long day. While she didn't want to eat alone with Jonah, Henry couldn't last.

When they finished assembling the bed and she'd put clean sheets on it, she let Henry pick out two books from those that were unpacked.

"Can I read to him tonight?" Jonah asked from the doorway, and she turned to find him casually leaning against the jamb. How long had he been standing there watching her? she wondered.

"Yes. I'll come tuck you in, Henry," she said, leaving the room. At the doorway she looked back to see Jonah sitting in the rocking chair with Henry on his lap. The little boy settled in his father's arms, and Kate suffered another pang for keeping the two separated. How long now would she have to live with guilt?

She hurried to her room to unpack some fresh clothes and shower.

Everything about Jonah was appealing, but she needed to constantly guard her heart and remember that this quiet country living would never last for him. To be happy Jonah had to be saving someone or handling some dangerous mission for his country. Getting out of Special Forces wouldn't matter.

She changed into cutoffs and a blue T-shirt, twisting her hair up on her head in a butterfly clip and going back to see if they had finished reading.

As he read and rocked, Henry looked up at Jonah. "You're my daddy? You're going to stay? You're not going to leave us?"

"No, Henry, I'm not going to leave you."

"Daddy," Henry said, running his tiny fingers along Jonah's jaw. Jonah's heart turned over. "I'm glad you're here."

"I'm glad, too, Henry," he said in a husky voice as a rush of feeling choked him. He tightened his arms slightly around his son and continued reading, hoping Henry didn't notice that he was getting emotional.

In minutes the boy was asleep. Jonah studied him, touching strands of his hair lightly, marveling in the child's perfection. Filled with love and awe, Jonah picked up Henry, carrying him to the new bed and putting him down gently.

Then he stood beside the bed. Jonah was fascinated with every facet of Henry, noticing his son's long lashes, his smooth brown skin, his small hands. He leaned down to brush a kiss on Henry's forehead.

"I love you, Henry, and will thank God every day that I found you," he whispered. He straightened and turned to discover Kate only yards away behind him, standing immobile with sadness in her eyes. She turned abruptly and left the room ahead of him.

When he found her waiting at the foot of the stairs, his anger soared, now that Henry was no longer around to witness his wrath. His gaze raked over her.

She was in cutoffs and she looked prettier than ever. There was something sultry and earthy about Kate, and the qualities had intensified in the last few years. Strands of her hair fell loose from the clip that held it pinned on her head. She always looked slightly thrown together, creating a casual, sultry air that had not changed with time.

When they entered the kitchen, she crossed the room. "What can I do to help with dinner?" she asked.

"I'll grill the steaks, and while we eat, I want you to tell me about Henry. Do you have a baby book for him?"

"Yes, I do," she answered.

"Fine," Jonah replied as he got greens for salad from the refrigerator. "I'll take care of the cooking. You go unpack his baby book so I can see it."

"Jonah, if we're tense and angry, he's going to pick up on it soon," Kate said. "You can't pretend to be friendly with me one minute and then seethe with anger the next."

"I figure the anger will go soon, because he's here in my life now, and I'm damn thankful for that. Just overlook the anger, or live with it the way I lived with yours when we were married."

She caught her breath and turned and left the room.

He swore silently and watched her walk away, mentally stripping away the cutoffs, looking at her long, bare legs and wanting her in spite of all she had done. He clamped his teeth so tightly they hurt, then turned to get a cold beer and start dinner.

Before they sat down to eat thick, juicy steaks on the patio, Jonah switched on the intercom.

"I want the device on," Kate said, "but Henry sleeps

like someone who has lost consciousness. He's out until eight o'clock in the morning. No nightmares or wanting a drink or wanting me in the middle of the night.''

"Well, if the unusual should happen, we'll hear him. Now tell me about him—everything, Kate."

She talked while they ate their steaks, a tossed salad and potatoes baked in a microwave oven. A cool breeze blew across the terrace, and she gazed over the turquoise swimming pool. Beyond the well-tended yard was a grand view of rolling hills, green pastures and, in the distance, a silvery pond. The Long Bar Ranch was a paradise—or could be, she thought, and she knew that when the time came, it was going to be difficult to move Henry away from here. She didn't want to think about that now. For the moment, they were here, and when she wasn't tied in knots by Jonah, she could enjoy the ranch, which was going to be so wonderful for Henry.

After dinner, at dusk, they cleared the table and then she spread out the baby book and scrapbooks. Jonah pulled his chair up beside her there.

Her skin tingled all over with awareness of him—his arm brushing against her, his fingers touching hers as they began to look, starting with pictures of Henry at the hospital where he had been born.

"Look at the thick black hair on him even as a baby!" Jonah exclaimed, staring at each picture with a joy that saddened her and heightened her guilt.

"Well, you and I both have thick hair," Kate said, and Jonah looked at her locks, picking up a handful in his grasp.

"Yes, you do," he agreed.

They sat side by side, his hand in her hair now and his face only inches away. His fingers had brushed her nape and his fist rested against her head, slight touches that were like dynamite near the flames of impossible desire. His dark eyes were momentarily free of anger and the only emotion smoldering in their depths was longing.

Once again her gaze locked with his. She couldn't move away, look away or even draw a breath.

While her heart thudded, she licked her dry lips. Why did he have this effect on her? Why had he always been so irresistible? Right now, in spite of all that was between them, she wanted to close that small distance between them and kiss him. She wanted him to wrap his arms around her and kiss her back. At the same time, she didn't want his kisses and never wanted to walk into his arms again, because it could only lead one direction—to more hurt than she had known before.

"Dammit, Kate," he whispered.

"I told you we couldn't live here together, Jonah! You were warned and you didn't pay any attention. Neither one of us wants to feel what we do," she said, unable to tear her eyes from his.

She started to get up to walk away from him. He did the same and they bumped against each other, shoulder to shoulder, hip against hip. He reached to steady her and then they looked into each other's eyes once more.

This time desire was an explosion between them, and longing was palpable. His dark eyes consumed her, and she could only tremble with need.

"Kate," he said, almost growling her name as he reached to pull her into his arms.

The most natural thing to happen, yet the most dangerous.

With all her being, she wanted to resist, to push against him, to race away, to say no. She preferred any of a hundred possible responses over the one she couldn't control.

Her hands flew up and she pushed against a rock-solid chest while she whispered, "No, Jonah! No, no—"

His gaze nailed her, stopping her words, immobilizing her. Searing and white-hot, a blatant desire was burning in his dark eyes like fires against an inky sky.

She knew he was going to kiss her because his intentions

were telegraphed in that look. And knowing it was enough to send her pulse galloping.

His head came down and his mouth covered hers in a hard kiss. His tongue stroked over hers, tormenting, tasting, exploring her mouth.

She thought she would faint. All at once it was paradise and hell. Heat kindled low inside her and spread. Desire made her shake, while her pulse roared in her ears, deafening her as his mouth claimed possession, an insistent kiss that she could no more resist than she could stop breathing.

Time was gone and the years fell away. She was back in Jonah's arms, kissing him. It had been five long years since they had been together. Five years of unfulfilled dreams, haunting memories, aching, empty hours. It had been so terribly long, and no one had ever kissed her the way Jonah did. Never in her life had kisses been this earth-shaking, making her world spin so crazily she felt as if she would fly off into outer space.

His strong arms wrapped around her and he pulled her tightly to him. Her softness pressed against his hard length and solid muscles. She wrapped her arms around his neck and stood on tiptoe and kissed him hungrily.

The shocks of the day were transformed into a longing and passion hot enough to consume them both. This wasn't what she wanted, and at the same time it was all she wanted. How could Jonah be even more exciting now than before?

His kiss conjured up a recollection of fiery lovemaking, the reawakening of a storm of passion.

This was something that shouldn't happen, yet it *was* happening, and she couldn't stop it. She wanted to keep on kissing him all night long. She had dreamed of his kisses, tried to forget them, fantasized about them, and now she was drowning in them. One of his hands was tightly knotted in her hair. The other arm was around her waist. Kate pressed closer still....

How long they stood and kissed, she never knew, for time was calculated in heartbeats and unbridled desire. Reason called dimly and was unheeded until she realized where she was headed—back into marriage with him. She didn't want that commitment, because her heart couldn't deal with the turmoil of being involved with him again.

When she pushed against Jonah, he stopped instantly, releasing her. He was breathing hard, unevenly, and Kate thought she saw a flash of anger in his enigmatic dark eyes.

As they stared at each other, battling emotions racked her, among them remorse and desire.

"That won't happen again, Kate," Jonah said.

"I could say that to you. I don't think I was the one who insisted we stay in the same house."

"We'll work it out. I'll look at the pictures on my own," he said, scooping up the baby album and scrapbooks and heading for the house.

She watched him go, his long legs covering the ground in swift strides. Suddenly she ached with need, wanting him more than she ever had before in her life. He was going to be a great father and love his son. He was a rancher now and might settle down. He must have enough money to be comfortable here, and must somehow know the ranch would sustain itself. Yet she knew Jonah through and through, and his life wouldn't be a settle-on-the-ranch-and-live-happily-ever-after story.

"I'm not going to love you again," she said softly, touching her tingling lips with her fingertips and wondering if there had ever been a time since the day they'd met when she hadn't been in love with Jonah.

And now, even if she wanted to let down her guard and go ahead and love the man, she had seen that spark of fury in his eyes when he had gathered up her scrapbooks and left.

She had committed an unforgivable sin in hiding the

knowledge of his son from him, and the accusations in his fiery gaze still singed her.

There would be no commitment from him, no turning back and forgetting their history. She suspected Jonah wouldn't forgive her for years.

She moved restlessly around the terrace, walking to the pool's edge and looking at the clear, calm water.

Finally, frustrated, angry with him and herself, still racked with guilt and burning with desire, she decided to go get her suit. Cold water and exercise would help douse the flames and calm the turmoil, and she could avoid Jonah, who was shut away somewhere inside the house, pouring over Henry's baby pictures.

Fifteen minutes later she dived into the water and swam the length of the pool. Shaking water from her face at the other end, she found Jonah standing there, watching her.

Chapter 4

Jonah watched Kate glide through the water, and his insides churned. He wanted to be in the pool with her, wanted her in his arms again. When he'd kissed her, it was as if he hadn't kissed a woman in five years—which wasn't true, but might as well have been. No woman's kisses ever mattered except Kate's. It had been heaven and hell to hold her once more.

He ached with wanting her, yet his anger made him keep a wall between them.

When she reached the end of the pool, she bobbed up in the water and he could see she was wearing a black halter top that revealed her luscious curves. His mouth went dry and he wanted to pull her up into his arms again. Instead, he clenched his fists and jammed his hands in his pockets.

"I called my folks and told them about Henry," he said, hating the huskiness in his voice and the ability she had to set him on fire just by being near him.

"I probably should have talked to them, Jonah." She bit

her lower lip. She hopped up on the side of the pool, then stood, hurrying to pick up a towel.

As she did so, he couldn't keep from staring. Glistening droplets ran down her sleek skin. She wore a black, two-piece suit that clearly revealed her figure—still great, even though she was so thin. The halter top clung to her lush breasts. Her tiny waist was bare, the black suit bottom cut low on her hips. Her stomach was flat again, looking the same as it had before childbirth. Her long bare legs took his breath, and as she crossed to a chair to pick up a towel, he couldn't help eyeing her round, sexy bottom.

"We'll see them tomorrow," he said, barely aware of what he was saying. He tried to get his mind back on what he had come out to tell her, and found it just as big an effort to tear his gaze away from her.

"We'll leave here around ten in the morning to fly home. I figured that would give you time for breakfast and to get ready."

"We'll have to be at the airport at eight, won't we?"

He shook his head, watching her skim the white towel over her body, and wanting to do that job himself. He wiped his sweating brow and knew he could use a swim in cold water, although even ice water wouldn't cool him down tonight.

"No, we don't have to be there until about half past nine. I've chartered a plane. Remember Boone Devlin?"

"Of course. No woman could forget him," she answered lightly.

"Boone has a charter service, so I called to get one of his planes. Since it's us, and I told him about Henry, he's coming himself. He wants to meet my son."

She caught her lower lip with her teeth, a slight frown creasing her brow. "I suppose he'll be angry with me, too. So I'll fly with two angry men and a child."

"Boone just wants to see Henry."

"You said Boone inherited a horse ranch. What did he do with it?"

"He hasn't done anything. I asked him, and he said that he's been too busy to deal with it yet. I know Boone. He's a procrastinator. He's going to sell his ranch when he gets around to it. He loves flying and probably gives little thought to the place. Both operations are already under fine management, anyway. Neither Boone nor I have to do anything to have it all click right along. I just happen to like ranching."

She nodded. "We'll be ready in the morning."

Jonah turned away, striding into the house and fighting the urge to stay outside with her. He wanted to go back and swim, but he knew that would be asking for trouble. Get away from the woman and forget her, he told himself. He went to the family room, sat down and pulled a baby book into his lap. Soon he was poring over it, lingering on each picture, looking at Henry when he was a year old.

As Jonah studied the pictures, he ached deep inside. He had missed all of this. "Dammit, Kate!" he snapped to the empty room, clenching his fists as he stared at a photo of Henry in a navy sailor suit. The toddler had a bib tied around his neck, chocolate cake on his face and crumbs squeezed in both tiny fists.

Jonah stared at the picture, trying to imagine the moment as if he were there, watching Henry taking fistfuls of his first birthday cake. He looked at photos of Henry in another outfit—red coveralls—where he was opening presents and wearing a paper hat. Jonah ached for what was lost, yet knew he shouldn't dwell on that, but just be thankful he had Henry now.

As he studied each picture, Jonah ran his hands over it lightly, as if by touching it he could get closer to that moment in Henry's life. By the time he finished, it was past two o'clock in the morning. He stacked the books neatly and strode to the exercise room to work out. An hour later, he plunged into the pool, swimming laps, trying to burn off hurt and anger and frustration, reminding himself constantly that Henry was part of his life now.

Tomorrow he would take his son home to meet all his relatives. When Jonah had told them about Henry, his mother had cried with joy, and his stoic, closemouthed father had bubbled with excitement—a rarity that could only be brought about by something monumental in their lives.

Jonah knew he needed to go to bed, but he didn't think sleep would come. Beneath all his excitement and turmoil and anger with Kate, desire still sizzled, and their kisses earlier had only fanned the flames. He wanted to be so bushed, he couldn't desire her or even dream about her.

When he finally went to bed, he tossed and turned. At last he threw back the sheet and walked out onto the balcony overlooking the terrace and pool. He stretched out on a chaise longue, looking through the wrought-iron railing to the pool and well-lit yard. A tall, stately live oak had lights high in the branches. As Jonah gazed at it, he realized he could hang a tire swing for Henry from one of the sturdy limbs.

Wondering what else his son might like, Jonah looked over the yard, then beyond, to the dark rolling hills. How his life had changed today! And tomorrow he would take Henry home with him.

The next morning he was in the kitchen when Clementine Blair, the cook, appeared. The diminutive woman, her brown hair streaked with gray, pulled on an apron, and when Jonah started to tell her about his guests, her brown eyes sparkled. "Your wife and your son are here! How peachy!"

"Ex-wife, Clementine," he said dryly, knowing very little about her and her views on life.

"Maybe not for long, Mr. Whitewolf."

"You can call me Jonah. And it will be for long," he added, wondering if his cook was a hopeless romantic.

As Clementine bustled around the kitchen, Marvella arrived to clean. He greeted the tall brunette who gave him a brief smile and he explained to her that there would be additional people living in the house. At the mention of ex-wife and child, she broke into a broad smile, exchanging satisfied glances with Clementine. He wondered if he had two romantics on his staff.

"A child! A little boy," Marvella said, smiling broadly as she left the kitchen.

Marvella had been gone only a minute when Kate appeared. Dressed in cutoffs and a T-shirt, she sauntered into the room and paused, smiling at Mrs. Blair.

"I just met Marvella," Kate told him.

"Good. Kate, this is Clementine Blair, my cook. Clementine, meet Kate Whitewolf."

While the women exchanged greetings, Jonah gazed at Kate. In her casual attire, she looked wonderful. Her hair was caught up on the back of her head with a clip, leaving tendrils falling around her face. She had a dewy, scrubbed look and he inhaled deeply, turning away before she saw the impact she had on him.

Over three hours later, they walked across the tarmac to a waiting plane so white it was dazzling in the sunshine. In jeans and a knit shirt, Boone Devlin stood waiting, his hands on his hips, wind blowing his thick hair.

As she approached the plane and its pilot, Kate's reluctance grew. At the same time she was aware that Henry's shyness had returned. When they'd left the ranch, he had become quiet, and she wondered if he was afraid of his first flight or afraid of the new grandparents and other relatives he would meet. Last night Jonah had given her a picture of most of his family, and she had tried to familiarize Henry with their names and faces. Now she wondered if she had just bewildered him. She also wondered how she would get through the day. Not only was she on edge around Jonah, she dreaded facing his parents. Minute by minute she was seeing what she had deprived Henry of, and that hurt even more.

Kate walked with Henry's hand in hers, Jonah on the other side of him. Looking incredibly fit and appealing, her ex-husband was dressed in a navy-and-red-plaid knit shirt and jeans, colors that emphasized Jonah's dark looks. His eagerness was as obvious as Henry's reluctance. And Kate wondered if she had hidden her dread.

As they approached the plane, she remembered Boone, who was, next to Jonah, one of the most handsome men she had ever known. And Boone knew his effect on women. He was a charmer, a rogue, but respectful of his friends and their women. In the past he had been entertaining to be around, friendly, never overstepping his bounds with her.

As she drew closer now, she could see anger in his gaze and knew, as she had expected, that Boone was furious with her for hurting his friend. She wasn't surprised, because these men were fiercely loyal to each other. That was easy to understand, since they had been in so many situations where their very survival depended on one another.

Smiling, the two friends shook hands. "Thanks for coming," Jonah said.

"Sure. I want to meet your son." He glanced over. "Hello, Kate," he said coolly, a reserved greeting that she knew was far different from what it would have been if she and Jonah were still married.

"Hi, Boone," she replied.

"Boone, this is Henry," Jonah said, dropping a hand on the boy's shoulder. "Henry, meet my friend, Mr. Devlin."

Boone shook Henry's hand and hunkered down to his level. "You're a big boy, Henry. How do you like living on the ranch?"

"I like it, sir," he answered politely.

"That's great. You look just like your daddy. So, are you ready to fly in my plane?"

"Yes, sir," Henry replied, looking beyond Boone toward the waiting plane with an apprehensive expression.

Boone stood. "If you want, Jonah, you can sit up front with me and buckle him on your lap. There's no wind and not a cloud in the sky, so we should have a smooth flight."

"Thanks, Boone," Jonah replied, glancing at Kate. She nodded, knowing she was going to have to let go and allow Henry to do all sorts of things with his father.

During the flight she rode alone, while the men and Henry were in the cockpit. As they flew north, the land below changed from green, rolling hill country covered with spreading oaks and sparkling rivers, to land splashed with mesquite, cactus and short grass. Dry riverbeds snaked across the flat ground and deep furrows cut the sides of arroyos.

After a smooth landing, as she climbed out of the plane, Kate was alone a moment with Boone, who gazed at her with that same smoldering anger. "Kate, you hurt Jonah as much as a woman can hurt a man."

"That hurt went two ways, Boone," she said, lifting her chin.

"Maybe, but keeping Henry from him—"

"I know I shouldn't have—" She broke off as Jonah and Henry climbed out of the plane and joined them.

"Thanks, Boone," Jonah said, shaking hands again.

"Thank you, Mr. Devlin," Henry said, enthusiasm lacing his childish voice. His shyness had vanished. "That was a cool ride!"

Boone laughed. "Anytime, Henry. Just get your dad to call me."

As they walked away, Henry turned to wave again at Boone.

Jonah got a cab from the airport to his parents' house. The moment she stepped out of the taxi, Kate's apprehension grew. Along with trepidation, recollections of better times bombarded her. She looked at the single-story, red-brick-and-frame house that held happy memories. Three mulberry trees shaded a green yard bordered with beds of bright pink and purple crepe myrtle, multicolored zinnias and riotous red petunias. Pots of flowers hung on the shady, inviting porch.

As Jonah opened the cab door for her, Kate took a deep breath. She dreaded the next few minutes and wondered if she would have to face the wrath of Jonah's entire family.

Stepping out of the cab, she smoothed the blue denim skirt of her sundress. She had worn a dress and sandals and let her hair fall loose. Thin golden bangles clinked on her arm, but she was barely aware of them.

Jonah rang the doorbell and then opened the door. ''Mom! Dad!'' he called.

They were there instantly—two tall, brown-skinned people with raven hair and that hawkish nose that both Jonah and Henry had inherited. The welcoming smiles on their faces took away a little of Kate's chilling dread. Neighbor Whitewolf was a powerful man with strong, well-shaped hands. Kate knew he had a large dental practice and enjoyed his work. Maggie Whitewolf was slender, striking, with large brown eyes and straight black hair. As she faced them, Kate was overwhelmed with emotion. She had missed seeing his parents, and memories of them were tied to happy times with Jonah.

While Jonah made introductions, they hugged Jonah and Henry, and when Kate looked into Maggie Whitewolf's warm brown eyes, the older woman held out her arms. ''Kate!'' she exclaimed, and hugged her tightly.

Kate could have fainted with relief. ''Forgive me, Maggie,'' she whispered as she hugged Jonah's mother.

''You're forgiven, Kate,'' she replied quietly. ''He's here now and that's what's important. I know you did what you had to do.''

Kate hugged Maggie again. "Thanks," she said, deeply grateful. She had always liked Jonah's mother, but never as much as she did at this moment.

Then she turned as Neighbor Whitewolf held out his arms to hug her. "Kate, it's good to see you. What a fine boy!"

She felt a tight knot in her throat, remembering too many homecomings when she and Jonah had been married, happy moments, warm and fuzzy times with his family. "Thank you," she whispered, not trusting her voice and fighting back tears over what could have been.

"Where's the rest of the family?" Jonah asked, looking around.

"They're coming in about thirty minutes," Maggie said. "We wanted to get to know Henry a little first. And let him see the house." She looked at her grandson. "Come on, Henry, we'll show you around and you can play with some toys that were your father's," she said. She motioned to Jonah and Kate. "There are cookies and drinks in the kitchen. Help yourself. The whole family will be here for lunch."

Enticing smells filled the house, and Kate walked with Jonah to the kitchen, more memories of happy times assailing her. She rubbed her brow. Everywhere she turned there were wonderful recollections, or Jonah himself, fanning the flames of an already fiery desire. They hadn't been together twenty-four hours yet, and she was already having difficulty coping.

When they entered the kitchen, she crossed the room to sit at the kitchen table. Ceiling fans slowly turned in the oversize kitchen, which was filled with simmering pots, covered dishes, pitchers of cold drinks. Everything about her surroundings was just like old times, except the most important thing of all.

Kate had lost all appetite, but watched as Jonah poured iced tea for both of them and sat across from her. "I'd go see what the folks are doing, but I know they want to get to know Henry, and in a few minutes he'll have so many new relatives around that his head will spin. Did you show him the picture and tell him about all of us?''

"Yes, I did," she said. "He can't keep from liking your family and his cousins. Jonah, your mom is her usual wonderful self."

"I knew she would forgive you," he said easily, running his index finger slowly over the rim of his glass. "Mom picks up and goes on, and she's so happy to have Henry. You'd think she didn't have a single grandchild, instead of having twelve of them now."

"Henry will love your parents."

"He's a quiet little boy, Kate."

"He's shy and he hasn't played with a lot of other children or been away from me very much. He'll probably come out of that some now that you're with him."

"Maybe so," Jonah said.

They heard a car and seconds later the back door burst open, and three of Henry's cousins poured into the room, throwing themselves at Jonah. In a few more minutes the house was filled with adults and children, and Kate knew any worries she'd had about Henry being overwhelmed or feeling shy were for naught. There were enough little boys about that Henry was overjoyed, playing with them as happily as if he had known them for years. When the women got lunch on the table, Kate looked out the kitchen window to see Henry playing ball with his cousins.

"When he gets to know us, I hope you'll let him come stay for a few days at a time," Maggie said as she picked up a bowl of potato salad to place it on the table.

"I think he'd love that," Kate replied. "Just let me know when you want him. It looks to me as if he'll want to come visit."

"I'm sorry about your parents, Kate."

"Thanks," she replied, looking into Maggie's brown eyes and wishing for something she knew she couldn't have.

During lunch, one of Jonah's brothers related a funny incident, and as everyone laughed, Kate looked at Jonah and her breath caught. It was the first real laughter she'd seen from him since their encounter yesterday, and it made him doubly appealing. His white teeth flashed and crinkles appeared in his cheeks. If only... The words hit her like a blow to her stomach. If only things were different! She tried to slam the door on that line of thinking. Then Jonah's gaze met hers and she looked away quickly, wondering how much her own eyes revealed her feelings.

It was late in the afternoon before they pulled away from the house in a large pickup of Jonah's. His possessions were loaded and tied down in the bed of the truck. By the time they reached the city limits, Henry was asleep in the back seat.

"You have a wonderful family," Kate said. In the close quarters of the front seat, she was only a few feet from Jonah and watched him as he drove. The day had been filled with moments of longing, and now to sit with him so close, she had to fight the urge to touch him.

"They are great. Henry seemed to fit right in."

"Yes, he did," Kate replied. "He's losing his shyness quickly. Or maybe he just feels at home with your family."

"They're his family, too, Kate. And kids are kids. Especially boys. Give 'em a ball to play with and they're happy."

Under former circumstances, it would have been a wonderful day, and she would have been relaxed, happy, eager to go home and go to bed with her exciting husband. Instead, she was on edge, fighting an attraction that wouldn't diminish. Every minute with him added to her need.

Why not toss aside her worries about his lifestyle and see if she could get him back? She was startled by the thought that had popped into her head. Immediately, she

rejected it. She thought it would take years—if not a lifetime—to get him to forgive her. And she really didn't expect him to stay on the ranch more than six months. If he
wasn't living life on the edge, he would get restless and
bored. Yet if she wasn't careful, she would be more deeply
in love with him than ever.

Kate studied his profile, doubly familiar because Henry
looked so much like him. Only Henry had childish features
and a child's jaw. Jonah's firm jaw and prominent cheekbones were those of a man, masculine and sexy. She looked
at his mouth, his full lower lip, and her insides tightened.
Her gaze dropped down over his bulging biceps, his smooth
brown skin, the jeans that were tight on muscled thighs.

When she looked up, her gaze met his before he turned
his attention back to the road. Her face flushed with heat
at being caught so blatantly studying him.

"You're not dating anyone?" he asked abruptly.

"No, I'm not. I never have."

"Not in five years, Kate?"

"I was pregnant most of the first year, had a new baby
the second one and then two sick parents after that. I really
didn't want to date. What about you, Jonah? Is there another woman in your life now?" she asked, trying to sound
casual and knowing she shouldn't care—not after five years
away from him. But in spite of reason, of telling herself
that she had to let go, and imagining that he had remarried,
at this moment she cared and couldn't keep from feeling a
rush of satisfaction when he shook his head.

"Nope. There's no one in my life."

"That makes us even more vulnerable to another hurt,
since we're living in the same house."

"I'll manage, and I'm sure you will, too," he said, a
muscle working in his jaw, and she knew he was enveloped
by his smoldering anger.

"Your mother and sisters-in-law are forgiving."

"They can probably see things more from your point of

view than my brothers, who probably see Henry's birth the way I do.''

"They were coolly polite and so was your father, but it doesn't matter, because they were all wonderful to Henry.''

"You know how my family loves kids and loves family. They're happiest when we're all together.''

"Do they mind seeing you move farther away?''

"They're accustomed to my being away—out of the country a lot of the time. And they're thrilled about the ranch. I want to have Mom and Dad come visit soon.''

"Anytime, Jonah. Henry loved being with them. I think he's missed my parents.'' She thought about all the nieces and nephews she'd met. "Your family is growing.''

"By leaps and bounds,'' he answered.

"Now, tomorrow, when I go to my new job, you're planning to keep Henry with you?''

"That's right. We need to hire a nanny for part of the time. I'll pay for one.''

"When I start work, I can share the expense.''

He waved his hand. "No. I'll do that. What hours will you work?''

"Fortunately, they have flex time. I can work longer four days a week if I want, and then take off Fridays. I'd like to see how that works,'' she said.

They discussed her job and then talked about Henry for a while. Eventually their conversation drifted on to various other topics, making the ride home seem brief. Jonah carried Henry inside and put him to bed, while Kate changed into her suit and went for a swim, then returned to her room.

She pulled on her cutoffs and a T-shirt and went to the kitchen to get a cold drink. When she looked outside, she saw Jonah swimming laps in the pool, and realized he had waited until she finished her swim before he got into the pool. She inhaled deeply, knowing he was right. They should avoid each other, yet how difficult it was to do!

As she watched him, he climbed out of the pool and picked up his towel. Her gaze raked over his muscled body and her pulse galloped. She turned away swiftly and hurried to her room. He hadn't chosen to join her in a swim, and she shouldn't hang around downstairs where he'd have to encounter her now.

In her room, she ran her hand across her forehead. What a day it had been! Yet in some ways she was glad it was over and Jonah's family had met her son. Henry needed that big family, with all its love and laughter. Jonah's parents would be wonderful for him.

Far into the night, Kate tried to read. She had her clothes laid out for the coming day—her first day on her new job. She was excited about the prospect, but its importance had diminished over the weekend. She sat on the balcony of her room and gazed at the yard and the land beyond it.

She fell asleep in a chair, and later when she moved to her bed, noticed the lights still blazed on the grounds surrounding the house. "You don't worry about the light bill anymore," she said softly, remembering how careful Jonah used to be, rigging timers on the outside lights and switching lights off when he left a room.

She stretched out in bed in the darkness, cognizant of the fact that she was once again under the same roof as Jonah, and from the moment of their encounter yesterday, her life had changed again forever.

The night was clear and dark as the big truck's engine broke the silence, and brakes hissed when the rig slowed and stopped.

A man hopped out of the cab of the empty truck and pulled wire cutters from his pocket. With decisive snips he sliced through the barbed wire and then climbed back into the cattle truck, revved the motor and rammed the fence post, toppling it. With a glance in the rearview mirror, he saw that the pickup was following him. How easy it all was! The only bad thing was he wouldn't be there to see their faces when they found out what had happened.

He had seen the rancher who lived here.

Jonah Whitewolf was in the house tonight. He and his brat and his beautiful wife. Arrogant, taking possession just as if he had earned his inheritance. Retired Special Forces. A lot of good all his fancy training would do him in this situation.

The man wiped his sweating brow. He was a pro at this now, he thought. They had practiced, starting up north and working their way down across Texas. The fools who worked for him had no idea what his true motive was. They thought he was doing it for the same reason they were— for the money. The money was icing on the cake, but that wasn't the real reason.

As he bounced over the rough ground, the man glanced around him. The night was perfect because of the darkness and the clouds that hid the sliver of a moon.

Motioning to his cohorts by waving his arm out the window, he led the way across open pastures. When he encountered another fence, he simply laughed and revved the motor, bursting through it and flattening it. The barbs wouldn't penetrate his thick tires. He knew exactly where to go, not caring that the big truck's engine roared and the trailer clanked and jangled with each rut and bump. There was no one around to see or hear him. Those cowboys didn't patrol the ranch—there had never been a need to guard it before tonight. Complacency was in his favor.

When he spotted the cattle, he grinned, and anticipation built in him. Everything was just as he had planned. While the rancher slept, the terror would begin.

The man slowed and stopped, cutting the motor and climbing out to give directions. He slid his hand over a scabbard fastened to his belt, reassuring himself that the knife was there.

Revenge was exquisite! Only one disappointment—the man who had caused all this was no longer alive to see it.

Monday morning when Kate went down to the kitchen, Jonah was already there with glasses of orange juice and slices of ham. The enticing smells of hot coffee and baking biscuits made her mouth water, but they weren't as tempting as Jonah. He stood at the stove, scrambling eggs. In jeans and a black T-shirt, he was sexy and appealing and looked as if he had had a long night's sleep, far different from her own experience.

"Good morning," he said. His smoldering gaze slid over her and she was suddenly self-conscious, hoping she looked all right in her lightweight, navy cotton suit.

"You look great," he said gruffly, and she gazed into his eyes. Blatant desire burned like a bonfire in their brown depths, giving her an additional jolt.

"Thank you," she said, wanting to add, "You do, too," but knowing she shouldn't. How many mornings in their marriage had she come into the kitchen to find him already cooking breakfast? And how many of those times had they made love right then or gone directly back to bed?

She took a deep breath, trying to bank memories that she had kept shut away for the past five years.

"What would you like for breakfast? Help yourself, and I'll have scrambled eggs in one more minute," he said.

"Thanks, Jonah," she replied, pouring a glass of orange juice. "When I get to work today, I'll call with my new number—just as soon as I have it."

He put down the spoon and turned, picking up a small blue cellular phone. "Here's an extra phone that I kept in the truck. You take it, since you don't have one."

"Thank you," she said, quietly pocketing the phone, knowing he would probably use it far more than she. She glanced out the kitchen window to see a barrel-chested cowboy striding purposefully toward the house. His gray

Western hat saw squarely on his head. "Here comes someone," she said.

"That's my foreman," Jonah said when he'd crossed the
room to look outside. "You need to meet him. From the
frown on his face, I'd guess there's trouble."

Chapter 5

Jonah opened the back door and ushered his foreman inside. "Kate, this is Scott Adamson. Scott, this is my ex-wife, Kate Whitewolf."

"How do you do," the cowboy said politely, removing his hat and running his fingers through his thick red hair.

"Sit down and have breakfast with us," Jonah offered, and minutes later all three of them were seated around the table with cups of steaming coffee, plates of hot biscuits and jelly, and scrambled eggs.

"We've had trouble," Scott announced abruptly. "We had rustlers last night."

"What did they take?" Jonah asked.

"A lot of cattle—all of the herd in the far south pasture are gone."

Jonah stood. "I'll call the Piedras County sheriff and then I need to phone my insurance adjuster."

"Sheriff Dakota Gallen's a decent man," Scott said. "You'll like him."

"As soon as I talk to him, I'll go look at the scene."

"I'll drive back up here and you can follow me. I've checked, and our equipment is intact."

"That may be because of the high-powered alarms around the barn and the house," Jonah said as he crossed the kitchen to pick up the phone and call the sheriff.

"Are you from these parts, ma'am?" Scott asked Kate, and she shook her head.

"Not at all. I'm from North Carolina. This is the first time I've been to Texas. I start a new job this morning in San Antonio."

"I hope you like it here."

"I thought rustling was something out of the last century," she said to the freckled foreman. She noticed his thick, blunt fingers, the freckles covering the back of his hands and wrists as he picked up his cup of coffee. Even though the weather was hot, he wore a long-sleeved blue shirt, and she guessed he tried to protect his skin from the sun.

"Rustling still happens. People can make a lot of money by taking someone else's livestock."

Jonah returned to the table. "The sheriff is on his way."

"If you'll excuse me," Kate said, standing, "I have to get to town. You're still all right with taking care of Henry?" she asked Jonah.

"Sure. Both Clementine and Marvella will arrive any minute now, and I'll be here all day and take him with me most of the time. Excuse us, Scott."

"I need to go, too. It was nice to meet you, ma'am," the foreman said, standing as she left.

After seeing Scott out, Jonah caught up with Kate and walked down the hall beside her, toward the stairs.

"You have a cell phone and you have my number, so you can call me anytime about Henry. Don't worry about him, Kate. I'll take good care of him."

"I know you will," she said, stopping at the foot of the stairs. Jonah faced her and straightened her collar, his fingers brushing her throat lightly. She met his dark-eyed gaze and wondered what he was thinking, unable to tell anything from his impassive expression.

"Good luck today with your job," he said.

"Thanks," she replied, thinking how polite they were being and wondering what undercurrents flowed around them. She suspected the only reason he was chatting with her was to reassure her about leaving Henry in his care.

"How late does he sleep?"

She glanced at her watch. "You're used to getting up very early compared to him. He'll wake up about eight o'clock."

Jonah nodded and strode away, disappearing back into the kitchen, where she heard his boots scrape the oak flooring. She went up to her room to get her purse and look at herself one more time, and then left the ranch.

When Clementine Blair arrived, Jonah returned to the kitchen. He waited until Marvella arrived to clean so he could talk to both women at once. When Marvella entered the kitchen, he addressed them. "Clementine, I know you aren't a nanny, and I've contacted an agency about hiring one. But this morning I need to leave Jonah here for a short time while I drive out on the ranch."

"That's fine, Mr. Whitewolf," Clementine replied instantly. Marvella nodded.

"Call me Jonah," he insisted, wondering how many times he was going to have to tell her, or if she would forever address him formally. "I won't be gone long."

"Don't you worry one minute. I took care of that precious baby, Jessie, when the Frateses were at the ranch, and I miss the child although I'm happy she has a new home now. I miss having a little one around, and it's super news that your son is with us."

"It's very super," Jonah agreed. "Okay, thanks. I have to meet the sheriff. We had rustlers last night."

"I heard," she said, and he marveled at how fast word

traveled around the ranch. Jonah suspected it reached surrounding areas and Stallion Pass just as swiftly.

"Two ranches a lot farther north have been robbed,"
Marvella added.

"Is that right?" Jonah gazed beyond them, through the
window at the yard. "When I decided to move here, I
thought it would be peaceful and quiet."

"It usually is," Marvella said.

"You both have my cell phone number, and be sure to
keep the alarm on when I'm gone," he said.

"I always keep that alarm on," Clementine replied, putting butter in the refrigerator and closing up a jam jar to
put it away.

"I better go," Jonah said. A short time later, he strode
outside to his truck. The sunny morning and deep blue
Texas sky did little to lift his spirits. He was angry that his
cattle had been stolen on his first week at the ranch.

When Scott Adamson drove past him, Jonah pulled in
behind Scott's shiny red pickup, following him across the
ranch until they reached the area where the rustlers had
struck.

Jonah climbed out and looked at smashed fences, high
grass beaten down where truck tracks cut across the green
pasture. "They didn't try to hide their tracks."

"They drove them from this pasture over to the loading
pens, got them loaded up in trucks or a big cattle truck."

"Let's drive there and look," Jonah said and climbed
back in his car to follow Scott to the pasture with the pens.

When he climbed out of the pickup this time, Scott hurried toward him. "That isn't all," Scott said. "I didn't want
to talk about it over breakfast and in front of your woman."

For an instant Jonah was taken out of his surroundings,
forgetting anger or worry about the theft. Your woman.
Kate hadn't been his woman for a long time now. The
statement startled him and gave him a pang that he

shrugged away. She wasn't ever going to be his woman again and he damned well better remember that.

Then he recalled what else Scott had said. "What else happened?" Jonah asked, a sense of dread gripping him.

The foreman pointed his long arm and index finger. "Over there. You have cattle with their throats cut."

"Oh, damn. That changes the crime," Jonah said, walking toward the scattered carcasses of dead animals.

"Sure as hell does," Scott drawled. "After the lawmen are finished, I'll get some of the boys and we'll take care of these carcasses." At the sound of an engine, he glanced around. "Here comes the sheriff."

Jonah waited with his hands splayed on his waist, watching the official, shiny black car driven by the Piedras County sheriff bounce over rough ground, slow and stop. A tall, rugged-appearing man climbed out of the car and slammed the door. On the passenger side, another uniformed man stepped out of the car.

While Jonah's hand was enveloped in the strong grip of the Piedras County sheriff, Jonah looked into assessing gray eyes. Without a word being said, Jonah liked the man. When the sheriff spoke, his voice was a deep bass.

"'Morning. I'm Dakota Gallen, and I've been wanting to meet Piedras County's newest resident. I'm sorry you're getting this welcome."

"Thanks." Next Jonah met Deputy Terry Haggard whose baby face and big, blue eyes made Jonah feel like an old-timer.

"When I called you, I didn't know about the slaughtered animals," Jonah said, leading the way to the carcasses of the slain cattle.

Gallen whistled. "This is a new twist—and one I don't like. There have been cattle rustlers at work north of here, but never any butchered animals. There are a lot of dead animals here. We've got something else on our hands now. You wouldn't think you've been in these parts long enough for anyone to have a grudge against you,'' Sheriff Gallen said, squinting his eyes and studying Jonah who shrugged.

Gallen circled the slaughtered animals and Jonah watched him. ''Do you think it was a cult thing?''

Gallen shook his head. ''Nope, because usually if it's a cult, they take organs. These animals just had their throats cut.''

''So someone doesn't like me and I've been here less than forty-eight hours.''

Beneath his broad-brimmed black Western hat, Gallen looked at him and Jonah gazed back, wondering what was running through the sheriff's mind.

''Could be a lot of things. It could be you, and someone who has a grudge followed you here. Could be someone who works for you that has stirred up the hate. Could be the ranch. Could be just killing for the sake of killing. Could be a warning of things to come in the county.''

''I hope it's not that.''

''Could be John Frates, although since he's deceased, that isn't too likely,'' Gallen continued. ''But it's possible. What about your ex-wife? Has she got any enemies?''

Surprised that the sheriff knew about Kate, Jonah shook his head. ''I don't think that's likely at all.''

''No boyfriends that would be riled up that she's staying with you?''

''You know a hell of a lot about my life,'' Jonah remarked, thinking it was not so different here from where he grew up. ''No, she said there aren't any boyfriends.''

Gallen shrugged broad shoulders. ''I like to know the people in my county, and news gets around in these parts faster than a wildfire in a gale.''

''If that's the case, you ought to get some clues soon about who's rustling cattle.''

Gallen became silent, slowly combing the ground around the carcasses and then around the smashed fences for any telltale signs. ''They've had a rash of rustlings farther north of here,'' Gallen said. ''There's been a professional gang in West Texas and we're beginning to wonder if they've just moved down this way. But there's never been any slaughtered cattle.''

''No leads as to who they are?''

The sheriff shook his head. ''Nope. They're getting bolder and more careless, though, so I expect them to make a mistake soon.'' He squinted his eyes and studied Jonah. ''I heard you're ex-military. Special Forces.''

''That's right,'' Jonah replied, becoming amused. ''Is there anything about me that you don't know?''

''I'm sure there is. I'm glad to know about Special Forces.''

''I'll be happy to help if I can.''

''I'm glad to hear that, too. Right now, just keep your eyes and ears open.''

''I'm new to this area, but Scott grew up here.''

''Both of you, just let us know if anything unusual occurs or you see any strangers. Those rustlings up north, they've been stealing equipment, too—at least last night you didn't have equipment stolen as well as cattle.''

''This ranch has a sophisticated alarm system,'' Jonah said.

''That's fine. We don't know if these are done by the same people, are copycat crimes or different groups. One rustling north of here had a different MO. The perp went into the house while the family was asleep at night. They disengaged the alarm. Family slept through the whole thing. I don't think anyone will come in on you while you're sleeping. But I wanted to warn you. If they have any sense at all, they won't try to slip up on an ex-Special Forces guy, but some of these perps are dumber than a post.''

''Sheriff Gallen, I don't think the ones you're dealing with here are so dumb. There's nothing here except tire tracks.''

"Which we'll try to trace," Sheriff Gallen said, shaking his head. "Call me Dakota. And can I call you Jonah?"

"Sure. You sound as if you think we're going to get to know each other better."

"I like to know everyone in my county. Hopefully, this is the only time I'll see you on business—or maybe again when we catch the rustlers."

Nodding, Jonah thought about Henry and Kate, Clementine and Marvella, the woman who kept the ranch house clean. There were two gardeners who tended the yard and they had worked for John Frates's father before they'd worked for the son. The same for the cook and the maid. Both had been with the family for years, so he trusted them, but he also wanted them to be safe.

"One man couldn't do this, get away so quickly and just vanish," the sheriff stated grimly, frowning as he squatted down to look closely at a track.

Walking back to his pickup, Jonah called home to check on Henry, who was eating his breakfast. Before he talked to his son, he promised Clementine he would be home within the hour. Soon Scott returned to work, but Jonah hung around, watching the deputy and sheriff search for anything left behind by the culprits. Finally the two lawmen told him goodbye, and Jonah climbed into his truck to return home.

As he drove back to one of the rough dirt roads that crossed the ranch, he glanced into the rearview mirror at the smashed fence and had an uneasy feeling. The slaughter of cattle had been evil and senseless. Sheriff Gallen had criminals on his hands more dangerous than garden-variety rustlers. It hadn't just been a robbery. The slain animals had to have been a message of some sort. A warning, revenge, pure hate... Jonah didn't know which it was, but he did know the culprits had nothing to gain by killing the cattle.

He was worried, because he wanted to be certain that Henry and Kate were safe.

Stop brooding about Kate, he told himself. "Yeah, right," he said aloud. She was causing him endless torment and almost total sleeplessness, and she hadn't been here two days yet.

He swore under his breath, thinking about her in town at her new job. She had looked luscious this morning—cool, more professional appearing than usual—and his pulse had revved the moment she'd appeared in the kitchen doorway.

And he did not want to have that reaction to her. He was angry with her, a simmering ire that flared with each reminder of how much he had missed of Henry's life and how unnecessary it had been. Yet now he was making up for the lost years. Henry was a delight, and Jonah was thankful to have his son living with him. He had to let go of his animosity toward Kate, he knew.

After his divorce he had decided that anger over the past was senseless. At that time he'd had to let go and get on with life, and he knew he needed to do that again now. Forgive Kate and forget about the past. Henry was here and that was what mattered, and if he had to remind himself of. that fact every day, he would, Jonah decided.

He made a mental list to check the alarms again, talk to the men about the rustlers and what the sheriff had told him, and caution Kate and the help about what had happened.

He had looked at his calendar this morning, still amazed by the changes in his life. He had an appointment with his accountant tomorrow morning, followed by an appointment the next morning with the financial planner, and after that a meeting with the stockbroker John Frates had used. Tad Chaya was the manager who kept books and handled the financial workings of the ranch. Jonah knew he didn't need to do much more than keep an eye on his investments, but he liked ranching and he wanted to be involved in it.

And how was he going to manage living under the same roof with Kate? Every time they were in the same room, sparks flew and both of them felt the electricity.

He wasn't getting into that trap again. And he knew that neither was she. Let the sparks fly—there would be no fires from them. During the week she would be gone all day, every day, until Friday. They could manage to keep apart in the evenings.

He gripped the steering wheel and swore. Stop thinking about her constantly!

On the way home, he passed Scott Anderson in his pickup, headed the opposite direction. They paused beside each other and rolled down their windows. "The sheriff's gone," Jonah said. "He said he would let us know if he gets any leads. I'm going to call the insurance man and I'll probably have to go back out there with him."

"Want me to wait to repair the fences?"

"No. Go ahead and start," Jonah said. "I think Sheriff Gallen will be finished with his investigation by the time you gather up the men and get the materials out there."

"Gallen's okay. If anyone can catch the rustlers, he can. Did he tell you he was in the Air Force? Special Operations?"

"No, he didn't."

"He's closemouthed about it, but Piedras County is lucky to have him for a sheriff."

Jonah nodded, thinking about the tall lawman, who had been all business.

"Remind me to tell you all about Piedras County's sheriff some day," Scott said with a grin.

"I'll do that."

"See you later, Jonah." The foreman drove away.

Jonah headed on home, thinking about Dakota Gallen. Special Ops. And now sheriff of Piedras County. Why would someone from Special Ops be buried out here in the boonies, working as a sheriff?

He shrugged aside the question, his thoughts returning to the slaughtered cattle. Someone was sending an unpleasant message. Who was it and why? What lengths would he go to, to get that message across?

A little over an hour after she left the ranch, Kate turned into the parking lot of her new office building, a three-story redbrick building that was neatly landscaped. She met fellow workers and was shown to her new office, a small room with windows facing south. It held a broad oak desk and a long table, wooden filing cabinets, two upholstered chairs and a drawing board. A new computer sat on one corner of the desk.

Within the hour she was poring over projects to familiarize herself with the company's clients.

While she worked, she kept glancing at the clock, wondering about Henry and how he was getting along with Jonah, yet knowing both were probably having a wonderful time.

Unaccustomed to being away from her son, she called several times during the day, getting Jonah every time. He would pass the phone to Henry, who jabbered excitedly about riding in a truck with his dad and riding on a horse with him. Late in the afternoon when she called, Jonah answered yet again.

"I don't think I'm missed," she said, "but I miss him. I'm not used to being separated from him all day. He sounds as if he's having a wonderful time."

"He seems to be," Jonah said, and his deep voice stirred too many memories of hours spent on the phone talking to him in the past when they were dating. Everywhere she turned, she was doing something that brought back memories of similar times with Jonah, and she realized there was little they had done together that she had forgotten.

"Right now we're in the pool."

"He's having such a super time, he won't even want to talk to me," she said. "We can talk when I get home."

"He wants to talk. Here he is."

"Mom! I can swim!" Henry exclaimed, and she could hear the excitement in his voice.

"That's wonderful! You learned to swim today?" she asked, wanting to pack up and get home to be with him, yet knowing Henry was receiving the best of care.

"Yes. I'll show you. When are you coming home?"

"In an hour I'll leave here, but it will be more than another hour before I get home," she said.

"Here's Daddy," Henry said, and he was gone. *Daddy. Jonah.* The words conjured up an image of the man, and she longed to be with the two of them.

"He thinks he can swim," she said when Jonah spoke.

"He can. You'll be surprised. He's not afraid to put his head underwater, and it was simple to show him a few strokes."

She sighed. "He didn't have a chance to learn when we were in North Carolina. I intended to sign him up for swimming lessons, but I would have had to go with him and I couldn't."

"It doesn't matter now," Jonah said. "He'll give you a demo when you get home."

"That's wonderful, Jonah, because now I won't have to worry so much about Henry being around the pool."

"I have an alarm I can set when we're out of the pool, one that will go off if anyone falls in. But now he can take care of himself enough to swim to the edge and get out."

"That's great, and he's so proud of himself." There was a pause, and she felt tension grow between them. "I'll be home in a couple of hours."

"Bye, Kate." The phone clicked and he was gone. She bit her lip and rubbed her temple as she replaced the receiver. How many times was she going to regret her past actions in keeping Henry from Jonah, who was proving to be a wonderful father for his son?

As she was closing up for the day, the account executive in the neighboring office, Mason Grant, paused at her door. He had shed his suit coat and removed his tie, and his white shirt was open at the throat. Thick brown hair curled over his forehead and he smiled at her as he leaned against the doorjamb. "Get through your first day all right?"

"Yes. I love it here, and the projects look wonderful. I'm just trying to learn about the clients I've been assigned."

"You're new to San Antonio, aren't you?"

"Yes," she replied, closing a bottom drawer and shutting down her computer.

"Come to dinner with me, and I'll show you around the Riverwalk."

She looked up at him in surprise. "Thank you, Mason, but I need to go home." She answered without having to give his offer any thought. "I'm staying with my ex-husband."

"Whoops, I didn't know that," Mason said.

"We're divorced, but this is my first day away from my son in a long time. Thank you so much, anyway."

At the mention of Jonah, Mason straightened up. "Okay. See you tomorrow," he said lightly. She stared after him when he left.

She could have gone out with him, and Jonah wouldn't have cared. She suspected he would have been happier, because he would have had Henry to himself longer. Why had she turned down Mason, who was a friendly and pleasant colleague? She had no obligation to Jonah. Far from it. He wouldn't care if she went out every night and married again in a few months. Except a marriage would complicate sharing Henry. He would care about that, but her dating? Never.

She hadn't even paused to think about the dinner offer.

She knew she didn't want to go out with Mason; she wanted to get back to the ranch to Henry. And was it just Henry she wanted so badly to see, or Jonah, too? She rubbed her forehead again. Was she still in love with him? Too in love to think of going out with anyone else?

Get up and go tell Mason that you'll go out with him. Go out and forget Jonah! That's what she should do, but she didn't want to at all. Why was she tied in knots over a man who was consumed with anger toward her?

She stood, still telling herself to march into Mason's office, accept the date and try to forget Jonah for an hour or two. Yet she couldn't. And if she went out to dinner, all she would do was think about Henry and Jonah and want to be back at the ranch.

Someday Jonah would meet someone, and when he did, he wouldn't hesitate to go out. She was certain he would marry again and he wouldn't look back, and she should try to get over him completely. And spending most of her time in close proximity to him wasn't going to help.

None of her logical arguments were to any avail. She picked up her purse and car keys and left the office, turning to look at it and feeling thankful for the job. With no rent to pay, she was going to be able to save a lot. Save a lot and fall more in love than ever with him—if she had ever been out of love with him even when she'd walked out on him.

When she reached the ranch and climbed out of the car, Henry came running, throwing his arms around her as she picked him up. She hugged him eagerly, glad to be home with him.

Jonah followed Henry outside and stood on the top step while he watched her. Father and son were in T-shirts and jeans, looking fresh after all that swimming. Her son was adorable, his father appealing. Henry smelled clean, and Jonah set her pulse racing the minute she saw him.

''Tonight we're going to a rodeo!'' Henry exclaimed in his high, childish voice. ''You'll go, too, won't you?''

She looked beyond him at Jonah, who stood in silence, and she guessed that he didn't want her to accept Henry's invitation.

Henry caught her chin with his small fingers and turned her face toward him. ''Please go! Will you?''

''Yes, I will,'' she said, wanting to share the experience of her son's first rodeo and wanting to avoid sitting home by herself, thinking about Jonah and Henry while they were gone.

''Then if that's the case, we'll eat soon,'' Jonah said. ''It's a small rodeo about thirty miles from here, but Henry's never been to one.''

''I want you to see me swim!'' Henry exclaimed. ''I can jump in and swim to the side all by myself!''

''You can?''

''You have time for a swim before dinner,'' Jonah said. ''I told Clementine to go, that I'd grill burgers.''

''Fine. Let's get our swimsuits on, Henry, and I'll watch you,'' Kate said, wondering what Jonah was going to do while they swam. Her pulse raced, and she tried to ignore him as well as her rapid heartbeat while she followed Henry into the house.

She showered quickly and changed into her black swimsuit, letting down her hair and grabbing a towel. When she walked out of the house onto the terrace, her heart missed a beat. Jonah was sitting on a chair at the side of the pool, talking to Henry while the boy paddled around in the water.

Suddenly Kate was conscious of how little her swimsuit covered.

''Mom!'' Henry cried, and when Jonah turned to watch her approach, every nerve in her body tingled.

She dropped her towel on a chair and jumped into the water, swimming close to Henry and finding the cold water delightful on such a hot day. She glanced at Jonah to discover his heated dark gaze riveted on her.

"Mom, let me show you how I can jump in!" Henry exclaimed, scrambling out of the pool. She moved to one side and watched as he took two quick steps and jumped, landing with a splash and sinking under the water. He bobbed up and paddled to the side, and she clapped her hands, a thrill coursing through her.

"That's wonderful, Henry! You can swim now!" She turned to Jonah. "It truly is marvelous!" she exclaimed with enthusiasm. "I've worried so much about him when he's been around water."

"Yeah," Jonah answered gruffly. He got up abruptly and left them, jamming his fists into his pockets as he strode into the house. She stared after him, her zeal dampened. In her happiness over Henry being able to swim, she had forgotten the circumstances.

"Watch me!" Henry piped in his high-pitched voice, and she turned back to her son, refusing to let Jonah's anger diminish her joy over Henry's accomplishment.

She paddled around the pool with Henry until Jonah came out to light the grill, and then she told Henry they should get out and dress for dinner. As he climbed out of the pool and began to dry off, she swam one quick lap, watching until Jonah went back inside before she came up out of the pool and grabbed up her towel.

All three of them ate together, their conversation centering on Henry, who basked in the undivided attention of the two most important adults in his life. Kate knew he had been a bit shortchanged the past few years, because she had been so busy caring for her parents.

As Henry chattered, both she and Jonah responded, seeming to hang on Henry's every word. Yet she was aware that they avoided conversing with each other. To her relief, Henry didn't seem to notice anything awry.

The minute they finished eating, Jonah glanced at his

watch. "We need to get going if we're to arrive there in time for the opening."

They carried the dishes inside and Jonah took Henry's hand. "I'll get him dressed to go."

Caught between dreading the evening and anticipating it, Kate nodded, hurrying to her room to dress in a red T-shirt and jeans, slipping her feet into a pair of old loafers. She belted the jeans and fixed her hair, letting it hang down her back in one long, thick braid. Feeling fluttery and excited, knowing she should be staying home and letting them go without her, she dabbed on perfume and put on a bracelet with silver charms. Next, she fastened dangling silver earrings in her ears. Already, tendrils of her naturally curly hair were springing free from the braid, and she gave up trying to control it. Swiftly, she applied blush and lipstick, and then left to find Henry. He was downstairs with Jonah and he wore a red shirt and jeans.

"Ready?" Jonah asked, eyeing her with one brow arched. He had changed into a long-sleeved, plaid Western shirt, and jeans that hugged his slim hips.

She nodded and took Henry's hand. He slipped away and skipped ahead of them, babbling about what he and Jonah had done during the day.

"He calls you Dad so easily," she said.

"I'm glad," Jonah replied tersely, and she fell silent, thinking he didn't want to talk to her.

All the way to the rodeo Henry chattered, and soon they were seated outdoors on bleachers, with Henry in the middle. Jonah explained the rodeo to him and within minutes the grand parade began.

Kate looked at her son, whose eyes sparkled. He leaned forward eagerly, watching everything and asking Jonah questions. He laughed at the clowns, and Jonah bought him pop and popcorn. She knew Henry was having a grand time.

And so was Jonah. His eyes were warm with obvious

love every time he looked at Henry, and he touched him often, draping his arm across the boy's shoulders, dropping his hand on his head or holding him in his lap.

The sun slowly set while they watched the bronc riding, the barrel racing and the calf roping. By the time the saddle bronc riding began, bright lights on tall poles had been switched on, lighting the arena almost as brightly as the afternoon sun. Finally they watched the bull-riding. When it was over, Jonah carried Henry on his shoulders walking back to the car, and ten minutes after they drove away Kate glanced back to see Henry slumped over, asleep in the seat.

They rode in silence, her thoughts in turmoil. At the ranch Jonah carried Henry inside, saying he would change him into his pajamas and tuck him into bed. She waited in the family room, and when Jonah entered, he turned as if to leave as soon as he saw her.

"Jonah, wait!" she said quickly. "There are some things I need to say to you."

"All right. What?" he asked curtly, hovering in the doorway as if impatient to get away from her. He stood stiffly, with his hands on his hips. "What is it, Kate?" he asked, and she could feel the wall between them and his still-smoldering anger.

"I can't ever say enough how sorry I am," she said, hurting with each word, yet knowing they had to be said. "I've hurt you and I've hurt Henry. You're a wonderful father for him."

"What's done is done, and we can't undo it. I'm trying to let go of anger and resentment. In time, with Henry around, I will. In the meantime, we ought to keep the hell away from each other."

She hurt, hearing the anger in his voice, yet knowing at the same time it wasn't anger that made him want to keep away from her. She could feel the volatile chemistry right now. In spite of all common sense and everything that had happened between them, she wanted to reach out and touch Jonah. She wound her fingers together.

"Thank you for all you're doing for him. And for teaching him to swim. That's a wonderful gift to him. Minute by minute he's losing his shyness."

"He's a great kid," Jonah said gruffly.

Kate wanted to cry out, "He is a great kid, and if only you had put us first in your life, we would be a family now!" Instead, she bit her lip and remained silent.

The phone rang, and Jonah crossed the room to answer it. When he did, she turned and left. As she walked out of the room, she could hear his voice lose all its gruffness and cold anger. The warmth that replaced it gave her a pang, because once, long ago, his voice had sounded like that whenever he talked to her.

Wondering if, in spite of what he had said, there was a woman in his life, she hurried upstairs to her room, which was a haven and a prison.

Feeling restless, she paced the floor, certain that sleep wasn't going to come, yet knowing she should try because she had to be at her job early the next morning. She moved to the window to look down at the pool, which glowed in the night like a bright turquoise jewel. It was empty, and she swiftly changed into her swimsuit. She would swim laps and then maybe she could sleep. She knew that Jonah didn't come out when she was in the pool, and he wasn't out there now.

She hurried through the silent house and crossed the terrace, dropping her towel and cover-up on a chair. She jumped into the pool just as Jonah surfaced and shook water from his face.

"Mercy! I didn't know you were out here," she exclaimed, startled and turning to the ladder to climb out.

"Come back, Kate," he said. "I just arrived. We can both swim. It's a big pool. You take this half and I'll take that half."

"If we both swim, we might not hear Henry."

"I'll crank up the intercom, and you'll hear him."

Jonah swam away from her and she stared at him in consternation. He climbed out, splashing water, and her gaze ran over his lean, muscled body, the black swimsuit outlining his firm bottom. Her insides clenched and desire heated her in spite of the coolness of the water. She knew exactly how that marvelous male body felt against hers, knew how he used it in lovemaking. She turned away and minutes later heard a splash as he jumped back into the pool.

She didn't want to return to her room, yet it was like putting dynamite and fire close together to stay in the same swimming pool with him. It was big, but not that big.

Clamping her teeth together, she began swimming as if she were in a race for her life. She swam laps without stopping, until her muscles ached. Once she glanced over to see his wet, muscled shoulders gleam as he easily sliced through the water.

Finally, she paused in the deep end and looked around to discover him nearby, watching her with amusement in his dark eyes for the first time since their initial encounter in San Antonio.

"You'd think a great white was after you," he remarked dryly.

"Maybe I feel like one is," she replied.

Jonah's brow arched. "Don't worry, it's not."

"I thought we were each going to stay on our own side of the pool and not talk or anything."

"Or anything?" he drawled, and suddenly she wondered if he was flirting with her. Startled, she stared at him.

"Kate, I need to talk to you, and couldn't tonight when Henry was with us, on the way home in the car," Jonah said, his tone changing abruptly. She knew if he had been flirting, it had been a slip he didn't intend. "I didn't want him to wake up and hear us," Jonah continued. "My folks used to talk when they thought I was asleep, and I heard all sorts of things I wasn't supposed to.''

She smiled slightly, feeling edgy, wondering what he wanted to talk to her about. She was unable to relax because he was too close, too bare, too masculine. He was strong and fit and the sexiest man on earth to her, and he was only inches away.

Chapter 6

"You heard Scott today—we had cattle stolen by rustlers last night."

"That sounds like something out of an old movie."

"Well, it happened, and it's happened in other counties north of here. I don't want you to worry, but you need to know. We have sophisticated alarms around and in the house, in the barn and outbuildings, and in every house on the ranch."

"You sound as if more is involved than rustling."

He shrugged. His raven hair was wet and plastered to his head, which changed his appearance, making him look more dark and dangerous. She was too aware of how close they were to concentrate well on what he was saying. They were in the deep end, where neither could stand on the bottom, and she clung to the side. He treaded water, barely moving.

"There was more involved. Scott didn't want to mention the subject in front of you or during breakfast."

She waited because she knew Jonah had bad news and was trying to get her braced for it. "And…" she prompted.

"They slit the throats of some of the cattle."

"No!" she gasped, chilled and revolted at the same time. "Why would they commit such a senseless slaughter, Jonah? The thieves have nothing to gain by doing that and you can't have lived here long enough to have made enemies."

"I don't know. I don't have any answers, but you're right, they had nothing to gain by slaughtering my cattle. That's a hate crime, so something else is going on. I don't know if the culprit got the wrong ranch, if he thought John Frates was still alive, or if the hate was directed at someone who works for me."

"That's dreadful!" Another chill ran down her spine, and he had her full attention now. "That's a far cry from stealing cattle."

"I know it is. I didn't intend to scare you by telling you. I just wanted you to know what was happening."

"Thank you for that," she said, glad to know but suddenly worried about Henry.

"Scott told me that the men will be on the lookout. Clementine said that when I'm gone, she keeps the alarm on. Someone will always be with Henry, either Clementine or me or Scott, who has two sons of his own."

Kate looked at the darkness beyond the well-lit yard. "It's so open out here and so isolated."

"It's safe. I can promise you that," Jonah assured her. He sounded so confident, so certain, yet she was still nervous. And she heard the note of steel in his voice, reminding her that he was accustomed to dealing with danger and it didn't frighten him. "I suppose you're right, but you can't keep people from getting onto your land. Last night proved you can't."

"No, but they won't be up here by the house. We have dogs and motion-detection lights and alarms. I'll have more lights installed for a wider perimeter. All seven houses on the ranch plus the bunkhouse have motion lights outside.''

''With you here, I know that there's no need to worry. I'm sorry you lost some cattle.''

''They'll be replaced. Now, jumping from that subject to another—when we arrived home from the rodeo, I got a call from my folks.''

She realized that was the call that had come when she'd walked out of the room. And now she knew why his voice had become warm and friendly.

''They would like to come see us this weekend, which translates to they would like to come see Henry.''

''That's fine with me. Henry will love them, just as he already loves you.''

''I called Boone to charter a plane for them, and he said he would fly them here himself. I invited him out to the house for dinner.''

''Jonah, this is your home. You do what you like. You don't have to run things past me,'' she said, surprised that he was informing her of his plans as if he needed her approval.

''I'm telling you because I don't want you to come home from work to find a houseful of people you didn't expect. On Friday night, I'd like to have a little get-together with some of my new friends and some old friends. I'd like to invite the neighbors.''

She smiled. ''Neighbors out here means people who live fifty miles away.''

''They're still neighbors.''

''Fine. I'll be glad to help in any way I can,'' she said.

''I'll have it catered and Clementine will be here to help. You won't have to do a thing.''

She tilted her head to study him. ''I know you made an above-average living and now you've inherited all this. You're chartering planes, having parties catered—this ranch must be very productive.''

"It is," he answered easily.

"Someday soon you'll start to date," she said, thinking of Mason asking her out today. As Jonah settled in this area, he would be meeting all sorts of people, Kate knew.

He shot her an unfathomable look, and she wondered what he was thinking. "We'll worry about my wanting to date when it happens," he said. "Right now, I need to familiarize myself with the ranch and get to know Henry. I've got a horse picked out for him."

"I hope it's gentle," she said, noticing that Jonah had changed the subject swiftly.

"Gentle as a lamb. I'm taking Henry to town tomorrow to buy him a pair of boots."

"You'll turn him into a cowboy."

"He's a Texan now. And if he's a cowboy, that's fine."

"I know it is," she answered. "You've already been so good for him." This time when he gazed at her in silence, she could see that familiar smoldering anger in his eyes. "Would you rather I stayed in the town during your party?" she asked.

"Hell, no. You don't need to do that. My folks'll want to see you, too."

"Your mother might want to see me. Your father acts cool, but Boone is more than cool. He's angry."

"Boone will be all right. You can keep Mom between you and him."

Kate had to laugh at that one. "I'm not hiding behind your mother!"

"Yeah. As if she'd let you," Jonah said, a faint smile tugging at the corner of his mouth. Kate remembered how easily he used to laugh, that deep, masculine laughter she so sorely missed. "Friday night when they get here, I'd like to ask Mike Remington and his wife over, and tell them to bring their baby girl, Jessie."

"This is your home, Jonah. You can invite anyone you want and do anything you want."

"Do anything I want, Kate?" he asked, his tone suggestive.

"As long as it's legal. But from your expression, you must be thinking of something that is off-limits, even to the homeowner."

"It's off-limits, all right," he drawled, and her suspicion that he was flirting deepened, sending her pulse rocketing.

"So what is this mysterious something you want to do that is so off-limits?" she asked curiously, knowing she should leave well enough alone.

"You always said I liked living dangerously and playing with dynamite."

"Yes, you did, and I guess you still do."

"So what in my life translates to living dangerously, to dealing with dynamite and all its risks?" he asked in a seductively soft voice.

Her mouth went dry because their conversation was opening doors both of them had long ago slammed shut. "I can't believe you're doing this."

"Doing what, Kate?" he asked with a devilish gleam in his eyes.

"We should swim away from each other, Jonah," she said breathlessly, unable to move.

"I'm not holding you. I think there's a foot of water between us," he said, but his words were a challenge and his dark gaze captivated her, turning on every nerve in her body. Then he drifted closer, and her pulse pounded when his arm circled her waist.

"We should keep our distance, Jonah," she warned again, but her voice had a tremor in it.

Jonah was torn with fury and desire. When she was only inches away, how easy it was to forget one and yield to the other. He suspected she was no more capable than he was of swimming away or even breaking eye contact. He was held by invisible needs that were as binding as chains. With all of his being he wanted her. In spite of common sense, in spite of anger, in spite of his lack of trust of what she might do, he desired her. And he liked flirting with her—it came as naturally as breathing, yet was as dangerous as running into a burning building.

His arm slid the few inches separating them, his hand went around her narrow waist and he was beyond the point of no return. Her skin was silky, pale and smooth. Drops of water sparkled on her long lashes, and her full red lips were so temptingly close! And that scrap of a swimsuit covered damn little of her. Every luscious curve was there for him to see, to remember, to desire.

The instant he touched her, he started shaking, and it took every ounce of control to keep from yanking her into his arms and holding her as tightly as possible.

"Jonah!" she gasped. Her cry was a protest, but her voice was laced with blatant longing.

He slid his arm farther around her bare middle. She was warm and wet and almost naked.

"Dammit, Kate," he said, his voice a husky rasp.

"Don't…" she whispered, but then he drew her close and their bodies pressed together, their bare legs tangling. He was aroused, hot, consumed by desire for her.

She bit off her words, her eyes going wide as she looked up at him, and he saw the flames in the depths of her hazel eyes. Her expression changed from surprise and wariness to a sensual heat. Her lips parted slightly; her breathing was fast and shallow. When her slender hands slid along his arms, he remembered how sexy and provocative she could be.

He didn't want to be attracted to her, to still love her, yet at this moment in time he had to hold her and kiss her. It was as if his life were at risk if he didn't get her into his embrace. Beyond measure, he wanted her, and though somewhere inside him an opposing emotion warred, desire won.

His head dipped down, his mouth covered hers and he

drowned in the softness of her lips, tasting her. One kiss, a kiss to die for...

Kate slipped her hands up his strong arms, feeling his hard shoulders, relishing how solid and muscular he was. Fire licked along her veins and she was shaken by his kiss, which stormed her senses and awakened long-dormant desires. Her breasts tingled, her insides heated, and she might as well have been in a free fall, plummeting into passion. She ached for him. All the pent-up craving of five years poured into her kiss as her tongue clashed with his.

His kisses set her ablaze with need for more, for all of him, for his hands and his mouth everywhere. Giving vent to the yearning that had torn her apart these past five years, she responded with a vengeance.

As if a dam had burst, sensations flooded her, and his reaction was just as intense. Giving and taking, they kissed eagerly.

What was she doing? Had she lost all common sense? Yet while her heart pounded, she kissed him passionately, held him tightly and wanted him desperately.

She moaned, trembling, her fingers tangling in his wet hair, exploring the strong, warm column of his neck. His manhood pressed against her and she knew he was aroused, desiring her just as she desired him. Yet what enormous barriers stood between them!

For a few more minutes she was going to ignore those warnings going off in her head. Relishing the flat, hard planes of his body, she pressed against Jonah.

His hand slipped down her bare back, over the scrap of wet swimsuit. How right it seemed to be in his arms, and how many nights she had dreamed of this! Too many hours she had lost sleep, while memories of his kisses tormented her. Yet with every second that she stayed here, holding him, she was losing her defenses and making herself vulnerable to the searing pain of separation she had gone through before.

Knowing she had to stop, she pushed against his chest. "No!" she whispered.

He faced her, desire blazing in his dark eyes, his jaw set. "I told you this wouldn't happen again, but when you get close to me…"

"We shouldn't swim together," she whispered, and turned, dipping under the water and streaking away from him as if she really were being chased by something terrifying. What she was trying to escape from was her own consuming hunger for Jonah, she knew.

Frantically, she climbed out of the pool, yanked up her towel and rushed into the house, hurrying up to her room, breathing as if she had run a mile race. In her bathroom, she stripped off her suit and showered, washing her hair and drying it. She pulled on a nightgown, then went to the balcony to look down at the pool. Jonah was nowhere to be seen.

They couldn't fight the physical attraction, but neither of them wanted a relationship. She didn't care to be involved with him again, and she knew he didn't want to be involved with her. Even when he kissed her, his anger still smoldered, held in check, yet there. She switched off the lights and went outside on her balcony again. It wasn't attached to his, thank heavens. She had never seen him outside, but she turned a chair so it faced away from his room, and she sat in the darkness, wishing her body would cool.

She rubbed her forehead, knowing she had to avoid Jonah. Their being together made for a combustible mix, a compelling attraction that neither of them could resist. Yet how could she avoid him when she lived in the same house and had to share Henry with him?

Why couldn't she forget Jonah? Get over him and not have her pulse race every time he came into the room?

She knew she would have to keep busy, spend as much time as she could away from him and practice more control when he was near.

And how was she going to sleep at night? So far at the ranch she had slept fitfully and only a few hours at a time. Maybe they could make a swimming schedule. She suspected he would laugh at that and not bother to remember the rules. Knowing Jonah, he would swim in his pool when he wanted, whether he was scheduled to or not.

The rest of the week Kate was busy at work, throwing herself into the job to keep her mind off Jonah. At night, she was careful to avoid being alone with him, and she suspected that he was trying just as hard to avoid her. As soon as one of them put Henry to bed, Jonah disappeared, and she didn't see any more of him.

On Friday evening, his parents and Boone Devlin were due to arrive at six o'clock, and the rest of the guests at seven. Feeling nervous, Kate slipped on a bright blue sundress that had a splash of roses embroidered across the skirt, with more roses along the square neckline. She wore bangles, dangling golden earrings, and had her hair caught up in a clip on one side of her head.

Slipping on tan sandals, she went to get Henry dressed. She found him in the upstairs family room and discovered that Jonah had already seen to Henry's bath and had dressed him.

"Don't you look super!" she exclaimed.

The boy smiled. "Look at my new boots," he declared happily, holding out a foot to show her classic hand-tooled cowboy footwear.

"They're great, Henry," she said, eyeing his blue knit shirt and new jeans. "You look so cute."

When he grinned and ran off, she turned to go downstairs. She walked through the kitchen, bustling with busy caterers. Outside, trays of colorful, tempting food covered tables set with bouquets of riotous red and yellow lilies, making the terrace look festive. On this cool summer evening, with the sun still above the horizon, the crystal-blue swimming pool made a vivid backdrop for the party.

The moment she stepped outside, Kate spotted Jonah talking to the cook. The men stood beside a large portable cooker where the ribs were grilling. A plume of smoke spiraled away from the black iron cooker, and the mouth-watering odor of ribs filled the air.

Kate barely noticed anything except Jonah, who looked incredibly handsome in a navy long-sleeved Western shirt, jeans and black boots. The moment she saw him, an electrical current surged in her. After their last passionate kisses in the pool, she was more susceptible to his appeal than ever, she knew.

When his dark eyes trailed down to her feet and back up in a quick glance, she tingled as if his fingers had skimmed over her. A moment later he left the cook and sauntered toward her, and to her chagrin, her pulse speeded up even more. They had been married for four years when they got divorced, yet she was reacting to Jonah now as she had all during their marriage and the months before.

"You look great," Jonah said impassively. There was a shuttered look to his expression, and she couldn't guess what he was feeling or thinking.

"Thank you," she said, pleased, yet remembering other parties when Jonah's voice had been filled with warmth. She recalled, too, how she had always been more aware of Jonah than anyone else at the party. And afterward...

She tried to tear her thoughts from those taunting memories. "You look handsome, and the house and terrace are gussied up like we're ready for a party. Henry is delighted with his new boots."

"Yeah. He likes them. I got him a hat today, too. You'll have to get him to show it to you."

"I'm sure he will," she said, excitement bubbling in her. All she wanted to do was stand and talk to Jonah, but she knew she couldn't.

"Boone called today and asked if he could bring a friend. I told him it was fine."

"Boone always has a friend," she said lightly.

"He likes the ladies and they like him." Jonah glanced beyond her. "Here they are."

Kate turned and crossed the terrace with Jonah to greet his parents. They had brought one of the other grandsons, Trent, and already Henry and Trent were talking. Trent was about an inch taller than Henry and had the same coal-black hair, though Trent's was long and shaggy.

"Hi, Kate," Boone said coolly. "This is a friend of mine, Lissa Anthony. Lissa, this is Kate Whitewolf, and this is the man I've told you about, Jonah."

Lissa flashed a dimpled smile at Jonah, while Kate turned to hug his mother and say hello to his father.

Maggie hugged Kate in return, and then Neighbor hugged her lightly. Kate wondered who Jonah took after, because he had none of the thickness of Neighbor's chest and shoulders, yet he was far taller than Maggie. Dressed in a red silk blouse and red slacks, Maggie looked her usual commanding self, while Neighbor, with his Hawaiian shirt and wide grin, looked as lovable as a puppy.

As they stood talking, Mike Remington and his wife arrived. Kate hadn't seen Mike since the divorce, but he seemed his same friendly self, which was a relief to her. His wife, Savannah, was amiable, and Kate held the little girl they had adopted.

"She's a beautiful baby," Kate said, looking at the child whose former room Henry now occupied. "It's wonderful that you two adopted her."

"Jessie is precious," Savannah replied. "We both adore her."

"Kate, where's this son that Jonah can't stop telling me about?" Mike asked, looking around. Kate called to Henry and Trent.

"I can tell which one is yours," Mike said dryly as the boys came running. "He looks exactly like a little Jonah."

"Yes, he does," Jonah's mother said, and within seconds Kate was introducing the children.

Soon Gabe and Ashley Brant arrived with their son, Julian, and their little girl, Ella. Julian immediately disappeared with Henry and Trent, while Ashley held Ella as introductions were made. Kate smiled when she greeted the black-haired, pleasant-looking woman. Gabe Brant was handsome, with the tanned skin of a cowboy. His brown eyes and welcoming expression made Kate feel at ease.

"Gabe is a neighbor," Jonah explained. "From one of the old families who originally settled this region."

"Glad to have you living in these parts," Gabe said. "You'll like it here, I think. In spite of the rustlers."

"Hopefully, they'll be caught before they do any more damage. Come in and get what you'd like to drink," Jonah told the Brants. "Both of you know everyone better than we do, with the exception of a couple of my friends and my parents. I'll introduce you to them."

They moved across the terrace, while Kate stayed near the door to greet other arrivals. Jonah had invited couples from nearby ranches, and children had been included in the invitations, so the noise level rose.

When Duane Talmadge and his wife, Hazel, arrived, Kate was the first to greet them. She held out her hand. "I'm Kate Whitewolf, Jonah's ex-wife," she said, shaking hands lightly with each of them. Tall and brown-haired, Duane had a scar that ran across his square jaw. He had the tanned, leathery look of a cowman who'd spent most of his life outdoors. His wife's auburn hair was graying, and she wore several large diamonds on different fingers.

Jonah appeared at Kate's side to meet them. "I've heard that you and John Frates were best friends," he said to Duane.

"We were close through high school and college. Then

he went on in the oil business, and I stayed on the ranch. He thought the world of you guys who saved him,'' the older man said.

"Come on in and help yourself to drinks and hors d'oeuvres," Jonah urged them.

"Thanks, Mr. Whitewolf."

"It's Jonah," he said simply, looking into the man's pale blue eyes.

As they told Kate they would see her later, and moved on with Jonah, another guest entered. Kate looked at a tall, rugged man with thick black hair. She smiled, greeted him and held out her hand, to have it shaken in a firm grasp.

"I'm Dakota Gallen," he said in a mellow bass voice that was deeper than most men's.

"I'm Kate Whitewolf. It's nice to meet you. I've heard Jonah mention you. You're the sheriff of Piedras County, aren't you?"

"Yes. And I'm sorry your arrival in the county has been marred by the incident last night."

"I'm sure you'd like to forget about it for a little while," Kate said, smiling at him. "Come with me and I'll introduce you to the few people here you don't know."

As she moved away from the door, Dakota Gallen walked beside her, telling her about the history of the ranch while they crossed the terrace.

"Do you know the Stallion Pass legend?" he asked, and she smiled but shook her head.

"An Apache warrior fell in love with a cavalry captain's daughter. The maiden and the warrior planned to marry, but the night the warrior came to get her, the soldiers killed him. According to legend, his ghost became a white stallion, forever searching for the woman he loved. The stallion roams this area, and according to the story, will bring love to the person who tames him."

"I'd think a lot of people would be scouring these hills for a white horse," she said, and he chuckled.

"What's odd is there have been wild white stallions around here off and on, going back to the legend, I guess. One of your guests has one now—Mike Remington."

"Mike does?" she asked, startled because she never thought of Mike as a horse person.

"Yes, he does. Maybe that's why he fell in love," Dakota said with a twinkle in his eye.

Jonah strolled up to join them. "What are you two laughing about?"

"I told Kate the legend of Stallion Pass."

"Mike has a white stallion from here," she told Jonah. "Did you know that?"

He laughed and shook his head. "Nope, but you're not going to get me to believe in that legend."

"Then you're not a romantic, Jonah," Kate said, gazing at him and knowing that wasn't true. Jonah used to do things for her that she thought were incredibly romantic. "I guess I have to take that back, though," she admitted. "You're a romantic. Just not enough of one to believe the legend."

"A horse is a horse," Jonah declared, "and not the ghost of any warrior. If you'll excuse us, Kate, I'll introduce Dakota to my parents." The two men started to saunter away, but Jonah turned back to her. "And I'll talk to you later about me not being romantic."

"That isn't what I said," she said, knowing he was flirting again. "You can be very romantic, but at the moment you have to be the good host."

"I'll show you romance, Kate."

She smiled and watched him as he rejoined Dakota and they walked away.

In the yard to the west of the terrace, Jonah had set up a volleyball net and a tetherball, and kids of various sizes already had games going.

Soon the party was in full swing, and while Kate was

busy talking to the rancher's wives, she forgot about any hostility from Jonah's friends.

As the gathering progressed, Kate tried to pay as little attention to Jonah as she could, yet it was impossible to stop being aware of where he was and what he was doing. Once she turned and he was standing beside her. "Are you enjoying the evening, Kate?"

"Yes. You have a great bunch of friends."

"Boone's being okay?"

"Yes. He's just a little cool."

"And Mike?"

"Mike is Mike, just like he's always been, except he's in love. I thought you said he and Savannah had a marriage of convenience," Kate murmured, watching a breeze tug at locks of Jonah's thick, black hair.

"In the beginning, when Mike told me about it, that's what his marriage was. Savannah's our attorney, and from that first day, I know he clashed with her. But then they decided to marry and adopt little Jessie. I guess Mike fell in love, which is surprising, because he seemed as much of a confirmed bachelor as Boone."

"I'd say he's in love," Kate said. "He won't leave her side, and he can't stop touching her or looking at her."

"I'm glad he's happy," Jonah remarked in a level, non-committal voice. He ran his finger along a thin strap of Kate's sundress. "Thanks for being my hostess, Kate. You're friendly with the adults and with the kids. All these kids might bother some women."

"I like having them around and I know your parents love it. They're definitely kid-oriented. And I'm glad to be hostess," she answered, aware of the faint touch of his finger, of the dark depths of his brown eyes. "It's a great party."

"Yeah," he said, still watching her, and she wondered what was going through his mind as they stared at each other. Kate didn't know why he stood immobile, but she was unable to move away.

"I'll see about the kids," she said at last.

She turned abruptly, annoyed with herself for letting him affect her so intensely. She crossed the lawn to watch the children play, yet as she strolled off, she was certain Jonah watched her.

By the time everyone was seated at round tables to eat tender ribs covered in barbecue sauce, the sun was setting and shadows stretched across the lawn. The air had cooled and a faint breeze had sprung up, making it a perfect summer evening. Kate sat eating at one of the tables, aware that Jonah was seated at another table with his back to her. He had been friendlier than usual tonight, and she wondered if it was because other people were around.

"How do you like your job, Kate?" Maggie Whitewolf asked, interrupting Kate's thoughts.

"I like it very much," she replied, taking a sip of water. "I'm busy trying to learn all the clients the agency has and get familiar with projects I've been assigned to take care of."

"When you get settled, and Henry knows us better, I hope you'll let him come visit us if he wants to," Maggie said.

"I'm sure the time will come when he'd like to visit, but it may take a little while. Because of my parents' illnesses, he's been very close to me. He's shy and unaccustomed to being away from me for long. But I know he'll want to visit you after a while."

"We can wait. He's an adorable little boy and I'm looking forward to getting to know him better."

"Thanks, Maggie, for just being you. You're a wonderful grandmother and mother-in-law."

"Thank you, too, Kate. I hope things work out for you and Jonah."

Kate smiled, hoping she hid the sadness that Maggie's remark brought. "Speaking of Henry, I don't see him, Trent or Julian." She eyed the children who had finished eating and were chasing each other across the lawn, but didn't spot the trio.

"They were up in Henry's room when I left them a little while ago. I can go check on them," Maggie said.

"Enjoy the party, Maggie," Kate replied quickly. "I'll go." Inside, she found the boys in Henry's room, where he was showing Trent and Julian his toys. They had a game spread on the floor between them.

"Are you boys okay?" Kate asked.

"Yes, ma'am," Henry answered without looking up.

When she saw they were engrossed in the game, she left to return to the party. As she reached an open door to the terrace, she heard Jonah speaking.

"Thanks, Boone, but I'm not ready to date."

"It's been what—five years, Jonah? You've turned into a monk."

"No, I haven't, and your offer to introduce me to someone must have a basis of good intentions."

"Oh, hell. It's none of my business, but I hate to see you fall in love with Kate for the second time—as if you were ever out of love with her," Boone added dryly in a voice laced with cynicism.

"Don't worry," Jonah replied, and Kate grimaced when she heard his bitterness. "I won't ever trust Kate again. And she's not interested in getting back together, because she sees me as the same danger-loving man she always did."

"Take care of yourself. The sparks still fly when you two get together, man. You may think you're over her, but—"

Wanting to cover her ears with her hands so she wouldn't hear another word, Kate turned and fled from the room, going to the dining room and entering the terrace from there, avoiding even glancing in the direction of Boone and Jonah.

I won't ever trust Kate again. Even though she didn't

want to fall in love with Jonah, and fought the possibility of having a relationship with him, the words hurt. Jonah's anger ran deep, so deep the rift between them would likely never mend. But that couldn't stop what she felt when she was around him.

And away from him. If he was so angry with her, why didn't he go ahead and date other women?

She saw Maggie talking to Savannah and Laurie, and she crossed the terrace to join them.

Jonah stood with a cold bottle of beer in his hand while he talked to Boone, but he watched Kate walk across the terrace to join others at a table. He had meant what he said to Boone—that he couldn't trust Kate. He didn't want to love her again, but he damn well wanted her. She looked beautiful tonight, different from the other women at the party. There were a lot of good-looking women here, but Kate stood out in her own special way. Her features were striking with her big, thickly lashed eyes and wide mouth. Her hair was worn in a dramatic do, swept up on one side of her head. Most of the women were in slacks, but Kate was in a dress with a wild splash of color across the front of the skirt. With every move, her jewelry clinked. Whether it was conscious on her part or not, Kate dressed to be noticed.

And he was noticing her, all right. It was hard to look anywhere else. Kate laughed at something someone said, and his insides clutched and heated. He desired her with a longing that was growing daily. And she was forbidden, off-limits. He wouldn't go back into a relationship with her. He didn't care to have that emotional commitment again, and she didn't want one with him. Yet he ached to take her to bed, to kiss her all night long, to stir her to complete abandon, as he knew he could. Memories set him ablaze and he had to stop thinking about her. With an effort, he tried to focus on the conversation of the group of guests who were standing beside him.

It wasn't thirty minutes before he was in a group that included Kate.

She was friendly and fit in with people, being the gracious hostess tonight, welcoming everyone, spending some of her time with each of the children, as well. If he didn't know better, he would guess her profession was teaching, because she was interested in children and knew how to make friends with them.

And Henry was blossoming, changing from the quiet child he had been that first day. He had been so excited to get his new boots today that he couldn't sit still on the ride into town and back. Jonah was totally fascinated with his son, and he'd already taken dozens of rolls of film of Henry. He had asked his dad to take pictures tonight. It still thrilled him to hear Henry call him "Daddy." Jonah wondered when the awe would leave him, or if it ever would. Henry was a treasure, and Jonah would be thankful every day of his life to know him.

Late in the party, he stood in a circle of men and the conversation switched to the stolen cattle. Dakota Gallen was in the group. "How far north have they had cattle stolen?" Josh Kellogg asked the sheriff.

"They've had rustlers this past year in West Texas and down through the area between there and here, but no cattle have ever been slaughtered except here."

"Must have a grudge against you or this ranch or someone on this ranch," said Wyatt Sawyer, another new friend and neighbor, echoing the sheriff's and Jonah's thoughts.

"We all need to keep up our guard," Gabe Brant remarked. "It has to be a random crime, though, because Jonah hasn't lived here long enough to make enemies."

"We don't know who we're dealing with here," Dakota answered.

The men nodded solemnly, and Jonah knew each one was lost in thought about his own place. And he realized it could be someone in the area with a grudge or a hidden purpose. For that matter, it could be someone at the party tonight.

He looked at the men surrounding him and wondered about them. Then he gazed across the terrace and saw Kate laughing, standing with a group that included several of the wives and two ranchers. Kirk Rivas was older, divorced and had a ranch in a neighboring county. Near him stood Duane Talmadge, neighbors and other men who had been cronies with John Frates. As Jonah watched, everyone laughed again and Kirk Rivas put his hand on Kate's shoulder.

Jonah hoped he remained impassive, but he felt a streak of dislike, and he wanted to cross the terrace and step between Kate and Rivas. He knew it was ridiculous. They had severed their ties five years ago, and she was free to date whenever she chose. He tried to look away and pay attention to the conversation around him, which had shifted to the next rodeo, but he couldn't resist glancing back at Kate and seeing Rivas still had his hand on her shoulder.

When she turned to walk away, Rivas dropped his hand to her arm, detaining her and saying something to her. Smiling at him, she answered and then walked away. Rivas stood, sipping his drink and watching her, and Jonah's urge to cross the terrace and put his arm around Kate grew stronger.

He knew his reaction was ridiculous. After not seeing her for five years, he had no reason for jealousy. It was just because they were back in the same house, spending hours together every day, that old feelings were surfacing, but he had to let go. He turned his back, trying to pay attention to the conversation of the men around him and failing completely. When he finally gave up and walked away, Kate was nowhere to be seen, nor was Henry. Jonah suspected she was somewhere with the boy.

The party ran late. Henry and Trent were playing so well together that Kate let them stay up an hour past their regular bedtime, but then Maggie said she would read to them and put them to bed. At eleven o'clock, Boone and his friend Lissa left, saying they would be back to pick up Jonah's parents on Sunday.

It was midnight when the last guests left, and as soon as they had gone, Maggie and Neighbor told Kate and Jonah good-night and headed upstairs.

The caterers had cleaned everything they'd brought, and the only evidence left of the party was the tables and centerpieces.

"It was a super party, Kate. I got to know some of my neighbors better," Jonah said, feeling relaxed and happy.

"It was a delightful party, and now Henry has all sorts of new friends in this area to play with." She started to walk away.

Without thinking about it, Jonah reached out to hold her wrist. "Wait a minute, Kate. We can keep a distance, but I'm not sleepy and I doubt if you are."

"Jonah…" she said, aware of his warm fingers lightly circling her wrist.

"Aw, let's sit out on the terrace for a little while."

"Against my better judgment, I'll join you," she said, unable to resist his invitation.

"Great." He led her through the house. When they stepped outside, music came softly over the intercom—the song they had considered special when they met. Kate still loved the song, and the moment she heard it, she remembered the first night she had heard it with Jonah. They had danced to it, wrapped in each other's arms and falling in love.

He must have remembered, too, because he turned to look at her. "Think we should risk a dance?" he asked sardonically.

"You can check your anger when you want, can't you?"

"Sometimes. I know I need to get over it. Anger isn't

productive, Kate. Come on. Dance with me," he said, reaching for her.

"Then keep a distance between us," she said, knowing she should say no, remembering the moments in the pool, yet longing to dance with him more than anything on earth.

He held out his arms, standing back with space between them, but that way there was nowhere to look except into his eyes, and that was as enticing as being in his embrace and pressed tightly against him.

"Jonah, we both desire each other, yet we don't *want* each other. A lot of it is because of old times, but if we don't keep our distance, it will lead to more hurt."

"Just dance, Kate, and enjoy the night. It's been a great evening," he said, and she wondered if he was even affected by their dancing.

They moved together easily, as if they had been dancing together for years. She remembered slow dancing with him, then passion and lovemaking. She tried to tear her gaze from his, but couldn't. His warm brown eyes were mesmerizing, holding her totally, stirring up feelings and needs she didn't want to acknowledge.

Why did he have such power over her? She was aware of his arm around her waist, his hand holding hers, and she suspected it was the most circumspect dancing he had done since the first time he had ever danced with a female.

Suddenly he turned her around, spinning her with one hand and then catching her close. She was pressed against him, her arm slipping around his neck while their bodies melded together. Banding his arm tightly around her waist, he danced with her, pressing his hips and thighs against her.

Her breath was gone, and her heart pounded. Their song was playing, the night was romantic and she was in Jonah's arms.

She was aware of the wonderful feel of his strong, lean body. His warmth in the cool night was inviting. She wound her fingers in his hair, knowing he was forbidden, yet relishing every inch of contact between them.

"Oh, Jonah!" she gasped, intending to tell him to stop, yet unable to. "I haven't danced in five years," she whispered, more to herself than to him. It was sheer heaven to sway with him, but with every brush of his hips against hers, she yearned to kiss and love him.

When the music ended, she stepped back, gasping for breath and looking at him. He was aroused, his manhood pressing tightly against his slacks, and her breasts tingled while her pulse raced.

"I should go—"

"No, don't. Come sit. We won't dance again. I think it was the song that got to both of us," he said easily.

She wanted to refuse him, because that was what she should do. At the same time, she didn't care to go sit alone in her room, so she nodded and followed him across the terrace.

In silence, he pulled two chairs around, leaving them yards apart. She watched muscles flex in his arms as he worked, her gaze running the length of him. What would he do if she walked over and wrapped her arms around him?

The question shocked her. It must be the night, the music and the hours they had cooperated and worked together. Then she remembered overhearing him talk with Boone, and she stiffened, hoping she could keep a wall between herself and Jonah. Whatever they did, he wouldn't ever trust her and he wouldn't ever change.

He turned and motioned to her. "Come sit with me, Kate," he repeated.

"For a brief time," she replied coolly. She sat down facing the turquoise pool, but her senses were focused on the man by her side.

Jonah sat in a chair and placed one foot on his other knee. He looked relaxed, as if he was feeling none of the turmoil and frustration that she was. And he probably wasn't, she thought.

"I enjoyed getting to know my neighbors tonight. You looked like you were enjoying yourself, too."

"It was a great party. Henry had a wonderful time, and there are a lot of children around here for him to be friends with. Although you live so far from everyone, I don't know how he'll ever see them."

"He will when he gets into school."

"We're going to have to talk about that, Jonah."

"Stallion Pass has a school and a bus comes by here. I can take him to the bus stop and put him on the bus, but since he's so young and this is his first year, I'd rather take him into town myself."

"You'll do that if we continue living here?"

"Yes. I can arrange my time," Jonah said easily, looking at her. "You look pretty tonight," he added quietly.

"Thank you," she answered, longing to reach over and touch his hand. Her pulse had skipped at his compliment.

The phone rang and he got up to answer the extension on the terrace.

Kate enjoyed the cool evening and paid no attention to Jonah, who talked in a low voice. In a few minutes, he replaced the receiver. "Kate, I'm leaving. Gabriel Brant's barn is on fire and they can use all the help they can get."

Chapter 7

Kate walked with Jonah as he entered the house. As she tried to keep up with his long stride, he told her about his phone conversation. "Gabe may have had cattle stolen— he isn't certain yet. Sheriff Gallen called me."

"Why would the sheriff call you?"

"He's calling all the ranchers who live in the vicinity of the Brant place."

"I'll bet he called you because he knows about your background and training in Special Forces," Kate said coolly.

"In the country, when there's a fire, everyone pitches in to help. It's not like a blaze in the city, where there are hydrants and plenty of water and fire departments to handle it."

"Sure," she replied, still certain it was because of his special training that the sheriff had called him. She looked at the grim set to his jaw and knew her questions were bothering him. "So the rustlers struck again, and this time not only took cattle, but set fire to the place. They're growing more dangerous, aren't they?''

"If it's rustlers, it looks as if they are," he replied.

"So once again, how safe is Henry?"

"I told you, he's completely safe here. I promise you. You know I'm not going to let anyone harm him."

She sighed and nodded. "I know you won't. I know I can count on you one hundred percent to protect him."

"There are some things I need to take with me, and I have to change clothes," he said, pausing at the foot of the staircase.

"Can I help? Your family is here with Henry, so I can go with you if they need more hands to put out the fire."

He gave her a faint smile. "Thanks anyway, but you stay here."

"You forgot to pat me on the head when you said that," she said, annoyed by his attitude.

He touched her cheek. "No, I had no intention of patting you on the head. You're plenty capable, Kate. I've never thought you couldn't rise to the occasion, and the last few years have shown that I was right. You took care of your parents and Henry without any help from others. I just think you should stay here with Henry."

"All right," she said, mollified slightly and wondering what he really thought.

He took the stairs two at a time, and she rubbed her forehead. There was someone in the area who was stealing cattle, burning barns, growing more dangerous. She shivered and looked at the windows and the lighted terrace outside. The house was a haven that made her forget there could be hurtful things in the world. Jonah wasn't invincible. Would Henry be safe?

As swiftly as the question came, she shoved it aside. Jonah would go to any lengths to protect their son. If he was around. Right now he was leaving them to go help someone else—so typical of him. Yet his parents were here and she was here, and Jonah had assured her about lights and alarms and his men. Even so, doubts nagged at her. Jonah had just inherited this place. He couldn't really know the men who worked for him, and which ones he could trust.

She tried to stop thinking about the possibilities of danger. Then Jonah was coming back down the stairs and she forgot everything else. He was in jeans, a black T-shirt and his black boots, looking dark, dangerous and handsome.

"You don't know when you'll be home," she said, suddenly having a moment of déjà vu, remembering too many times when she had told him goodbye and watched him leave, terrified because he was going into harm's way. Only this time she wouldn't be kissing him goodbye.

"No, I don't, but don't expect it to be soon. Fires like this, unless contained right away, are difficult to get under control."

In silence they gazed into each other's eyes, and she guessed that he was remembering other goodbyes, too. She turned abruptly. "Take care of yourself," she said stiffly, hurting to the core. There was an insurmountable barrier between them, and she needed to walk away and not give him another thought tonight.

Ten minutes later, alone in her room, she knew it was impossible to get him out of her mind and impossible to forget about the fire and the danger and the loss to his friendly neighbors. Switching off lights, she walked out onto the balcony, where she could see a red glow in the inky night sky. She guessed it was the Brants' fire.

Sitting in the darkness, she mulled over the entire day, thinking about the friends and neighbors she had met, remembering the children who had come with their parents tonight. Henry had new relatives and friends. He was delighted with his cousin Trent, and Kate was glad that he was getting to know his big, friendly family.

She looked at the red glow in the sky and could imagine

Jonah in the thick of the struggle, helping out, directing others. *I'll never trust Kate again.* Even though she knew it shouldn't matter to her what Jonah said, his hurtful words rang in her ears.

They'd separated five years ago—five long years—yet here she was, still hurting because of him. Would she ever get over him, or was she destined to love him always?

She didn't want to answer that question.

Her attention went back to the fire, and she pictured Jonah and the others struggling desperately to beat out the flames. And somewhere out there in the dark night was the arsonist—or arsonists. If the fire was connected to the rustlers, then it meant more than one person was involved. A group bent on destruction and hurting others. The rustling had to be for monetary gain. But the barn burning and the slaughter of Jonah's cattle—those crimes were evil and had to have been done with only one motive in mind: hatred.

She shivered and rubbed her arms, wondering why anyone would hate the open, friendly people around here. Why would anyone dislike Jonah? Unless it went back to his days in Special Forces.

Dark shadows across the lawn looked sinister. Anything could be hiding in the blackness. In spite of Jonah's reassurances that the ranch house and other buildings were safe, she could not shake the feeling of vulnerability. Why had he been a target? Because of John Frates? Because someone else had wanted Jonah's inheritance? Because someone who worked for Jonah was out to get him?

She sat outside until she fell asleep. When she awoke it was dawn. She stretched and went inside, to lie down and go back to sleep. It wasn't until seven-thirty, when she went downstairs, that she learned Jonah would not be home today.

Through the night Jonah battled the blaze, along with ranchers and hands from several counties. There was only a light breeze, which helped the situation. It was after dawn when they began to get the fire contained, and by noon the next day the blaze was out. Only smoldering embers remained, blackened land and the smoking ruin where the barn had stood.

With his sleeves rolled high, his shirt unbuttoned to the navel and drenched with sweat, Sheriff Gallen walked over to Jonah. Carrying a canteen of water, he offered Jonah a drink. "Thanks for working all through the night," he said.

"Glad to help out," Jonah replied, wiping his own sweating brow and taking a drink. He wiped the mouth of the canteen with a bandanna and returned it to the sheriff.

"I'm starting to wonder if it's someone with a personal vendetta against people in this region."

"Do you have any clues yet?" Jonah asked.

"Nothing substantial. The tire tracks we took from your place gave us the brand, but we can't run down where they were purchased or when. We don't have any other leads, although we'll go over this area inch by inch. The firemen took samples of ashes to test. The rustlers will make a mistake sometime soon, and we'll catch them. With several perps involved, it's more likely one of them will make a mistake."

Gabe Brant joined them. Covered with dust and soot, with his T-shirt torn, he raked his fingers through his wavy brown hair. "Thank you both for all your help."

"We all need to help each other in this kind of thing," Jonah said.

"Brant, you don't know anyone who has a grudge against you, do you?" Dakota Gallen asked.

"Not that I can think of, but there are bound to be people who are less than enthused about me. I'm a rancher, a cattle buyer, an employer, a businessman: I've made decisions that various people haven't liked, and my dad before me did things to make enemies. But as far as someone who hates me enough to do this sort of crime? No, I can't think of anyone."

"What about you, Jonah?"

"Hell, he hasn't lived here long enough to make any enemies," Gabe remarked dryly, before Jonah could speak.

"No, I haven't. You need to ask Scott Adamson or my ranch manager. They would know a whole lot better than I do if someone had a grudge against anyone on my spread."

"Is there anyone who might feel cheated out of the inheritance of the Frates ranch?"

Jonah shook his head. "As far as I know, the only people who might have questioned our inheritance were John Frates's in-laws, and I'm sure they're not into cattle rustling. Right now, they're in a rehabilitation center."

"At present, the rustling seems to be concentrated in this area," Dakota said. "Piedras and Lago Counties. The crimes are getting worse, the perps bolder. You two have been struck, so you shouldn't be hit again, but it pays to stay alert. Just keep your eyes open and report anything unusual to me. We've got to catch them soon, because the damage is escalating and I'm afraid someone is going to get hurt."

Jonah and Gabe nodded, and shook hands with the sheriff before he turned to walk away. Jonah went back to help put out the last smoldering embers.

During the morning at the Long Bar Ranch, Jonah's parents took charge of Henry and Trent, playing with the boys in the family room. Kate was restless, eager to hear what was happening with the fire. From television she learned that the firefighters had the blaze under control, and she sighed with relief, wondering if she would ever stop worrying about Jonah.

The family was at supper Saturday evening when Jonah arrived back at the ranch. Kate heard the clatter of his boots, and then he swept into the room and her pulse jumped. He looked dirty, disheveled and grim, and he had a cut across his cheek and another on his arm. She had to fight the impulse to get up and try to take care of him.

In spite of his grim expression, he seemed anxious to clean up and join them at the table. When he reappeared, his wet hair was combed smoothly back from his face. He was dressed in fresh jeans and a clean white T-shirt, and he looked as if he had had a peaceful night's sleep instead of staying up all night fighting a fire.

He grinned at Henry and spoke to each one of them, but in spite of his cheerfulness, Kate sensed something was bothering him.

Whatever it was, she guessed that he didn't care to discuss it in the children's presence. Later, after Trent and Henry had gone to bed, Jonah was cheerful with his parents. It was only a few minutes past ten o'clock when they retired, and Kate was finally alone with him. Out of habit, she started to leave the room, but Jonah motioned for her to stay.

"I want to talk to you," he said solemnly.

They were in the family room, and she sat on a cool leather chair. As soon as she was settled, Jonah sat in another chair and faced her. "We got the fire out today, but it was deliberately set, and some of Brant's livestock were stolen. The things happening in this area aren't like ordinary rustling. No one gains from setting a barn on fire."

"Does the sheriff have any leads?"

"None. But don't worry. If I have to leave Henry with Clementine, I'll get one of the men to come up here to the house to stay," he said. While he talked, he pulled off his boots, tugging them from his feet and setting them beside his chair. As he did so, her mouth went dry and her heart began to thump. Memories assailed her of watching him remove his military boots, and then his belt and shirt....

She took a deep breath and tried to concentrate on what he was saying.

"Since we've been hit already, the sheriff doesn't think it's likely we'll be robbed again, but I don't feel as certain about that."

"Why don't you?"

He shook his head. "No tangible reason. Just an uneasy feeling that we're being targeted for some specific reason. I don't think it was a random thing, and Gallen doesn't, either."

Kate looked through the glass doors. "This house is so open. Anyone with binoculars could see all through it."

"Through the downstairs. Not upstairs. Kate, I can find the decorator who furnished the house, or you can. Or you could select something yourself. But I'm thinking it might be safer to get some shutters, or blinds, or whatever they do for windows. Not in here, because this room opens onto the terrace and we use it constantly, but some of the other rooms."

"I agree," she replied, relieved that it had been his suggestion. "It worries me to have the house so open."

"Do you want me to see about it, or do you want to do it?" he asked.

She was astonished that he would turn decorating his house over to her, a temporary resident. "I'll look into it and let you know before I do anything."

"You do whatever you like. We both have Henry's best interests at heart, and you have great taste, so don't even check with me. Just go ahead and get something. Cost is not a problem."

"That's the first time I've ever heard you say that," she remarked, wondering how lucrative the ranch operation actually was, and if there was oil or some other source of revenue on it.

He smiled at her. "I've got some benefits from the military, plus the ranch."

"Jonah, with these attacks on ranchers in this area, I'm concerned about the new nanny. I know you'll check her out completely."

"Don't worry about it, Kate. I can have friends run background checks on her, and whoever I hire will be so squeaky clean she could work in intelligence. I'll be damn careful when I hire someone to take care of Henry. And as I've said, I don't intend to leave him with a nanny all the time. I want him with me. But I can't keep asking Clementine and Scott Adamson to watch him for me."

"I agree."

"I may wait until they catch whoever is committing the crimes, though, before we hire the nanny."

"They may never catch the criminals," she said.

"After a while I'll go ahead and hire someone, but I'm not in a rush. I told the agency that."

"In a way, that's reassuring to not have a stranger in the house. I know my uneasiness is partly because these last years I'm accustomed to being with Henry."

"You've done a great job with him, Kate."

"Thank you," she replied, surprised and pleased to have him say so.

"Tomorrow, I'm going to start checking out security for the place. The house comes first, and then the other buildings. We're reasonably secure already."

"Then you are concerned about safety!" she exclaimed, and a shiver of fear slithered over her. If Jonah was concerned, there was sufficient cause to be. "Is there anything you're not telling me?" she asked.

"Nope. I just know I can make this place more secure, and I intend to do so."

"And you'll carry a gun?"

"Yes, I'll pack, but don't worry about that, either. The minute I enter the house, the pistol goes on a high shelf in my closet."

"You're really worrying me now," she said.

"Let me do the worrying," Jonah said. "I promise I'll keep you and Henry and the others safe here on the ranch."

She nodded. "I found more pictures of Henry that you haven't seen. Would you like to look at them?"

"Sure," he answered, and she stood.

"I'll get them and be right back." As she left the room, her spine tingled and she suspected that if she turned around, she would find him watching her.

Minutes later, when she returned, she found Jonah on the terrace. He had poured them both tall glasses of iced tea, and she sat beside him at one of the tables and placed a scrapbook in front of him. "Thanks for the tea," she said, and she picked it up and took a long drink, feeling the cold liquid go down her throat. "I was thirsty."

Jonah pulled his chair close to hers and reached out to open the scrapbook. Her attention was diverted from the album to the man beside her. She could detect his tangy aftershave, see the cut on his cheek at close range, touch him easily if she wanted to. As he began to thumb through the photos, she explained where each had been taken.

They looked at pictures of Henry playing in her folks' backyard, pictures of Henry with her ailing parents, one with her dad in his bathrobe, his arm around Henry's shoulders.

"That was the last photo of Dad," she said quietly.

"I'm sorry you had to go through all that alone, Kate," Jonah said gently. He turned to look at her. He was only inches away and his dark eyes were filled with sympathy that made her remember that terrible time a few months back. The loss of her parents still hurt, and she compressed her lips, trying to control her emotions. Jonah's response had caught her off guard.

"Thanks. It's over now," she said stiffly, without looking at him. She had made it through that time without too much grieving because of Henry, but at Jonah's quiet statement, she remembered those last days and how badly they had hurt. But she didn't want to cry in front of Jonah or lose control.

"Kate," he said softly, and turned his chair, wrapping his arm around her. "I'll bet you kept a stiff upper lip for Henry's sake and bottled up all your grief. Didn't you?"

She nodded without looking at him. "The pictures brought it back," she whispered.

Jonah pulled her against his chest. "You know, it's okay to cry and it's permissible to grieve. You'll have a tougher time getting over their loss if you don't grieve."

"It's just hard to look at the photos," she whispered, sitting stiffly with her head pressed against Jonah's chest, her hands gripping the chair as if she had to hang on for dear life.

She fought the tears that welled up, startled that he was being so kind. His hand stroked her head lightly, and as she gained control of her emotions, others surfaced. Kate became aware of being pressed against the wrought-iron chair, her head and hand against Jonah's chest. She could hear his heartbeat, strong and steady.

"Jonah," she whispered, and leaned back a fraction to look up at him. She was instantly lost in his dark-eyed gaze.

"Ah, Kate, we can't leave each other alone even though I know we both want to," he whispered, putting his finger beneath her chin and tilting her face up.

"Besides that, we're out here in the light, in plain view of the house and everyone."

He stood, taking her hand and leading her into the darkened family room, where he turned to pull her into his embrace. But she had had a moment to shake off the spell that his dark gaze had spun around her.

"Jonah, no. Not out there, not in here. You regret it every time you kiss me. I regret it, too. We—"

"Come here, Kate," he said, pulling her close. His mouth covered hers, and she was soon hopelessly lost in his sensual magic.

Her blood pounded and her insides heated. Desire was a tormenting flame, bursting to life and making her tremble. She slid her arms around Jonah's neck and clung to him, moving her hips against him, desiring him and hearing only the wild thumping of her heart. He kissed her as if he were going to devour her, a tantalizing kiss of seduction. Teasing, tempting her, he kissed her thoroughly while he held her.

Need possessed her, overwhelming her, and she slid her hands across his shoulders and down his arms, exploring every inch of muscle and flesh. She was starving for him, aching with longing.

She wanted to drop her hand to his hips, to touch him intimately. Her common sense and caution were being burned away by his hard, passionate kisses, blanking out her thought processes. Kate felt his own hands trailing lightly over her, with devastating effects.

She moaned softly, a whimper of reluctance, a soft cry of need. "What are we going to do?" she whispered, before his mouth covered hers again and all thought fled.

Jonah's hands slipped beneath her shirt and stroked her breasts lightly. Kate trembled, desire turning to white heat. She gasped, gripping his shoulders while he pushed away her lacy bra and cupped her breasts, his thumbs circling her nipples.

A tremor shook him, and then another, and she realized they were destroying each other, careening in a direction neither wanted, yet were powerless to change. Even though she knew she shouldn't, she desired him with all her being.

"No, Jonah," she whispered, and pushed against him. She looked up at him and saw his dark eyes burning with blatant desire.

"We're not going there again," she said. "It hurt before and it'll hurt now. You don't want it and I don't want it. Not without love. And you can't say you love me. You can't say you trust me."

When a shuttered look crossed his features, she knew she was right. She saw the muscles clench in his jaw and his chest expand as he took a deep breath.

"And you damn well don't love me, Kate, or you never would have left me," he said, with so much bitterness she winced. He turned and strode away, and as she watched him go, she hurt so much that tears spilled over and ran down her cheeks.

Why was she crying over him? Was she still so much in love with him? Could she ever get over that love when she was living in the same house with him?

She didn't think a day had passed since she'd left him that she hadn't thought about him. Why did they have such a volatile chemistry between them when neither of them wanted it?

She wiped her cheeks and walked to the window to look outside. She should move somewhere else. The instant the thought came, she rejected it. Henry was happier now than she had ever seen him. She was going to save so much money, and that would help her and Henry later.

Kate resolved to make a greater effort to avoid Jonah. If they didn't see each other, there would be fewer opportunities for moments like the one that just passed. "Stay away from him completely," she told herself. "That's what he wants."

She saw him cross the terrace. He was in his skimpy swimsuit and his muscles flexed as he walked. Her gaze ran over his bare back, his taut buttocks, his strong thighs and long legs, and her heart pounded again as if he had touched her.

She wanted him physically with all her being. She was starved for his lovemaking, aching to be kissed and caressed and held in his arms, and to explore that marvelous male body of his. The pure joy of sex had been rapture in their marriage.

She watched him drop his towel and take a leaping dive

into the pool. He swam with long, powerful strokes while she stood mesmerized, unable to walk away, remembering too much, recalling sensuous details that had her tied in knots and hurting.

"I don't want to love you again, Jonah Whitewolf!" she whispered fiercely, before she turned and rushed from the window. She ran to her room to take a cold shower. Then she pulled on a T-shirt and shorts and headed to his workout room, needing to do something physical to get her mind off Jonah and cool her fevered condition. Every nerve was raw with desire for him.

In the exercise room, she climbed on a stationary bicycle and began to pedal and push, working furiously as if she were in a race. A race to forget tormenting memories sexy enough to tempt her right back into his arms.

Her muscles began to ache, and she had to laugh at herself. At Jonah's, too, because she suspected his muscles, and more, ached as well. She stopped pedaling and dropped her head on her arm, her laughter changing to hopeless tears of frustration.

Jonah turned and floated on his back, breathing deeply from the exertion of swimming lap after lap. He thought about the slaughtered cattle and the Brants' barn. Was it random or was someone deliberately selecting certain ranches to strike? Was it someone he knew?

He heard the phone ring, swam to the edge of the pool and climbed out, grabbing his towel as he answered. He talked briefly to Sheriff Gallen, making an appointment to see him early Monday morning. When he'd hung up, he glanced at his waterproof watch. It was almost two o'clock in the morning, but he knew he wasn't going to sleep, even after a night lost fighting the fire. Jonah headed to the cabana to change into jeans, a T-shirt and boots.

Minutes later he saddled a horse and headed across the

ranch, knowing it was a futile gesture to ride out in the night, but curious if he might see anything amiss.

An hour later, Jonah was still riding quietly along the fence line. The nearby county road, an asphalt ribbon cutting across the land, had few turns in this part of the country, and he could easily see when a car approached. Only he knew he wasn't watching for a car. He was looking for a cattle truck and a pickup. They had learned that much.

But nothing more. None of the stolen cattle had shown up at any markets yet.

Jonah peered into the darkness, knowing that somewhere out there someone was filled with hate directed toward the Long Bar, its owner or occupants. He had a bad feeling that the worst was yet to come.

Chapter 8

The man sat swishing amber liquid in a glass, while his blue eyes peered at a map spread on the table before him. He had drawn a circle around the Long Bar Ranch. Also circled were other ranches in the area—the Brant place, the Big Windy Ranch belonging to Duane Talmadge, the S Bar Ranch of Wyatt Sawyer. The man tapped the map with his pen and raked a hand through his long, blond hair.

Slaughtered cattle and a burned barn. That was little or nothing to these ranchers. Cattle could be easily replaced. The barn was more serious. But not serious enough. There had to be more.

He thought of all the old-time ranchers in the area—Rivas, Kellogg, Brant. The Sawyer kid, the black sheep of the Sawyer family, who had inherited a ranch his father never intended to give him. More power to him; he was off the list.

Kellogg... Nope, he didn't want to tangle with Kellogg. The Brants...Gabriel Brant, with his wife, Ashley. The man wrote ''Brant'' on a piece of paper.

Slaughtered cattle were nothing. A mosquito bite. No, he could do better than that. Another strike against the Long Bar—one that would put fear in all the ranchers' hearts. The man carefully printed Kirk Rivas's name on a list. Rivas: three divorces and two teenage sons who had left home. The girlfriends didn't matter.

Rivas, the Long Bar and the Brant ranch. And Duane Talmadge. Duane Talmadge would be last. The crème de la crème of crimes against the ranchers.

But he'd start with the Long Bar Ranch on the first night with no full moon, and this time it wouldn't be just slaughtered cattle.

The man turned to look at a calendar. Two nights from now. Two nights from now they would still be worrying about the burned barn and they wouldn't be on the lookout for anything else. At the thought, the man gripped the glass until his knuckles were white. The slaughter and the barn burning were just a beginning.

He toyed with the list in front of him. Put them in order of importance: Talmadge, Rivas, Long Bar, Brant. Let them worry and let them suffer, as he had worried and suffered. Let them wonder. They would never get it, and soon he would be safely away. Even now they would never search in the right direction and find him.

He laughed. "Now, you bastard, I'll pay you back!" he exclaimed in a loud voice. Gulping down his drink, he threw the glass across the room. It hit the brick fireplace and shattered into a hundred glittering pieces, and he laughed again. He was safe, absolutely safe, from this vantage point. He could watch, wait and strike, and when he was finished, he would vanish forever.

This week he would return to Frates's place—the Long Bar. It was time for payback.

The man got up, knocking over the chair. He tilted the bottle and drank, feeling the tequila burn his throat. He slammed down the bottle and turned to stagger to the bed, sprawling across it.

As he lay there, he thought of the burning barn. He had stayed behind to watch all the hands running back and forth. He'd watched Brant giving orders and jumping in to try to save a structure that was already lost. There were horses in it and they had gotten them out. Next time, he would see to it that they didn't.

It was time to get serious. His practice runs were over. Whitewolf, Brant, Rivas and Talmadge.

The man hissed, thinking about what he intended to do. He wanted them to pay and pay and pay.

At ten o'clock Monday morning, Jonah drove to Stallion Pass. It always surprised him that this small Texas town had so much wealth. The prosperity showed up in many ways, from the reproduction turn-of-the-century lampposts on each street corner to the ornate Victorian courthouse in a tree-shaded square that held fountains, park benches and a gazebo. Surrounding the square were office buildings, boutiques, elegant shops and galleries. The original hotel, now over one hundred years old, stood on the square.

Stallion Pass had been a cattle town, then a railroad town. Later, when a rich oil field had been discovered just beyond the city limits, the boom had continued.

In recent years Stallion Pass had developed into a haven for artists. Streets running off the square were lined with art galleries.

Jonah slowed and parked in front of the ornate courthouse, then went inside to look for the sheriff's office. He walked on marble floors past offices with frosted glass doors. Some original brass spittoons were still in the building, and high ceilings held slowly-turning fans.

He stopped at the reception desk and told the uniformed man there who he was. He was directed to an office that had Sheriff Gallen's name on the door. Knocking lightly,

Jonah entered and found Dakota Gallen sitting behind a desk in the spacious room.

"Dakota," he said in greeting.

The sheriff dropped his pencil on the papers spread on his desk, got up and came around to shake hands with Jonah. "Thanks for coming in."

"Sure. I didn't mind stopping by your office. I had some errands to run in town, anyway."

"Have a seat," Sheriff Gallen said, pulling another chair around to face Jonah. His tan uniform was wrinkled and his office was cluttered, but one look at his lively gray eyes refuted the notion that he wasn't well organized. "You're wondering why I asked you to come to my office," he said with a friendly smile.

"Yes, I am. I've told you everything I know."

Dakota leaned forward with his elbows on his knees. "I've looked up your Special Forces record."

"You must have friends in high places," Jonah remarked with wry amusement, and Dakota shrugged.

"I wanted to check it out. And it's impressive."

"Thanks," Jonah replied, suspecting the sheriff's own record might be just as impressive or more so.

Dakota nodded his head. "I know how highly trained you are. Would you let me deputize you?"

"What the hell for?" Jonah asked with a laugh.

"I want your expertise. You don't need to report in for work or anything like that, and I'll ask you to forgo getting paid."

"That's no problem."

"I didn't think so. Being a deputy would give you official status for the investigation, and if you find the culprits, you would be authorized to act."

Jonah's first thought was of Kate, and then he clamped his jaw tightly shut. She wouldn't be happy with whatever he did, anyway. And it no longer mattered what she thought. He thought about Henry and knew he would do whatever was necessary to keep him safe.. "I'm thinking about my son."

"I don't want you in any danger. You don't have to go after the culprits. It's just to give you the authority to check things out."

"And to act if I find someone rustling cattle."

Leaning back in his chair, Dakota nodded. "That, too, which would put you in danger. If you've had enough of dangerous situations, say no."

Again, Jonah thought about Kate, and knew she would hate it if she discovered he was a deputy. He stood. "You know, I think I'm going to turn you down. Out at my place I offered to help, but I wasn't thinking about going so far as to become a deputy. That's too official. I got a divorce over my being in Special Forces. My ex-wife and I aren't reconciled. We're just together because of our son, but I don't want to fling this in her face."

Dakota's expression was impassive, and he shrugged. "That's fine. Just thought I'd try. You can still call me if you hear anything or get any leads."

"Sure. Thanks for thinking enough of me to ask."

"I enjoyed the party Saturday night."

"Thanks." Jonah paused at the door. "Do you see any pattern to the crimes?"

"Not so far. You and Gabe Brant don't have much in common except for owning ranches in this area. He grew up here. You didn't. He knows nearly everyone for three or four counties around. You hardly know anyone. I can't imagine why anyone would have a grudge against you. It has to be your ranch or your men or something else."

"Or maybe it's just random hate," Jonah said.

"I don't have any leads," Dakota continued. "I did learn that the fire was set, and not very cleverly done. They just poured gasoline all around, tossed a match and ran." He reached out and picked up a paper from the stack on his desk. "We did get a description of the tires and some possibilities about make and model. They drove a pickup and a cattle truck.''

Jonah took the paper to read about the brand and size of tires, what vehicles they would fit.

''You can't find where the tires were purchased or any leads to these vehicles? A cattle truck is a big, noticeable item.''

''Nope. Nothing so far. And no cattle with brands from the Long Bar or the Brant ranch have turned up at any feedlots or cattle sales.''

''So what do you think they're doing with the stolen animals?''

''They could be crossing the border somewhere and selling them to our neighbors to the south. The border is patrolled, but there's no way to cover it all the time,'' Dakota said.

Jonah shook his head. ''Well, there may not be a pattern to which ranches they've robbed. Or even a reason for burning the barn. These creeps may just be destructive.''

''Keep your ears open, and thanks for coming by.''

Jonah told him goodbye and left. As he drove away he thought about Dakota's offer and his own refusal. He'd do whatever he could because he wanted the culprits caught, but he didn't want to be a deputy. And he didn't think he would be any more help if he was.

For the next week Kate saw little of Jonah except at suppertime, when they both sat down to eat with Henry. She made arrangements for carpenters to come install shutters on the downstairs windows, and when the job was finished, she felt more secure.

Two nights during the week she had to work late, but Jonah and Henry waited to eat with her when she got home. Some nights Jonah would take Henry to swim, or would tuck him in bed, and she would leave the two of them alone. Other nights she would do something with Henry, and Jonah would disappear.

Wednesday of the following week, she saw Jonah and Henry in the corral when she came home. Both father and son were in T-shirts, jeans and boots. Henry was riding a bay, the horse slowly circling the corral, while Jonah watched him. Henry looked so small on the large animal, but he sat up straight and was smiling, and she knew he was happy.

As she walked toward them, Jonah turned and sauntered to the fence. She was aware of his steady scrutiny and she twisted a wayward tendril of hair back into place, even though others had escaped the bun behind her head and she knew taming them all was hopeless. She had already shed the jacket to her navy suit.

"Hi!" she called to Henry, who waved.

"Mommy! Watch me ride!" he exclaimed. "We're going out on the ranch tomorrow and I get to ride Butter."

"That's great," she called. "Butter?" she asked Jonah, who rested his arms on the top of the fence and gazed at her impassively.

"You look excited, Kate. Did something special happen at work?"

"It's not fair how you always can tell if I'm happy or sad, while I don't have a clue how you feel or what's on your mind."

"Well, it doesn't really matter anymore," he drawled, while she stared at him, tempted to turn around and walk back to the house and not say another word. But then she looked at Henry and changed her mind.

"I did have a super day. When I took this job, they assigned particular clients to me and certain projects. There was one ad campaign they had been preparing for a long time, the campaign was for a company called Design Landscape Gardeners. The week I started work there, I was placed on the team working on the Design Landscape campaign. Well," she continued, feeling fluttery now, because he looked so unapproachable. "What I'm working on now is a colossal assignment and will mean a lot of money for my new company."

"That's great," Jonah said quietly. "And a bonus for you? That's the way it used to work."

"Actually, yes. I'll receive a bonus."

"Congratulations. That's great, but I don't think that's what you walked over here to tell me."

Jonah being so prickly wasn't making it any easier to talk to him. Once again, Kate was tempted to turn around and walk away. Since they saw little of each other, the chasm between them seemed to be growing larger. She looked again at Henry, who was smiling and leaning forward to pat the horse. Taking a deep breath, she glared at Jonah, who gazed steadily back.

"No, that isn't what I came over here to tell you. The office wants to celebrate this deal and two others that have happened this year, plus the company's anniversary is coming up. Therefore, they are having a party and an open house. I'm to present an award to one of the men and someone is presenting an award to the team which includes me."

"Congratulations again, Kate," Jonah said politely, as if he were talking to a total stranger on the street.

"I want Henry to come see my office and I want him to see me when my team gets this award."

"It's fine with me," Jonah said with a shrug.

"Well, it concerns you, too," she stated, becoming exasperated and trying to think of some way to avoid including Jonah. "I'll be busy with the clients and with the party. I thought maybe you could bring Henry and take him home."

Jonah's brow arched, and his eyes narrowed slightly. He turned to watch Henry riding around the corral. "I reckon I can do that."

"Jonah, if I could think of any other way, I would. I don't want to send Henry with just anyone."

"Nope. I'll do it, Kate. Don't worry about it. Just tell me when and where you want us to be. And how do I dress him?"

She bit her lip and looked at her son. "He's got some Sunday slacks and a white shirt, if he hasn't outgrown them. He's got one sport coat. The party is Friday afternoon. It starts at four o'clock, the awards will be around six o'clock and the party is over at half past seven. There will be hors d'oeuvres, but Henry better eat something before he comes."

"I'll take both of you to dinner afterward," Jonah said.

"You don't need to do that," she replied stiffly and turned to go.

Jonah watched the sway of her hips, and when he thought she was out of earshot, he swore softly. The minute she had pulled up and stopped, his pulse had started racing. When she'd swung her long legs out of the car and walked toward him, his insides had turned to jelly. Her hazel eyes had sparkled and she had looked bubbly and desirable, but he had doubled his fists and tried to remember to keep distance between them.

She wanted him to take Henry to a party to see her get an award. Jonah would be happy to haul Henry around, but he was trying with all his might to avoid Kate and stay as far away from her as possible.

And doing so had helped. At least he was getting a few hours sleep each night. He knew he had been a jerk with her just now, but they needed dissension to keep the distance between them.

He put his chin on his hand on the fence and openly watched her walking to the house. He remembered moments like this when she had gained a big client or finished a project, and how they would go out and have their own celebration.

He clenched his teeth and turned around to focus on Henry. Forget her, forget her, he told himself. On Friday he would take Henry to her office and sit with him and watch her get an award. He'd let him look around, and then he and Henry could get the hell out of there.

Or if she wanted to bring Henry home herself, he would leave him with her. Except Jonah had invited her to dinner, an offer that had popped out as if he didn't have control over his own speech. At least she'd had enough sense to turn him down.

"Daddy, look! He's trotting!" Henry exclaimed, and Jonah turned to watch his son, thinking again how much Henry had changed since the first few days he had come to the ranch. When he began to learn to do a few things, like swimming, he seemed to gain more confidence to do others.

Kate spent Thursday evening trying to decide what to wear for the celebration at her office. Jonah had Henry outside swimming with him, and while she was alone, she wanted to get everything laid out for Friday.

She tried on first one outfit and then another, finally deciding on a simple black dress. She was nervous and wished she could attribute it to being so new to the company and having an award presented to her team. But she knew exactly why she was on edge, and it had nothing to do with her new job and everything to do with Jonah. He was cordial enough, and every evening they ate dinner together with Henry, but all conversation was focused on their son and they communicated very little with each other. She knew Henry was too young to notice whether or not his parents conversed with each other. He probably enjoyed all the attention, in any case.

As soon as dinner was over, either she or Jonah would take Henry for the evening, and the two adults would rarely see any more of each other until he went to bed, and then only briefly to tell Henry good-night. Kate had never encountered Jonah in the pool again, and she wondered if he had given up swimming alone while she lived with him. Most likely he swam when he knew she wasn't around to join him.

Jonah couldn't sleep and paced restlessly around the family room. He turned on the television, gazed outside across the terrace at the pool and finally went up to his room. He glared at Kate's closed door. He thought about her constantly and could not get her off his mind.

After he'd put Henry to bed, Jonah had exercised tonight for over an hour. He had been swimming enough to exhaust most people, but he still knew he wasn't going to fall asleep. Switching off the lights in his room, he yanked off his T-shirt and went out on his balcony to sit. Seeing that Kate's balcony was empty, he thought about her in bed. Images of Kate caused him more turmoil than ever. He tried to think of something else, but found it difficult. Finally he dozed, waking again far into the night.

He sat in the darkness, relaxed, not wanting to get up and move. But finally he went inside and happened to glance out a bedroom window that beyond the yard held a view of the barn. A flicker of light caught Jonah's attention, and then it was gone, so quickly he wondered if he had imagined it.

He pulled a chair to the window and sat down, staring out the window at the darkness beyond the well-lit terrace and pool, to the area near the barn. For a long time he saw nothing. Jonah was just about to give up and go to bed when he saw a flicker of light again. This time he was certain of it. Instantly he ran across the room, jamming his feet into running shoes. He got his pistol down from the shelf in his closet, tucking the weapon into his jeans, then turned to rush across the room. He paused at his desk to jam a cell phone into his jeans pocket and grab his walkie-talkie.

Wanting to catch whoever was out there, he raced downstairs, moving through the darkened house with the ease of a cat, because he knew the layout and his eyes had adjusted to the darkness. As he ran, he activated the walkie-talkie and pressed the button.

"Scott, can you hear me?" he asked in a low voice.

There was a short burst of static and then he heard his foreman's sleep-filled voice. "Jonah?"

"Yeah. I saw a light by the barn. I'm leaving the house, heading for the corral."

"I'll go there, too."

"You get up the road in case someone tries to leave in that direction." At the back door, Jonah stopped to turn off the alarm and reset it, so he could leave and still have it turned on while he was outside.

Light surrounded the house, and he sprinted across the yard, vaulting the fence. As soon as he was out of the range of the floodlights, he hugged shadows, running to the far side of the barn. The door was slightly ajar and Jonah moved with stealth.

He stepped inside, standing immobile, allowing his eyes to adjust to the darkness. Then he listened with all his senses alert. Who was in here? he wondered. Was this the rustler and arsonist? Jonah tried to catch any scent, any sound of someone who might be in the barn with him. There were no horses in the stalls, so the silence was total.

As he stood listening, Jonah detected a faint ticking. There were no clocks in the barn, and he wasn't wearing his watch. He crept forward with care, remembering where a light switch was. When he reached the switch, he hit it, illuminating the barn.

His gaze swept the area to reassure himself that he was alone. The instant he decided there was no one in the barn with him, he tried to find the source of the ticking, listening carefully and moving toward the faint sound.

His gaze almost slipped right past it, but he finally noticed straw loosely covering what looked like a box. Dropping down on his knees, he brushed away the straw and found a briefcase. When he placed his ear against it, he realized it was a bomb.

Chapter 9

Jonah yanked up the briefcase by the handle and ran to the door, racing out the far side of the barn away from the house.

He sprinted into the field behind and then swung his arm, putting all his strength into the toss and pivoting so that his whole body and all his muscle was behind it as he tossed the briefcase high in the air and let go. It sailed into the darkness, while he spun and ran back toward the barn.

The explosion knocked him off his feet. A deafening blast shook the ground, followed by a wall of air barreling into him. A fireball illuminated the pasture with blinding light, followed by a thick plume of smoke rising skyward.

Jonah hit the ground, but then he was up, running for the house, because he could imagine what the blast would do to Kate and Henry.

Yanking out his cell phone he dialed 9-1-1, and the minute he heard the voice of the dispatcher, he said, "This is Jonah Whitewolf. Get Sheriff Gallen. Someone just tried to blow up my barn. I don't think he's had time to get away from the ranch. As far as I know, everyone is all right.''

He broke the connection to call Scott Adamson on the walkie-talkie, but before they could connect, he saw the foreman sprinting toward the house. Adamson seemed to spot him at the same time and veered toward him.

''What the hell happened?'' he called as he approached Jonah.

''Someone put a bomb in the barn. I found it in time to pitch it out into a field.''

''Hellfire!''

''I've called the sheriff and I want to get to the house. You check on the men and get some to fan out and search for the bomber—he wasn't far ahead of me. Get someone else to call Clementine and the others and let them know what happened.''

Scott was already gone, running back toward the bunkhouse. Jonah stretched out his legs and sprinted toward the house, swearing under his breath. Nearly every light in the house was on, and he could imagine Kate's fright and anger. And he suspected that, some way or another, she would blame what had happened on his past and his dangerous lifestyle in the military.

If the Brants' barn hadn't burned, he would wonder himself if it were someone out of the past with a vendetta against him. But the Brant rustling and barn burning had to be tied to the slaughter and rustling of his own cattle, and now the attempted bombing.

Hot anger made Jonah grit his teeth. How he would like to catch the culprit! He worried about Henry and Kate and everyone who worked for him, although he suspected his men could take good care of themselves and would welcome a chance to catch the creep.

Jonah unlocked the back door and went inside. He was

sprinting toward the stairs when he met Kate coming toward him.

She wore a blue cotton robe that covered her from her chin to her knees, but his mouth went dry because he knew she wore little beneath it. Her hair fell loosely around her face and he forgot the bomb, the intruder, everything except this incredible-looking woman. And then he gazed into her eyes and saw only anger.

"What happened, Jonah?"

"It was a bomb."

"Oh, my gosh!" she exclaimed, still looking furious. If she felt any fear, it was well hidden. Knowing Kate, she probably was angry. She always met life head-on, and he had never seen her cower from anything, which made it harder for him to understand why she hated his being in the military.

"Where's Henry?" he asked.

"I told you—Henry sleeps. He slept right through it," she replied.

"Thank heavens," Jonah exclaimed. "I was worried that I would find him crying and you wringing your hands, but I should have known better."

"Where was the bomb and was anyone hurt?"

"I happened to be awake and saw a light out on the grounds. I dressed and went down to see about it, and found the door to the barn open. When I slipped inside, I could hear ticking, so I switched on the lights, followed the sound and found a briefcase. I yanked it up, carried it outside and tossed it."

"I thought you said you had fancy alarms on everything," she said, frowning at him.

"It's my guess, and we'll find out soon, that whoever planted the bomb also knows how to dismantle alarms."

"Oh, my word! So we're not safe here."

"Yes, you are," he said grimly. "I'll see to that. I'll have more alarms installed and maybe get some of the men to patrol the grounds at night until they catch the culprits. We'll keep a couple of the dogs up here in the yard at night so they'll make noise.''

''Jonah, I'd think this was someone from your past if it weren't for the Brants' barn.''

''I agree,'' he said. ''But since they got the Brants, it must be something else. It might not have anything to do with me. It may be someone else on the ranch.''

He raked his fingers through his dark hair and it sprang back into place. ''Soon Sheriff Gallen will be here and I'll need to talk to him. In the meantime, let's go get a drink.''

She glared at him, and he knew she was blaming him for what had happened, but she nodded and walked beside him, and when she did, all problems seemed to fall away. The scent of her perfume enveloped him, and longing struck him again with the force of a blow to his body. Her blue robe was circumspect, but he wondered what was beneath it—probably a silky gown. Her head came to his shoulder and she was temptingly close.

When they entered the kitchen, he headed for the refrigerator. ''Sit down and I'll get you something. What would you like?'' he asked.

When she didn't answer instantly, he glanced around and sucked in his breath. Her hazel eyes had darkened with unmistakable desire, fixed on his bare chest. He turned to face her squarely, standing only yards from her as he put his hands on his hips.

''Maybe we should forget the drinks,'' he said, fighting his own internal war. ''I'm worried about the danger out there, but that's nothing compared to the danger in here.''

Her gaze flew up to his face and her cheeks flushed, and he wondered what thoughts had been running through her mind. He moved closer, tilting up her chin. ''How I'd like to know what you're thinking,'' he said quietly.

''Probably the same thing you're thinking,'' she whispered. "And shouldn't be. Let's get that drink, Jonah, or separate now."

He knew she was right and he turned, but it took all his willpower to keep from trying to flirt with her or even just to reach for her.

"I'll have orange juice," she said, and walked around the kitchen table to sit, watching him.

He poured two glasses of juice and sat down across the table, knowing they needed to keep a barrier between them. They needed to keep the state of Texas between them, yet he wanted Henry here with all his heart.

"I ought to be out there helping the men look for the bomber."

"Go ahead. I'm not holding you."

"Like hell you aren't," he answered with amusement, and her brows arched while her lips curved in a faint smile.

"I'm not touching you," she replied in a saucy voice. "I'm not wearing anything sexy. I've told you to go, so why do you think that I'm holding you here?"

He couldn't resist, leaning toward her over the table. "I know what I see in your eyes, Kate. That's unmistakable. And I'd give half the ranch to know what you're wearing under that robe. Whatever it is, there's not much of it, and my memory still serves me well. What you're wearing is sexy, all right, even if it is buttoned to your chin."

"That's your overactive imagination," she said, but her cheeks had flushed again. She took a sip of her orange juice and set down the glass, running her long, slender fingers over the smooth surface. He could remember those fingers moving over him, and he caught her hand in his.

"You have beautiful hands, Kate."

She pulled away and stood abruptly, picking up her glass of orange juice. "Jonah, we're just tormenting each other. I shouldn't have agreed to this drink, and you don't have time for it."

As she started to walk out of the kitchen, he got up and

moved with her. "I'd try to talk you into staying here with me, except I need to get a shirt and get out there to meet the sheriff," he said. "The firemen will be here and probably the media. I have to leave you, Kate, so what will one quick kiss hurt?" he asked, unable to keep from taking her in his arms. "We won't have a choice. It can't go beyond a quick kiss."

"Jonah, that's like an alcoholic saying just one quick drink," she protested, but her voice was breathless, and she was rooted to the spot.

He took the glass from her hands. Her eyes were huge as she looked up at him.

"That just adds to the torment. I thought we were going to avoid each other."

"Well, we didn't tonight, and the torment's not going away and I want to kiss you," he said, leaning down. "Kate, did it ever occur to you that I'm out of the military and I may have changed?"

"Jonah, you know the—"

His lips brushed hers, and she gasped and stopped talking. Her arms wrapped around his neck and her eyes closed and he knew she wanted to kiss as badly as he did. He ducked his head down again, this time covering her mouth firmly, his tongue going into her mouth.

The impact was a hot blast to his insides, turning him hard in an instant.

The kiss lasted seconds or minutes. He didn't know how long, except that it was far too brief. Then she pushed against his chest and broke away.

"I told you we shouldn't," she gasped. Her hair was tangled around her face and now her robe was in disarray and her lush curves evident. Her lips were red from their kisses, her cheeks flushed with color, and he wanted her.

"Damn straight we shouldn't," he snapped, "but we are!" He kissed her again, hard and thoroughly, feeling her body soften and press closer. She thrust her hips against him and tightened her arms around his neck, moaning softly.

Her kisses scalded him, making him ache, and he knew he would be worse for this. But she was irresistible.

"I want you, Kate!" He ground out the words, unable to keep from saying them. He ran his hands over her back and waist, sliding one hand around to cup her breast, while he shook with need.

Never had he wanted a woman, or even Kate herself, as he did at this moment. He had missed her, ached for her, and now that she was standing in his arms, he didn't want to stop or let go for any reason.

He reached down and caught the hem of her robe, grabbing the hem of her nightgown, too. He slipped his hand beneath them and then his fingers brushed her flat belly and slid up to cup her warm, soft breast.

He groaned, aching to take her right now, here in the kitchen.

Kate trembled and moaned, stroking his back, his head, his shoulders. His hands were demolishing her thought processes and all logic.

"Jonah," she whispered, kissing his throat, and then he leaned away. He bent down to push her gown and robe higher. His tongue stroked her nipple, and she thought she would faint from the sensations he stirred.

He pushed her back, shoving up the gown and robe to cup both her breasts and circle her nipples lightly with his thumbs while he looked at her. "You're beautiful, Kate," he said in a husky voice.

Lost in a world of feelings, she couldn't answer him. She ran her hands over his chest, touching his hard nipples.

"Jonah!" She looked into his eyes before he bent his head to take her nipple into his mouth, his tongue, hot and warm, circling the sensitive tip. While she clutched his shoulder with one hand, she slid the other down his chest and lower, unable to resist touching him. Her fingers ran over his bulging blue jeans. She didn't think he could feel her slight touch through the heavy denim, but she heard his gasp and then his hands were at his belt buckle, unfastening it.

When she grabbed his hands, they looked into each other's eyes. "I have to go now, Jonah. You said the sheriff was on his way."

Jonah wrapped his arms around her and leaned over her, kissing her passionately once more. Her toes curled and she held him tightly, dimly wondering if he had even heard her.

Her bare breasts were pressed against his bare chest and she could feel their hearts pounding, while her pulse roared in her ears.

His kisses were devastating, escalating their need and desire and compounding their problems, but she couldn't stop.

Why did she respond to him like this? Why did he have to be the only man on earth so incredibly appealing, special and sexy to her?

She pushed against him and it was like pushing against a rock wall, and then she wasn't pushing, but was running both her hands all over him. He picked her up and she locked her arms around him, and then realized what she was doing.

"Jonah, you have to put me down!" she gasped.

He let her slide down until she was standing on her feet again. When he released her, she opened her eyes to meet his gaze. "I hear a car," he said gruffly. His words didn't register at first. She touched his chin in a caress, trailing her fingers along his jaw to his ear.

"Oh, damn, Kate! I want you." He held her shoulders. "I have to run. Tell the sheriff I'll be right back."

Jonah hurried out of the room, and she looked down at her blue cotton robe that was a thin, summer-weight garment. Even as she was thinking that she ought to run and change, someone banged on the back door.

Trying to straighten her clothing, she hurried forward, peering through a window to see the flashing lights of the sheriff's car. She knew she must look as if she had just been kissed. Her lips tingled and Jonah had needed a shave, his bristly jaw rubbing her sensitive facial skin. Her robe was a wrinkled mess she tried to smooth with her hands.

Taking a deep breath, she opened the door to face Sheriff Gallen, who gave her a sweeping glance. "Evening, Kate," he said, touching his finger to the brim of his gray Western hat. "Sorry you've had trouble again."

"Jonah's coming," she said. "He had to get his shirt. Come in."

"I'm glad no one was hurt," Dakota said, stepping into the entryway and turning to her. "That's the first consideration. Tell Jonah that I'll head on toward the area where the bomb exploded. Firemen are not far behind me. Jonah can join us when he's ready."

She heard Jonah's footsteps—he was wearing his boots—and knew he was coming through the kitchen. He appeared, his gaze meeting hers for an instant before he turned to Dakota Gallen. The moment Kate looked into Jonah's eyes, her heart thudded. He might be going out with the sheriff to survey the damage, but his thoughts and desires were still with her. He wanted her, and it showed in his compelling gaze.

"See you in a little while," he said gruffly. He brushed a kiss on her cheek, startling her, because they weren't alone and because he didn't usually kiss her casually, either alone or in front of someone else.

She watched the two tall men cross the yard, the bright lights causing long shadows as they walked. She heard a siren and saw a pumper engine coming up the drive. She couldn't see the site of the explosion when she was downstairs because the barn hid it from sight.

Thank heavens Henry had slept through it all, she thought, dreading even having to tell him about it and wondering if they should. Maggie wanted Henry to come stay with them for a few days, and Kate wondered if that would be best. She knew Jonah would keep him safe here, and she knew just as well that she and Jonah should not stay alone in the house.

"Did it ever occur to you that I'm out of the military and I may have changed?" She remembered his question. Had he changed, and was she not giving him a chance? Giving them a chance as a family?

Everything in her wished that were true, that he had changed and had given up taking risks and jumping in to do wild things to help people in dire straits. But she couldn't believe it, and tonight was a perfect example. He had run out after the bomber, found and carried the bomb from the barn, risking his life in the process. No change in him there.

The way of life he had led was so ingrained in Jonah that she couldn't imagine he would ever change.

She climbed the stairs and headed to Henry's room to check on him again, pausing at her son's bedside to look at him. Love filled her. He was a wonderful boy and she was thankful to have him. And thankful now that he had Jonah, who was a fine daddy for Henry.

She left, going to her room and switching off the lights before stepping out on the balcony. The firemen were dousing the last sparks and small flames left from the blast. They had set up temporary lights to illuminate the site, and her knees went week when she saw how much territory the blast had scorched.

She couldn't see the entire area because part of it was hidden by the barn, but she could see enough of the crater and burned grass to be amazed at the amount of damage. The explosion would have easily leveled the barn, she suspected. Would it have taken out more than that? The garage was nearby, the corral adjoined to the barn; they both might have gone in the blast.

She shivered. Somebody out there had a deep hatred of someone or something at the Long Bar Ranch. It couldn't be Jonah, because he was too new to the area, but a bomb was deadly and in earnest.

Should she get Henry away from the Long Bar? She thought of what a wonderful time he was having here, and she really did believe Jonah would keep Henry safe.

"He's not a miracle worker," she whispered into the darkness as she sat on her balcony and watched men moving around in the distance.

She needed to save all the money she could, look for a house in town and move away from Jonah. But when she did, there would be a custody battle over Henry. That thought depressed her and she knew she was better off staying on the ranch. Just avoid the rancher...

So much easier said than done. Times like the party—great moments, and then afterward, when they had danced and she had wanted to love him and be loved by him—those incidences seemed to happen often and become more devastating each time they occurred.

She thought about Mason from her office and his dinner offer. She could no more date someone else than she could stop breathing. "Oh, Jonah!" she whispered, running her hand across her brow and feeling caught in an impossible situation, one filled with danger.

Trying to shove aside memories, she went to her room to get dressed and go downstairs. Before long the house might be filled with lawmen, and she wanted to know what was going on and whom they suspected. Or if they still had absolutely no leads.

What was the connection between Gabriel Brant and Jonah—or the Long Bar Ranch? She couldn't imagine that Jonah was a prime target. That would be as ridiculous as someone thinking the grudges were against her.

She hoped the lawmen came up with something soon. The Brants had lost their barn and cattle. Jonah had lost cattle and tonight had nearly lost his barn and his life.

She vowed to shore up her resistance to him. No "quick" kisses that hadn't been quick, but had tied her heart to him more strongly than ever. This was the man she had loved so wildly and desired so intensely. Yet he was still drawn to danger. It was an impasse. No changes; he was impossible to live with. And almost impossible to live without.

Hang on, she told herself. Time always passes, and months from now she would have money saved and more options.

Months from now... By then she might be more hopelessly in love with him than ever before.

Jonah stood at the edge of the burning grass. "I know a little about bombs. Can I tag along at the crime scene with your men?"

"Glad for you to do so," Dakota said. "I saw in your military record that you're a bomb expert."

"Of sorts."

"I don't have a bomb specialist, and we can get one up here from the San Antonio PD, but it'll take maybe a day— if I get one at all. We haven't had much need for a bomb expert in Piedras County."

"That's a plus. Also, I want to check out the alarm I have in my barn, but I think I know what I'll find."

"And that is—?" Dakota prompted.

"We're dealing with someone who knows how to dismantle sophisticated alarm systems."

"Well, hell. I don't know why I expected this job to be peaceful."

"Also, I think it was just one person tonight. The rustling had to have involved more than one, to butcher that many cattle and steal as many as they did. But the barn burning and this explosion tonight had to have been one individual.''

"I agree. We've just got to discover what connection you and Gabe Brant have. Tomorrow I'd like to come out and talk to each of your men. I don't see how you can possibly be the target, unless someone expected to get this inheritance and you took it from him.''

"I sure didn't take it from anyone. I'm still in shock that I inherited this ranch.''

"You may not even know. I'll check with Savannah Remington.''

They moved apart, and Jonah pulled leather gloves and a bandanna from his pocket. He began to comb the area of the blast, picking up bits and pieces of what had been the bomb. He planned to give them to Dakota to send to San Antonio for analysis, but in a short time he began to have an idea what kind of bomb it had been.

He placed the pieces he found in a row on the bandanna. As he knelt over them, Dakota walked up. "Is that the bomb?''

"Yep. What's left of it. Can you get an analysis?''

"Yes. I'll take it to town tonight.''

"I have an idea about it. It's a relatively simple bomb, and he used an ordinary clock for the timing device.''

"You were right about the alarm in the barn. You can check it out, but I looked at it and figured it was dismantled by someone who knew exactly what he was doing. We dusted it for fingerprints, but couldn't find any, and I don't expect to find any anywhere else.''

"So you have someone who knows how to build a bomb, how to dismantle an alarm and has a cattle truck. And is wearing gloves while he works.''

"That's right. Pretty specific, and we ought to get some leads out of it somewhere. My men are looking for footprints, but we haven't had any rain for about two weeks and the ground is too hard to get footprints.'' Dakota gazed toward Jonah's ranch house.

''I hope he sticks to barns and doesn't try to get into houses,'' Jonah said.

''If he knows how to dismantle an alarm, that changes how safe everyone is at home,'' Dakota stated grimly. He stared at the burned area. ''I'd like to stop at the house and talk to your ex-wife. I need to rule out anyone in her life, even though it's unlikely. It always comes back to Gabe Brant, and that means it's not someone out of your past or your ex-wife's.''

''I agree. I didn't know Brant until I moved here. The connection has to be something to do with growing up or living around Stallion Pass.''

''I'll go on up to the house and talk to your ex. Unless she's gone back to bed.''

''She's probably up,'' Jonah said flatly, trying to avoid thinking about Kate in bed. ''I'll continue looking for any bomb fragments. Or anything else I can find. I'll quit before you go, and give this to you to take to San Antonio.''

''Thanks.'' Dakota turned and strode toward the ranch house, his long legs covering the distance easily. Jonah was tempted to join him. He'd rather be back with Kate than out in the darkened, burned field, searching for bits and pieces of metal and explosives to give to the sheriff.

Squaring his shoulders, he went back to work, scanning the area. He hunkered down, looking carefully at every inch of ground.

A half hour later, he stopped, tied up his finds in the bandanna and headed toward the house. He met Dakota coming out.

Jonah handed him the bandanna. ''Here you go,'' he said.

''I didn't learn anything from your ex-wife. She's as puzzled by all this as we are, and there are no jealous boyfriends in her background.''

Jonah nodded. He enjoyed hearing the sheriff declare there were no men in Kate's life, even though she had told him as much herself.

"If you learn anything, let me know what you can," Jonah said. "We're on the front lines out here."

"I know you are. It's great you found that bomb and tossed it tonight before it could hurt anyone or do any damage. Keep in touch."

Jonah watched the sheriff climb into his cruiser, turn around and head up the drive to the county road into town.

As Jonah walked to the house, he looked up at the bedroom windows. Kate's room was dark, and he suspected that even if she were awake, he wouldn't see her again tonight.

He smiled at the thought of Henry sleeping through an earthshaking blast. Kate had been right—the kid slept through anything.

Tomorrow would be Friday and he was taking Henry to see Kate get her award. He dreaded the evening, but she deserved whatever she got, and it was important for Henry to see his mother's office and watch her receive such an honor.

When his folks learned about the bomb, they'd want Henry to come stay with them. He didn't know whether Kate would let him go this soon or not, or whether or not Henry would want to. Jonah suspected the boy would be happy to be where he could play with his new cousins. He and Trent had been inseparable when the family had visited.

Jonah entered the quiet house. When he passed Kate's room, her door was closed. He thought about their kisses earlier. In its own way, kissing Kate had been as risky as dealing with the bomb. Yet he couldn't leave her alone, and just thinking about her was getting him all stirred up again. She was desirable, impossible. He wanted her in his bed. And she half wanted to be there—he was certain about that.

Inhaling deeply, he went to his room to shower and change into swim trunks. Downstairs again, he sauntered through the house and made a running dive into the pool, where he swam laps until his muscles ached and he was exhausted. Then, as he lazed in the water on his back, he thought about the bomb tonight. If he had run out when he had seen the first glimmer of light, would he have caught the bomber? For the hundredth time, Jonah wondered what the tie was between him and Gabe Brant. He couldn't imagine, and so far no one else could figure it out, either.

On Friday, Jonah got Henry ready to go to Kate's office. He buckled the child into his seat in the rear of the car and climbed behind the wheel.

Henry's conversation jumped from cows to a book he liked, and Jonah drove, chatting with his son, dreading the next few hours.

"Daddy, how come you never kiss Mommy?"

Startled by Henry's question, Jonah glanced in the rearview mirror to see the boy looking at him, waiting for an answer.

"Henry, your mommy and I aren't really back together, even though we live in the same house. We're divorced. Mommy has told you that before."

"No, you're not divorced. You're together," Henry insisted, staring at the back of his father's head.

"Yes, we're divorced, Henry," Jonah explained patiently, "and someday, you and Mommy will move away from the ranch and then you'll spend part of your time at the ranch with me and part of the time in town at your home with Mommy."

Henry was silent, and Jonah looked back to see tears spilling down his cheeks. Mentally, Jonah swore. He hated having to tell Henry the truth, but there wasn't any other option. He watched for a place to park, signaling and turn-ing onto a county road. He pulled off on the shoulder of the road and parked, getting out and opening the back door of the car to unbuckle his son's seat belt. "Come here, Henry," Jonah said gently.

He took the little boy in his arms, standing beside the car and hugging him. "I love you with all my heart, Henry, and I'm not going out of your life and you're not going out of mine. You'll live at the ranch a lot. And you'll have Mommy and me around so much that you won't notice the difference. I promise you, we'll both be around all the time, just not together in the same house like we are now."

"I want to stay like we are now," Henry cried.

"I'd like that, too, son. Henry, you know what?"

Henry looked up, wiping his eyes. "What?"

"You look really spiffy and cool for Mommy's party. Let's not worry about something that isn't going to happen for a long, long time. Tonight, we're going to her party and we'll all be together. We'll go home together and we'll stay just like we are now for a long time. Let's think about that this evening. You look super for Mommy's party, so let's forget the other stuff and go see Mommy's office, okay?"

"Okay," Henry said, taking a deep breath.

Jonah smiled and hugged him. "That's my boy." He helped get him buckled back into the seat, then climbed behind the wheel again. On the way into the city he talked about Henry's horse, Butter, and the other animals, hoping Henry wouldn't worry about having to leave the ranch.

Had the boy ever asked Kate why she didn't kiss Daddy? Jonah wondered as they sped toward San Antonio.

Chapter 10

That morning Kate had gotten up an hour earlier to shower, wash her hair and dress with care. As the day wore on, she grew more nervous and knew it was because Jonah was coming. She half expected to see Henry arrive in Scott Adamson's charge, so Jonah wouldn't have to come to her office and spend so much time with her tonight.

But at five-thirty, in the crowded lobby of the office building, she looked across the room and saw Jonah and Henry.

Kate's heart lurched, because Jonah was the most handsome man she had ever seen. In his navy suit, white shirt and red tie, he looked suave and more appealing than ever. Henry was in his only sport coat, a white shirt and tan slacks. His hair was neatly combed, and standing there with his hand in Jonah's, he looked adorable.

As Kate threaded her way through the crowd to them, she saw Jonah glance around and then spot her. The moment they looked into each other's eyes, her insides became fluttery.

As he impassively watched her approach, she wondered again what was running through his mind. He could easily hide his feelings—something she could not do.

"Hi," she said to him, then bent down to kiss Henry lightly and pick him up. "You look very handsome, Henry, and I'm glad you're here."

"This is your office?"

"This is where everyone works, and then I have my own office where I work. C'mon. I'll show you and Daddy." She set Henry on his feet and led the way, conscious of Jonah walking behind her. She still felt uncomfortable anytime she had to call him "Daddy" for Henry's benefit.

Mommy, Daddy and baby. What would have happened if she hadn't walked out on Jonah?

She jerked her thoughts away from a question that had plagued her through all the years of separation. She didn't want to think about that. It was done, and she couldn't go back.

Her spine tingled, as if Jonah's eyes were on her, yet she told herself she was being silly. He probably was looking around, and the last thing on his mind was her. Unable to resist, she glanced over her shoulder and found his gaze sweeping over her.

She turned around, and then they were at her office, where she stepped inside, waving her hand. "See, Henry, there's my desk and here are ads I'm working on and these are layouts. There's my drawing board."

"Great office," Jonah said, lounging in the doorway. "I saw a bar. I'll get a drink while you show Henry everything. Can I bring you something?"

"They're serving champagne and plain punch. If you can carry them, why don't you bring two cups of punch for Henry and me?"

"Sure," Jonah replied. When he was gone, she sighed. He didn't want to be here, and she wished she had been able to think of some way to avoid having him come.

"Can I look in your desk?" Henry asked.

"Of course," she answered, circling the desk to sit and lift Henry onto her lap.

After looking through her drawers, Henry hopped down to walk around the office. When he climbed up on the stool to sit at her drawing board, she gave him a sheet of paper.

With care, he drew stick figures, each one having a large head and a big smile.

"Excellent, Henry," she said, watching him draw, looking at his small fingers holding the pen tightly, his tongue tucked in the corner of his mouth. She wondered if Jonah had forgotten their drinks, yet she knew he hadn't. Jonah never forgot anything. He just didn't want to come back to her office.

"It's you and Daddy and me," Henry exclaimed proudly.

The figures had big smiles, and she hoped that Henry felt that way about his parents and didn't sense the tension running between them.

"Believe it or not," Jonah said from the doorway, "I ran into someone I know."

"I believe it," she said, smiling at him. "Everywhere you go, you do. I want to hear who, but first, come look. Henry drew a picture of us."

Henry gazed up at Jonah and she felt a pang at the look of expectation on her son's face and the love in his eyes for his father.

"Hey, kiddo, that's super! That's me, isn't it?"

Henry grinned, pleased by Jonah's reaction, and turned to look at his picture. "Yes."

"And there's Mommy and there you are. I didn't know you could draw so well, Henry. I like your picture! Here's your punch."

"Henry, come sit at my desk to drink your punch," Kate said, and Jonah handed him the cup when he was seated.

"There's a guy out there, Les Williams," Jonah said,

giving the other cup of punch to Kate. "We were in basic together. He's one of this company's clients now. He has a printing company."

"Yes. I know the company, but I don't know him."

"Nope, that was before your time, Kate. Are you keeping Henry's art? If not, I think I'll put it in a frame and hang it in my office at the ranch."

"Go ahead. I have a lot of Henry's drawings."

"May I have the picture you just drew, Henry?" Jonah asked.

The boy nodded, handing the paper to him solemnly. "I'll draw one for you, too, Mommy."

Jonah looked at his newly acquired gift. "I'll put this drawing up somewhere so it doesn't get wrinkled, and take it when we leave. If you two will excuse me, I'll go see if I can find anyone else I know."

Kate nodded and watched him go, knowing he was trying to stay away from her and that that was the wisest course.

Thirty minutes later everyone gathered in the large reception room at the front of the office, and the president of the company called for attention.

Jonah sipped slowly on the first glass of champagne he had taken. He didn't care for champagne, nor did he care for punch. All evening he had tried to keep distance between himself and Kate, but it wasn't what he wanted to do. When she and Henry had been alone in her office, he had wanted to stay and talk to them, to look at Kate's work, but he knew he should get away.

Now her boss was making a speech, and Jonah found it impossible to pay attention to the man. He watched Kate, who stood only a few feet away, slightly in front of him, with Henry at her side.

She looked beautiful. When he entered the office and had first seen her, she had taken his breath away. She wore a simple black dress that revealed her knockout figure. The skirt ended above her knees and showed a lot of her long, fabulous legs. Her hair was pulled up, looped and pinned on her head, and he longed to run his fingers in it and let it all tumble around her face and over her shoulders, the way he liked it best.

He was torn between wanting to go back to the ranch and get drunk and see if he could numb himself to all he was feeling, or take her to dinner after this was over. Neither choice was appealing. He wasn't given to drinking heavily, and liquor wouldn't supply anything except a few hours' relief, followed by a headache. If he took her to dinner, that would be tough on both of them.

Jonah's attention was caught when the president of the company called four employees up front, including Kate. Jonah took Henry's hand to keep him at his side while Kate moved through the crowd to the front of the room to stand with her team.

Picking Henry up so he could see, Jonah moved closer to the wall to keep from blocking the view of anyone behind him. Along with the others, Kate was presented with a plaque, and the president spoke about what a great new employee she was and what a fine job she was already doing. Jonah barely heard, because he was too busy watching her and thinking about her.

The dress molded her figure and she looked dazzling, poised and self-assured. He realized she wasn't as gaunt as she had been when they had first seen each other in the drugstore, and he was glad. He ached, wanting her, wanting a family, wishing she felt differently about him and his lifestyle. They could be a family.... He stopped his thoughts, knowing he couldn't look back or wish for what he wasn't going to have. She was unhappy with him for running outside after the intruder. But if he hadn't, his barn would have been blown up.

Would Kate have been happy if he had cowered in the house and let the police handle the whole thing? he wondered.

As his gaze drifted over her, from top to bottom and back up, she turned to face everyone to make her presentation to a co-worker, flashing a brilliant smile that turned Jonah's insides to jelly.

He could remember when she had smiled easily and often, smiles that had melted him, enticed him. With a few exceptions, the only time he saw her smile now was around Henry. Jonah clenched his fists. She had him tied in knots all the time, each minute of each hour of each day. He would walk out now and wait in the hall, except he needed to hold Henry and let him see his mother.

Every muscle in Jonah's body felt tense. He was hot and bothered, and he couldn't tear his gaze from Kate.

Finally, it was over and she came toward them, holding her plaque and giving them a radiant smile.

"Congratulations, Kate," Jonah said, fighting the inclination to reach out and hug her.

"Thanks."

"Congratulations, Mommy," Henry said, echoing what his father had said, and she laughed. Her eyes sparkled, and her white teeth were even, her lips full and tempting. Taking a deep breath, Jonah wished he could stop staring at her.

"Thank you, Henry."

She turned to Jonah. "I can take Henry now, and I'll take him home with me. You don't have to stay any longer, but thanks so much for bringing him and keeping him while I got my plaque."

"Let's go to dinner, Kate. I'll take you and Henry out so you can celebrate."

She blinked, looking startled for a moment, and he was startled himself. The words had popped out, when earlier he had decided he wouldn't offer to take them to dinner and had dismissed the idea.

"That would be great, Jonah," she replied cautiously. "I don't have to stay here any longer. I'll tell my boss thanks and goodbye and then I can go. Let me take Henry with me.''

Jonah nodded and moved toward the door, waiting there until they returned to his side. He held the door open, catching a scent of her perfume as she walked past him.

''Where would you like to eat?'' he asked, remembering her favorite was Italian and trying to think if he knew any Italian restaurants in the city.

''There's a place everyone at work talks about, but I haven't been there,'' she said, naming an Italian restaurant, and in a short time, Jonah located it from her directions. They went inside the cozy establishment to find an accordion player singing Italian songs. Baskets of flowers hung from rough rafters across the ceiling and tables were covered in red-and-white checkered tablecloths with a glowing candle centered on each.

The three of them were seated near a fountain. As with their dinners at home, he and Kate gave their full attention to Henry, yet Jonah was keenly aware of her. He ordered a bottle of red wine, and during dinner, when he refilled her glass, he looked across the candlelight into her eyes. For a moment the world fell away and he was alone with Kate.

He could drown in her wide gaze. Desire burned like green-and-gold flames in the depths of her luminous hazel eyes. He poured her wine slowly, watching her as she gazed unblinkingly back at him. Jonah's body responded and he ached for her, wanting to set down the wine bottle and reach across the table and take her hand.

Tearing his gaze from hers, he set the bottle down with great deliberation, watching what he was doing. When he looked up, she had dipped her head and was looking at her plate. She had one hand in her lap and the other on the stem of her wineglass.

He couldn't resist, and reached across the table to touch her fingers. The instant he did, an electrical charge ran like lightning over his raw nerves. She inhaled and looked at him sharply, but didn't draw her hand away.

"I'm glad about your plaque and bonus," he said.

"Thanks. I sort of fell into it, but I'm glad, too."

"You look breathtaking tonight." Ravishing, radiant, sexy. He wanted her more every day.

"Thank you, Jonah. You and Henry look very handsome," she said, smiling at their son.

Jonah leaned back and released her hand, trying to turn his attention to Henry and get his mind off Kate.

When they left the restaurant later, Kate paused. "My car is at the office. If you'll drive me there, I'll get it and I can take Henry home with me."

"Naw. I'll get one of the men to come into town and pick it up. There's always someone coming and going. Let's go home together."

Kate nodded, his words making her tingle. *Let's go home together.* If only that's exactly what they could do. That moment during dinner when Jonah had poured her wine... The desire in his eyes had been unmistakable. And he had covered her hand with his, watching her, talking to her as if he cared and the whole evening hadn't been a social chore for him.

Kate knew she should insist on getting her own car and driving home separately, but she didn't want to do that. Instead, she slid into the seat of his vehicle and watched Jonah check that Henry was buckled into his seat, then get behind the wheel. By the time they reached the city limits, Henry was asleep.

"He's sleeping," she said, turning slightly to look at him, then twisting to look at his father. Her gaze ran over Jonah's profile, down his broad shoulder and arm to his hands on the wheel. The evening had been wonderful, and some of the usual strain of being around him hadn't been present. She knew she was as bubbly with excitement as if she were on a first date with him.

"There's something I wanted to talk to you about, but I thought I should run it past you when Henry wasn't around before we ask him," Jonah said. "My mom called this afternoon, and I told her about the bomb."

"She probably wants you to move off the ranch?"

Jonah laughed. "Nothing that drastic. I guess she thinks I can take care of myself, and ditto for you, but she wants us to bring Henry to stay with them for the coming week."

Kate looked back at her sleeping son and wondered if she could get through a week of separation from him. "I've never been away from him that long, Jonah. Not at all until I started work, and that's only through the day."

"Does that mean you'd rather he didn't go? Do I tell Mom no?"

"No, I'm just thinking out loud and telling you how I feel. I think it would probably be safer for him to go."

"Do you think he'd want to? From what you've said, he's never done anything like that before. Of course, if he didn't want to stay, I'd just go right back and get him. We could fly up anytime."

"I think as far as Henry is concerned, he'd love it. He and Trent were inseparable and he likes your parents. I think he's missed my parents and now he has yours. Henry will probably be happy to go, and as you said, we can go get him if he doesn't like it."

"So I can tell her yes, and we'll take him up there to-morrow?"

She studied Jonah's profile again, then his hands on the steering wheel—competent hands, strong hands. Magical, seductive hands when he wanted them to be.

"What about us, Jonah? Should I move to a hotel room until Henry gets back?"

Jonah laughed softly. "Hell, no! We can stay out of each other's sight."

"We can, but will we? We've failed miserably at that so far."

"I don't think we've failed miserably. Maybe a few slips, but we'll manage. Henry asked me tonight why I never kiss you."

Startled, she stared at him. "What did you tell him?"

"I told him that we were still divorced, which Henry argued with me about. I told him that someday you would move to a house in town and he would live with you part of the time, and part of the time with me on the ranch."

"And what did he say to that?"

"He started crying, so I pulled over and hugged him and told him that we would be together just like we are now for a long time, and we shouldn't worry about changes that would come later. That was okay with him."

"Oh, mercy!" Kate rubbed her brow, wondering once more how much she had hurt a lot of people, including her son, by walking out on Jonah.

He took her hand in his. "Stop agonizing about it, Kate. I didn't tell you that to make you fret or to make you sad. I just thought you ought to know because he may start asking you questions, too, like why don't you kiss Daddy."

"He probably will. I've hurt so many people, Jonah. I've hurt Henry and I hate that."

"I guess you did what you thought you had to do. That's what we all do. Now stop stewing about Henry, because he cheered up, and you know how children are. He will have forgotten all about it by tomorrow."

"Maybe," she said, biting her lip and unable to keep from thinking about it.

"Looks like you work with friendly people at your office," he said.

"Are you trying to change the subject?" she asked, amused and wondering if he was handling her just as he had Henry.

"Nope, but I don't see any point in dwelling on that incident any longer."

"Yes, I do work with great people. That makes it better

to go to work. I like the job and I like the people. Everyone has been adither over the bomb on your ranch.''

''That's the hot news item in these parts. I hope the bomber sees the headlines and learns that his plot failed and all he blew up was a field of grass that needed to be tilled, anyway.''

''I think that's what you told one television reporter. You may just aggravate the bomber even more, but I know that doesn't frighten you.''

''Nope, it doesn't. And I've had alarms put in the house and barn today that no one is going to dismantle easily. We have two different systems on the house. If someone tries to dismantle one, the other will go off while he's working on the first. If the lines are cut, the alarm goes off. We're covered, and so are the other houses and structures, including the barn. I've let Clementine and the others know, so they should feel safer.''

''Have you heard anything from Dakota?''

''Nope. Nothing yet.''

Jonah turned into the ranch and they rode in silence to the house, where he carried Henry inside. ''I'll put him to bed, Kate. Meet me in the kitchen and we'll have a cup of coffee.''

''No, Jonah. You and I both know we need to stay apart,'' she said, and moved away from him, hurrying to the stairs. Once in her bedroom, she closed the door and sagged against it. She wanted to be with Jonah, wanted to have that coffee with him, wanted to walk into his arms and love him all night long! Wanted to go back to him....

I'll never trust Kate again. Those words were enough to remind her that she couldn't ever go back.

And Henry asking why he never kissed Mommy. Sooner or later Henry was going to ask her why she never kissed Daddy. She put her hands over her face and wondered if she had made the greatest mistake of her life when she'd walked out on Jonah.

Tomorrow she was going to take Henry to his grandparents, then she was going to return home with Jonah, and just the two of them would be here. How was she going to survive? And how could she resist him?

She thought about him running out after the bomber—how she had hated always worrying about him. She didn't want to go back to that constant anguish, and somehow she knew that Jonah would always do something that would distress her about his safety.

Has it ever occurred to you that I might have changed? Remembering his question, she knew he hadn't. He was still the same through and through. Yet she couldn't stop wanting to be with him. Tonight had been wonderful, moments when all their differences had fallen away and they had enjoyed being together as a family, even with their attention almost totally on Henry. She crossed the room to get ready for bed, knowing sleep wasn't going to come easily.

Just as Kate guessed, Henry was eager to visit his grandparents, so early Saturday morning she packed a bag for him and a small one for herself, because she and Jonah would spend Saturday night with his family.

The drive was longer than the flight had been, and Henry was excited, chattering cheerfully all the way. Kate had a good time and knew that Jonah and Henry did, as well. And at his parents, all the other relatives came over. Trent brought a backpack, because he was going to sleep over with Henry.

In some ways it was like old times, wonderful times, except that night Kate slept in a bedroom by herself and she knew Jonah was on a sofa.

She lay in the dark and thought how marvelous the day had been and how she loved his family. And she knew she might as well face the fact that she loved Jonah and probably always would all of her life.

Should she try to get their marriage together again? As swiftly as she asked herself that question, she knew the answer. Jonah wouldn't. *I won't ever trust Kate again.* His words would haunt her the rest of her life, too.

What a muddle she had made of everything! She loved Jonah, Henry loved Jonah and there was no going back. She had fought being with him, tried to forget, tried to resist, but it was useless and she knew why. She loved the man with all her heart.

Would she love him when he started doing dangerous things again?

She couldn't answer that question, because she hated it every time he rushed into danger. She had hated living with that constant threat.

She rubbed her forehead and felt caught in the same dilemma she had been in when they were married. If they went back together now—if he ever would—could she live with his willingness to take risks?

She didn't think she could if it was like it had been before. With Henry, she would worry even more when Jonah did something risky, because not only would it mean her losing Jonah, it would mean Henry losing the father he adored.

And Henry adored Jonah. There was no mistaking the bond that had swiftly forged between father and son. It was mutual and permanent. Thank goodness Henry had none of that penchant for doing daredevil things. She knew Jonah saw his son as shy and quiet, but Kate was thankful for Henry's caution.

She stared into the darkness. "I love you, Jonah Whitewolf," she whispered in the empty room. "I always have and I always will." She might not want to be married to him, but she had to admit that she loved him still, and there was little likelihood that was ever going to change.

It definitely wouldn't change as long as she was living

in the same house with him, seeing him daily, doing things with him constantly.

She ached with wanting him, yet couldn't get up and go to the kitchen or swim or sit on the balcony at his parent's house. She was stuck in the bedroom, unable to sleep, facing the truth for the first time in a long time about her feelings for Jonah.

It was late Sunday afternoon when they kissed everyone goodbye. Dressed in shorts and a black tank top, Kate held Henry tightly. "Be good, and call me anytime you want. Daddy gave you a cell phone to keep while you're here, and you can call on that. I love you."

"I love you," he said, kissing her cheek. She hugged him tightly and set him down, watching as Jonah hugged him in turn. Her heart lurched at the sight of father and son together. Jonah was in a T-shirt and jeans, Henry dressed the same. Henry's thin arms wrapped around Jonah's neck tightly.

Then Maggie hugged Kate. "Don't worry about Henry," the older woman said quietly. "If he gets unhappy, I'll call you."

"I don't think he's going to miss us at all," Kate said, smiling at her mother-in-law.

"There are a lot of little boys here for him to play with."

Nodding, Kate turned to hug Neighbor. She hugged other relatives, kissed Henry again, and it was another ten minutes before they were in Jonah's car, driving south on the sweeping highway bordered by endless fields of grass. In the far distance, sky and earth meshed and were indistinguishable.

Overhead, its wings spread wide, a hawk circled on warm air currents high above the rush of cars on the interstate, and Kate marveled at this new state she resided in, so different from North Carolina. Texas and Jonah were synonymous to her. Texans were so friendly, yet as tough and enduring as the land beneath their feet.

"I meant to get away an hour earlier so you wouldn't be pressed getting up to go to work tomorrow," Jonah remarked.

"I'll be fine. We'll get home about ten. You know, I've been thinking. I keep scrapbooks of Henry's pictures, so we ought to start getting two copies of everything. I can keep one for you, too."

"Sounds fine to me. It was a fabulous weekend, Kate."

"Yes, it was, except I'll bet you didn't sleep much on that short sofa."

"I slept on the floor," he admitted.

She laughed. "Sorry, Jonah. I had the bed."

"Which you didn't offer to share," he teased.

"At your parents'? I don't think so!"

"We've shared one there before plenty of times, and if we had, my back wouldn't have a crook in it today."

"We were married then, and I don't think your back has a crook in it at all."

"Want to see?" he asked.

She laughed, feeling bubbly and exhilarated. "No, I don't! You keep your hands on the wheel, or let me drive."

"I might let you drive, and then I can sit and look at you while we talk."

"Jonah, you're flirting again."

"It's harmless and makes the drive a lot more interesting. And if it makes you laugh, that's great! I'll meet you in town and take you to dinner tomorrow night."

"I thought we agreed that while Henry is gone, we were going to try to avoid each other."

"It's just to eat dinner, which you have to do anyway. Come on, Kate, lighten up. I'm trying to get over the anger I felt. Help me out here."

She stared at him in consternation. "I want you to get

over your anger toward me, but at the same time, you and
I have…'' Her voice trailed away and she bit her lip.

"Have what?" he asked, his brow arching as he glanced
at her and then looked back at the road. "What, Kate? I
can't wait to hear the rest."

"You know good and well that we have this chemistry
between us that's like dynamite. We ought to keep a million
miles between us."

"That's dull and careful and far too practical. Life is
meant for living. And we can bank some of that chemistry.
Look at us now—we're doing all right and having a
friendly conversation. Nothing more."

"That's because you have to drive this car," she remarked dryly. "If we were sitting on your terrace at home,
I don't think things would be so circumspect."

"I'll bet they would. I'll wager the price of dinner tomorrow night. Wanna bet me?"

She had to laugh at him. "Jonah, you're hopeless and
you're going to do what you're going to do whether it's
wise or not."

He grinned. "Isn't this a lot better than driving home not
speaking to each other?"

"Yes, of course it is," she said softly, feeling her resistance weakening. It hadn't been even twenty-four hours
since she had promised herself to be extra cautious around
him this week. Yet they were in the car and he had to keep
his hands on the wheel and his attention on the road. The
minute they reached the house, they'd need to go their separate ways. If they couldn't resist each other when each of
them was hurt and angry, it would be impossible if they
had no buffers between them. This friendly atmosphere was
the road to seduction and hurt.

"Penny for your thoughts."

"I'm thinking we just increased the risk for more heartache."

"By being friendly? I don't think so, Kate. Life is meant to be lived, not spent in anger."

"So forgive and forget and trust again?"

He drew a deep breath and became silent, and she knew that she had just brought his anger back. But it had been a happy interlude.

"See, Jonah, friendship is only skin deep."

"You used to be the best friend I had in the whole world," he said gruffly, and she noticed his fingers had tightened on the steering wheel.

"And you were mine," she said.

For another twenty minutes they rode in silence. Kate found herself wrapped in thoughts about Henry, remembering something funny he had told her the night before.

"Jonah, last night when Henry said his prayers at bedtime, he had a line wrong. He said 'deliver us from eagles.'"

Jonah smiled. "Did you tell him he doesn't need to pray to be delivered from eagles? It's evil that he needs to worry about?"

"Yes. He asked me if evil was someone trying to bomb our barn."

"Do you think he's frightened about the bombing?"

"No. It doesn't mean much in his life, and he slept through it."

"I don't know where he gets that sound sleeping. Not from you or me or anyone in my family. I guess your dad could sleep through most things."

"That he could. Clementine is the one who is upset over it."

"I know she is," Jonah answered. "I've given her and Marvella more time off. Both women will come in just once a week for now."

As the miles sped past, they talked about Henry, and Jonah's nieces and nephews. They stopped along the road to get sandwiches, and soon conversation was back on a friendly basis. But there was no more flirting, and the talk was the same as it would have been between two casual acquaintances. Yet Kate was relaxed and enjoyed the ride with him.

By the time they reached the ranch, it was dark. When they entered the kitchen, Jonah turned to her. "Let's swim and have a cold drink. I know you're not going to sleep this early, and I'm not, either."

When she hesitated, he said, "C'mon, that's a big pool."

Knowing she was once again tossing aside all promises she had made to herself, she nodded. "Why are you always so irresistible?"

His brows arched, and he crossed the room to her, setting her pulse racing. He stopped only a foot away, entirely too close. "I'm not the irresistible one, Kate. That's you. I can't stop flirting or wanting you or dreaming about you or a million other things. We both know we should avoid each other, yet neither one of us wants to do that. I damn well don't want to tonight. I'll miss Henry and so will you. It's as if he's been in my life always. So let's swim like crazy and maybe wear ourselves out enough that we won't want to make love."

"Oh, Jonah!" She looked into his dark eyes, which blazed with desire. He trailed his finger along her cheek and his touch was electric, causing her nerves to quiver and her skin to tingle.

"Dammit, Kate, it's impossible," he whispered, and she saw that he was going to kiss her.

Chapter 11

He stepped forward and wrapped his arms around her.

She gasped, looking up at him, and then desire raged like wildfire, heating her and making her tremble. Pent-up longing was impossible to hold back.

He bent his head, his mouth coming down to cover hers. She opened her mouth, her tongue stroking his while she wrapped her arms around his neck and pressed against him.

His arms tightened and he moved closer, pulling her close in his embrace. With the first masterful stroke of his own tongue, her body turned boneless and desire became all-consuming, tearing at her and making her want him more than she ever had before in her life.

Wrong or right, hurt and heartache, it no longer mattered. She wanted his loving and wanted to love him.

As if a dam had burst, all her longing pounded through her veins, setting her pulse racing.

"Jonah, Jonah!" she exclaimed, while her hands slid along the strong column of his neck. Her fingers tangled in his thick, straight hair. She wanted to explore and touch him everywhere, as if she had never done so before in her life.

She pressed her hips against his, feeling his hard arousal. He wanted her—his kisses were proof of that. Scalding kisses that made her hot and shaky and eager.

All those promises to herself of resistance were going up in smoke. And she didn't care. She loved the man and she wanted to love him and be loved by him.

Desire was white-hot, blazing uncontrollably in her, burning away caution. She wanted to love him the rest of the night. She wanted his kisses and his hands on her, his body on hers. She had to kiss and touch him everywhere.

"Jonah," she breathed, gasping and then kissing him again. His hands slipped over her back and down to her buttocks, and she moaned. Every touch, each kiss was fuel on a fire already raging out of control. How could she want him this badly?

His arms tightened, and he leaned over her, causing her to cling to him, her body molding to his as his kisses devoured and inflamed her. His tongue stroked hers, deeply and passionately, making it clear that his desire was overwhelming, too.

She shook, stunned by the force of their attraction.

"Kate, I want you," he muttered, almost growling the words as his tongue traced the curve of her ear and his warm breath caused more tingles.

She ached for him deep inside, wanting all of the loving he could give her. His hands drifted slowly over her bottom, tugging her tank top out of her shorts. He stepped back, pulled the top over her head and flung it aside.

With the same desperate movements, her fingers shaking, she pulled his T-shirt out of his jeans and over his head, looking into his eyes. She saw his surprise and knew he had expected her to say no or push against him or give some token of resistance. He hadn't ever guessed that she would want him as desperately as he seemed to want her.

He wound his fingers in her hair and tilted her head up to look down into her eyes, and she gasped at the hot desire in his gaze. "You want this, don't you?"

"Yes!" she cried. "Oh, yes, I want you!"

"Kate—" He broke off to kiss her once more, demolishing all reason. When he raised his head again, his dark brown eyes pierced hers like laser beams. "What we do to each other," he said, as if the words were forced from him. His fingers tightened in her hair, and she didn't know whether anger or desire was driving him now.

"What we do to each other is ecstasy," she murmured, trailing her tongue across his chest, running her palm over one nipple while her tongue stroked the other one.

He inhaled sharply and dropped his hands to the waist of her shorts, quickly unfastening them and pushing them away. He unsnapped the clasp of her lacy bra, removed it and stepped back to cup her breasts, looking at her with so much desire and heat that she quivered and wanted back in his embrace.

"You're the most beautiful woman on earth," he whispered, and bent his head to take her nipple in his mouth, to bite gently, to lick and tease while she gasped with pleasure, an exquisite torment.

She wrapped her fingers in his hair, closing her eyes and letting her head fall back, momentarily riveted by sensations that shot through every inch of her and then pooled low, a raging desire.

"Jonah," she gasped, leaning forward to nip lightly along his neck and shoulder, her hands running over his upper arms, feeling the taut, powerful muscles. She dragged her palms over his muscled chest and down over a flat, washboard stomach that was as muscled as the rest of him.

With fumbling fingers, she tugged open the buttons of his jeans and pushed them away. She hooked her fingers in his briefs and pushed them down, sliding her hands along his strong thighs.

"Jonah!" Gazing at him, she snagged his wrists so that he couldn't touch her. She knelt, her tongue flicking out, trailing along the inside of his thigh, while her hand wrapped around his thick shaft and she stroked him.

He moaned and a tremor shook him when she trailed her tongue higher, then along his hard length, taking him in her mouth.

He slid his hands under her arms to lift her up, and when she looked into his eyes, her heart thudded with the hunger she saw mirrored in his gaze. He wrapped her in his embrace, kissing her senseless again.

Jonah shook with desire. He wanted Kate as he had never wanted her before, knowing that he was finally letting loose all the pent-up longing he had kept bottled up for so long.

His shock when she had indicated she wanted him still reverberated through him. He'd expected the resistance and reluctance he had gotten ever since their divorce. But it was gone. She was wild in his arms, giving back as much as she got, driving him to a point where it was an almighty struggle to maintain his iron control.

But he wanted to keep that control and make this last. She might not ever yield eagerly to him again. Yield and give with a total, passionate response that all but melted his insides.

She was breathtakingly beautiful, her body so incredibly desirable. He was rock hard, hurting, ready and wanting her, yet he wanted so much more. He had dreamed of this moment for over five years now, longed for it. Imagined it when he had been stuck in dangerous situations where he had to just sit and wait.

Now the time was here and he wanted it to last. He wanted to savor every second of it and every inch of her luscious body, which she was offering so eagerly.

Her hands were all over him, driving him wild. Every touch, every movement, every kiss from her sent his pulse racing and his heart pounding. Did she know that, at this point in time, he would do anything for her?

"Kate," he said in a husky, low voice. He doubted if she even heard him, and it didn't matter. He had said her name for himself. He wanted her, wanted her softness to envelop him. He wanted to take her to heights of passion she had never experienced before.

He slid his arm around her waist, tugging off her lace panties and pulling her to him. His fingers slipped between her thighs, fondling her intimately. She gasped and closed her eyes and her head rocked back while her hips thrust against him repeatedly. Kissing her, he rubbed her while she clung to him, her fingers biting into his shoulder. When he took her over the brink, she cried out.

The more he excited her, the more she excited him. Years fell away. She was here in his arms, letting him love her again, only this time more passionate than ever, as if starved for his loving.

Heaven knew he was starved for hers! How he wanted her! He wanted to bury himself in her heat and end the torment.

Her eyes flew open and the desire in those hazel depths shook him. He wrapped his arms tightly around her waist, and when he did, she wrapped her legs around him.

He groaned, letting her slide down his length, and then while kissing her, he picked her up.

Determined to have her in his bed, he headed for the stairs, taking them easily while she turned to trail kisses along his neck and shoulder. She teased his ear, her tongue a hot, wet torment that stirred more erotic feelings.

He lowered her to his big bed, coming down beside her to bite her ankle, then drag his mouth up the inside of her silken thigh. Tomorrow might be filled with regrets by both of them, but he would worry about that later. Tonight, Kate was his, not only willingly, but eagerly, wanting him just as he wanted her. That was a treasure he had only dreamed about, a memory to keep forever and a relief from the hell he had been going through.

He paused to look at her soft, tempting body, so creamy and pink.

"You're beautiful," he repeated, and leaned down to continue his gentle assault on her inner thigh. She cried out with passion and dug her fingers in his hair, moving him where she wanted him.

Kate gasped with pleasure as Jonah's tongue stroked her where his fingers had been, driving her to wanton abandon. She thrashed beneath him, wrapping her long legs around him, wanting him inside her.

Here in his bed, she knew she had crossed lines and let go of all barriers. And he knew how she felt—she had made that clear to him tonight. She knew what she wanted and she wasn't holding back, and remorse would not be part of this night. She was ready to give of herself totally and take from him the same way.

She gasped with pleasure, then wriggled away and pushed him down on the bed. "Let me kiss you," she ordered, bending forward, a curtain of hair hiding her face from him as she trailed her tongue over his nipples and chest.

She continued kissing his marvelous male body, her tongue drifting across his flat belly, down to his throbbing manhood, which she licked and stroked while her other hand caressed his powerful thighs.

Groaning, he sat up, cradling her against his shoulder. Then he turned her, placing her on her back and moving between her legs. "Still protected, Kate?"

When she shook her head, he moved away, crossing the room to open a dresser drawer. He was magnificent and she couldn't stop looking at him. She slid off the bed and crossed the room to come up behind him, pressing against his warm, hard length, her arms going around him.

"I want you, Jonah."

"Ah, Kate, how I want you, darlin'." He turned swiftly to hold her and kiss her, then picked her up and carried her back to bed.

Once again he moved between her legs, opening a packet to get out protection.

She drank in the sight of him—male, hard, ready for her. She held out her arms and draped her legs over his thighs. He lowered himself, coming down to enter her.

She felt his thick, hard shaft penetrate slowly, and she had to move, desire compounding to a driving force that made her lose control. She was Jonah's completely, yielding, loving him, holding him tightly against her and relishing the warmth and hardness of his body as he slowly filled her and swept her to new heights.

"Jonah!" she cried, seeing lights exploding behind her closed eyelids as hot desire consumed her.

United, with all differences burned away in passion and one driving force motivating them, they moved together. She gripped his shoulders, relishing holding him close. Her long legs were locked around him and she yielded completely. Urgency carried them along, higher and higher until they crashed over a brink and release came.

She held him tightly, feeling his body shudder as he moved with her. She kissed his throat. "I love you," she proclaimed softly, certain he would be lost in passion and never hear her. And if he heard, he wouldn't care.

He slowed, finally letting his weight down on her. He kissed her lightly, showering kisses over her shoulder and throat, her forehead and cheek, her ear.

"You're stunning, Kate. You're wonderful. I want to hold you in my arms all night long."

"I want you to hold me all night and I want to hold you," she said, turning her head. He looked into her eyes and her breath caught at the tenderness she saw there.

After making love, she expected he'd be satiated, soon returning to his distant self. She wouldn't have been surprised if he had regrets. But she didn't expect to look into his eyes and see desire blazing as if they hadn't yet made love at all.

She tightened her arms around him and pulled his head down to kiss him. When she did, his mouth opened and his tongue touched hers, his kiss an affirmation of the closeness they had just felt.

"Jonah, I'm glad."

"So am I, Kate," he answered solemnly. Holding her close, he turned so they were on their sides, facing each other. "You're fantastic."

She smiled and ducked her head, kissing his neck, and he pulled her into his embrace.

He sighed, holding her and stroking her back. "I think my bones have turned to soup."

She laughed softly and kissed his throat again, trailing her fingers over his chest. "I don't think so."

"Kate, stay here with me tonight."

"I will."

He moved away to look at her, playing with her hair. "Do you have to go to work tomorrow? Any chance of calling in and telling them that you have to stay in bed?"

She laughed again. "No, Jonah, I'm not calling in and telling them that. Let's not worry about morning yet."

"Good enough," he said, trailing kisses over her forehead and down her cheek. "You're perfection, Kate."

"Then you're blind," she answered dryly, but his words pleased her and his kisses thrilled her. She was glad he wanted her to stay in his bed, glad he wanted her to skip work tomorrow, even though she didn't think she should when she was so new to the company. "After a while we should call Henry and tell him good night and that we're home now."

"I think it's already past Henry's bedtime, but we can let Mom know that we're back at the ranch. Although she doesn't expect me to check in with her,'' he added with amusement in his voice.

"She might not expect it, but she'll like it.''

"We'll do it in a little while. Right now, I just want to hold you and touch you and look at you," he said, caressing her shoulder.

"That's fine with me," she answered, trailing her fingers over his smooth back, feeling the solid muscles. She let her hand slide down his firm buttocks, to his thighs, sprinkled with short, dark hairs.

She knew they were both skirting issues about how this night of loving would change their relationship, but at the moment, she didn't want reality to intrude on her euphoria. And she suspected that he didn't, either.

"So much for staying alone in the same house and avoiding each other," she said.

He grinned. "This is infinitely better."

"I'd have to agree with that one. You're a very special man, Jonah."

"How so?" he asked.

"You're a fantastic father and an awesome lover, and when you want, you can be fabulous to be with.''

"Hot damn, darlin', you'll turn my head! I don't remember such praise when we were married.''

"Maybe I was more into reality then. Or less appreciative.''

He smiled at her. "You're a seductress and I think you planned every minute of this night.''

"Jonah Whitewolf!'' she exclaimed indignantly, and then she saw the glint in his eyes and knew he was teasing her. "If anything was planned, I wasn't the one who did the planning.''

"Like a lot of good things, tonight was completely spontaneous.''

"That's because we're like fire and dynamite when we get together. The explosions happen.''

"Then you're fire, because you set me off every time you're in the same room."

"You've hidden it well," she said, running her index finger along his shoulder. "You know we just compounded our problems tonight."

"Maybe. Maybe we solved some. You could move in here with me and solve some more."

"Right," she remarked dryly. "Solve your lack of sex."

"That's right, baby," he drawled in a husky, seductive voice, and she laughed while he nuzzled her neck. "Next time I can go slower and give you more pleasure."

"If you go slower and give me more pleasure, I'll disintegrate."

"We'll try and see," he said softly, running his hand along her hip and up to cup her breast.

She caught his wrist to stop him. "You're supposed to be too exhausted to be interested in that right now."

"Who says? I'm interested. I'll show you."

"Jonah! I need to clean up a little, too."

"Then we'll do that together. One of those hot, sexy, seductive baths. Come on." He stood and leaned down to scoop her into his arms and carry her to his big bathroom. In minutes he had water pouring into a round tub, and he took her hand, leading her down the steps.

"This is very fancy," she said, eyeing the mammoth tub and luxurious decor.

"That it is. Absolutely fascinating," he said, his gaze drifting over her nude body. He leaned down to take her nipple into his mouth, flicking his tongue over the taut bud.

She inhaled and clung to his shoulders. "A bath, Jonah. We were going to bathe, remember?"

He raised his head and his eyes had darkened with desire. Climbing the rest of the way into the tub, he sat and pulled her down. She straddled him and faced him, looking into his heated gaze.

''So soon?'' she whispered, aware that he was hard and ready again.

''That's what you do to me, Kate,'' he said solemnly. He framed her face with his hands and looked at her, and she felt as desired as a woman could possibly be by a man.

Jonah leaned forward to kiss her and she was lost again, her body responding instantly, making her ready for him. But he kissed and caressed her, lingering the way he'd said he would, to make this time even better for her.

When the bathwater reached their waists, he paused to turn off the spigots. Still intrigued and excited, she ran her hands over his magnificent chest, which now gleamed with water. She wasn't going to tell him she loved him, because he wouldn't tell her he loved her in return, but she did love him, and every kiss, each caress, was an outpouring of what she felt for him.

She leaned down to trail her tongue over his nipple and hear him groan before he pulled Kate up to kiss her, hard and long.

Finally he tugged her over him, his shaft entering her, and his fingers stroked her intimately, touching erogenous zones. When he kissed her hard, a blinding spiral of need drove her to a frenzy.

Release burst inside her and she collapsed over him, just as he reached his own climax. Satiated, joyous with love-making, she clung to him. She had no idea how much time passed before he turned her, pulling her onto his lap and holding her close in his arms with her back against his chest.

''You're decadent and wicked, Jonah,'' she said softly.

''And you love it, you wanton little seductress,'' he said, nuzzling her neck.

She leaned back against him. ''I could purr now.''

''Just wait a little while and I'll give you a real reason to purr.''

She laughed and twisted around on his lap to look at

him. And then she remembered their differences in outlook, the problems, and knew that this was an accident—a brief, euphoric interlude.

He gazed back solemnly, and she wondered if he was thinking the same thing. Their love was hopeless, their relationship at an impasse neither could change. This interlude of ecstasy was only that, an interlude. It had changed nothing, had done nothing except satisfy their lust. She leaned her head against his chest, knowing they hadn't solved any problems between them, but had merely compounded and complicated them.

"Don't let tomorrow intrude yet, Kate. This is too great."

She sighed. "That's difficult to do, but I agree and I'll try. We really got ourselves in deeper, and complicated our lives even more."

"I don't think so. In the long run, I think things between us will be better."

"Jonah, that's a real stretch. We'd better stop now."

"You're right," he said, standing with her in his arms. She yelped as water splashed and sloshed. Jonah carried her out of the tub and set her on her feet.

"Now we can dry each other off," he said, handing her a thick, fluffy navy towel. He took one himself and began to dry her body with slow, seductive strokes.

She did the same to him, still relishing every touch and caress. Her pulse was racing again and she tingled, wanting him, when just five minutes ago she hadn't thought she would again tonight.

"Turn around, Jonah, and I'll dry your back," she said, running the towel over his smooth skin, down over his narrow waist, his trim buttocks. She started to dry his legs and he turned.

"Kate," he whispered, dropping his towel and tossing away hers, pulling her into his embrace to kiss her again....

Through the night they loved, until Jonah fell asleep in

her arms at dawn and she knew she would miss a day of work. She was exhausted and she didn't want to leave the house or the bedroom.

She wouldn't think ahead. Seize the day and worry about tomorrow later, she told herself. There was plenty of time for heartache on down the road, but right now, she wanted to love him, and for him to love her.

The night had compounded desire instead of satisfying it. She couldn't understand her own reactions, but she wanted him. She twisted slightly, moving carefully to raise up on her elbow and look at him while he slept.

He was the most handsome man on earth to her and she could never see him any other way. He had been a warrior when she'd met him, and she'd known what she was going into when she married him. But at the same time, she hadn't known how devastating it would be to live day after day with him in constant danger.

She touched his hair lightly, wanting to run her fingers over his firm jaw, looking at his thick lashes, glad those lively dark eyes were closed, because they missed nothing.

His shoulders were broad and strong, his arms muscled, his chest like a rock. Her gaze ran down his bare length and her pulse skipped. He was a magnificent male, so incredibly special, yet at the same time so hopelessly determined to do what he wanted to do.

She wrapped her arms around him and lay down again, holding him close against her. "I love you, Jonah," she whispered, knowing that if she wanted to be honest with herself, she would admit it to him. But it wouldn't solve anything. Jonah didn't trust her, and he wouldn't really care whether she loved him or not, because love was useless without trust.

I may have changed... Again she recalled what he'd said, but she knew better than that. He hadn't changed one tiny degree or he would never have run outside the other night after the bomber.

No point hoping for miracles. She didn't know where the two of them were headed, but she didn't see marriage looming in the future. Not without trust.

She sighed and pressed against him. Take what you have right now, she told herself, knowing tomorrow would be filled with more heartaches.

She dozed, stirring only when erotic tingles made her shift and move her hips. She opened her eyes to find Jonah leaning over her, his tongue circling her nipple slowly while he caressed her with his free hand.

With a sigh, she turned, wrapping her arm around his neck and pulling him down for a kiss, and within minutes they were making love as if it were the first time all over again.

Later, she called her office to tell them she wouldn't be in, and returned to Jonah's waiting arms. "You're causing the decadence here," she said.

"It won't hurt you to miss one day of work. I'll call Scott after a while and let him know that I'm busy all day. And then, my beauty, I'll have my way with you."

"Is that a promise?" she asked, and he grinned.

"Kate, we could live together this way."

She started to answer and he put his finger on her lips. "Don't say anything yet. Think about it." He moved his hands. "And while you think about it…" He leaned down to kiss her and she promptly forgot everything except him and his mouth and body.

It was noon before she stepped out of bed, yanking at the sheet to wrap it around her. "I'm starving for food. I'm going to shower and then I'm going to eat. I'll be happy to feed you if you don't want anything complicated."

"Fair enough," he said, his gaze drifting over her. He slid off the bed and crossed to her. "Now that that decision is made, give me a good-morning kiss."

"Not on your life, mister! I know where that leads. You wait until I get some food." She turned and fled. "We need to call and talk to Henry, too,'' she called over her shoulder.

When she had showered, she dressed in clean cutoffs and another blue T-shirt.

Downstairs, Jonah was on the kitchen phone. He talked a moment and motioned to her. "Come talk to Henry. I don't think he's missing us as much as you suspected."

She picked up the receiver and said hello, hearing Henry's childish voice. "Mommy! I'm having a cool time. We're going swimming this afternoon."

"Great! You can show Grandma and Grandpa how well you swim. I miss you."

"I miss you, too," he said, but he raced over the words.

"We'll hang up now. I'll call you tonight, Henry." She replaced the receiver to find Jonah watching her. He had jeans on and was bare-chested, with his feet in loafers. She was conscious of her appearance as his gaze drifted slowly over her. He reached for her to pull her onto his lap. "You look beautiful."

She sat down and wrapped her arms around his neck and wished there were no tomorrows to worry about. "Jonah, could we both trust again—you trust me to stay, and I trust you to cease taking risks?"

Chapter 12

He gazed at her in silence, his dark eyes unfathomable. "I don't know whether I can give you an answer, Kate. We can try, and see how it works out. What would be the harm in that? We still want each other, so why not try?"

She realized the implications of his question. Get back together. Could they work it out? Would he really change? Would he ever trust her? Could she stay worthy of that trust?

She trailed her fingers along his jaw. "I'm willing to try," she said quietly, her heart pounding because she was going to risk everything for him again.

He wrapped his arms around her and kissed her exuberantly. When he released her, he looked at her with a solemn gaze. "Okay, Kate. Move in with me, into my bed and into my life."

She inhaled deeply. "Jonah, I hope—"

He kissed her once more, stopping her words, and the next time he raised his head, he repeated his question. "Will you move in with me?"

"Yes, I will," she said, making a commitment that both thrilled and frightened her.

"Oh, Kate, how I've wanted you!" he exclaimed, tightening his arms around her.

As if he were the only solid thing in her world, she held him and kissed him, but she wished the words he had said were *I love you* instead of *I want you*. She was committed now and she hoped that things worked out, and she was wrong about him tiring of ranch life.

"We'll just have to take each day as it comes," she said, and he arched a brow.

"You don't sound very sure," he said.

"I'm not and I don't think you are, either."

"I guess not," he said, "but in the meantime, life will be better and Henry will be happier."

"True. And in the meantime, right now, I want to eat. I feel like I haven't eaten for three days."

"C'mon, darlin', and I'll feed you. You know, you could take the whole week off and just loll around here with me."

She laughed. "Don't be ridiculous, Jonah! A week off a job I just started?"

"Ah, Kate. Your laughter is the best sound in the world. How I love to hear you laugh and see your eyes sparkle. Every smile is a gift for me."

"That's mutual. You're sexier than ever when you laugh."

"I can't buy that one," he said, grinning at her. "You don't have to work, Kate. If we get back together, you don't have to keep that job," he said in an earnest voice.

"For now, I'm keeping my job, at least until we see that this is what we want," she said, moving off his lap.

"Suit yourself, darlin'." In minutes Jonah had fried slices of pink ham, prepared fluffy yellow scrambled eggs, poured orange juice and coffee. Kate had made toast and set the table, and when they sat down across from each other to eat, Jonah took her hand.

"I want to hang on to you. I want to make sure you're here with me."

"I'm with you and I'll go back up to bed with you after we eat."

"There went my appetite for food—"

"Sit down, Jonah! I said after we eat."

Grinning, he plopped back in the chair and picked up her hand again, brushing kisses on her knuckles. "I'll just nibble on you for breakfast."

"You'd better eat your ham and eggs or you'll be starving soon and you'll have to get out of bed again."

He grinned and started eating. When he did, she took a bite of eggs. "These are wonderful, Jonah," she exclaimed, closing her eyes while she chewed.

"They're just eggs. Kate, I want to tell you something."

"And this ham is delicious. Everything is wonderful."

"Kate, can you tear yourself away from food a moment and listen to me?"

She opened her eyes. "Sure," she answered, drinking her hot coffee. "What is it?"

"I didn't see any reason to tell you before, and I didn't want it to make a difference in our relationship."

She stared at him and wondered what he hadn't told her that he didn't want to make a difference. "What is it?"

"Don't look so worried. It's good news. When I inherited this ranch, that wasn't all. Each one of the beneficiaries inherited money, too."

"Well, that's wonderful, Jonah. That's how you can afford the catering and chartering planes and all. That's great."

She bit into her toast, spread with raspberry jelly. "I was starving."

"So I noticed," he drawled. "Kate, it was over a million dollars."

Her mouth fell open and she stared at him, stunned. Her

appetite fled and she felt dazed. "Over a million? Plus this ranch?"

"That's right."

"Mercy, Jonah! That's an enormous fortune!"

"Yes, it is. I have a financial advisor and lawyers and an accountant, and I'm trying to get more of the inheritance into charities. Kate, I can do all sorts of things for Henry."

"Oh, mercy!" She was still stunned, unable to grasp that Jonah now owned so much. "Maybe that's why someone tried to blow up the barn. Maybe someone hates you for that inheritance."

"I've thought about it. I don't know if Gabe Brant inherited that much from his father."

"That's a lot of money," she said, barely thinking about Gabe or the bomb. "Over a million dollars. Your family didn't say anything."

"I told them I hadn't told you and I wanted to wait."

"Were you scared that I'd go back to you for the money?" she asked, feeling indignant.

"No, not at all. Just the opposite. I know how independent you are and I thought the money might run you off for good."

"Mercy!" she exclaimed, still stunned.

"So you see, you don't have to work if you'd rather stay home with Henry."

She thought about that for a moment. "For now, let's keep things the way they are," she said, and he nodded.

"Kate, if there is anything you or Henry need, just tell me."

She closed her eyes, momentarily taken aback when she thought how she had saved and struggled and sold all the furniture that she and Henry had, plus her parents' things, to make ends meet and pay her parents' medical bills.

Jonah reached over to take her hand again. "I'm sorry for the difficult time you had."

"See, there you go again," she said, trying to get a grip

on her emotions. "You know exactly what I'm thinking. I never have a clue with you."

"That wasn't too hard to guess. And I mean it—anything you want, just get it."

"There is one thing, Jonah, since you obviously can afford it. My car is in constant need of repair. I don't have to have anything newer, but I'd like something that I'm not always pouring money into and that runs when I need it."

"I think we can take care of that," he replied, and she saw the amusement in his expression.

"Now don't go out and buy some expensive, brand-new car."

"I'll get you a car that's reliable. How's that?"

"It's great. Over a million…!"

"You forgot to eat, and your eggs are getting cold."

"So they are," she said, returning to her breakfast. She tilted her head to study Jonah. "I might look into schools and see what would be best for Henry, because now there are possibilities I wouldn't have considered before."

"I think that's great. I've been told that Stallion Pass has an excellent school system."

"I'll check into it. You're not driving a new car, either."

"I'm driving the one I inherited, and my pickup. I got everything that went with the ranch, plus the money."

"I just can't get used to the idea. What about Boone and Mike?"

"They each got the same amount."

"That's amazing. All because you saved the man's life." Jonah nodded. "Now that you're not so interested in eating anyway, come here," he said, taking her hand and pulling her around the table to his lap. He wrapped his arms about her.

"If you kiss me, I'll taste and smell like ham and eggs."

"Do you think I care?" he asked before his head dipped down and her answer was lost.

* * *

Midweek, Kate was eager to leave work and get home. She had taken two days off, spending them in Jonah's arms. She was in love with him all over again, loving him more than she ever had before. She appreciated him more, loved him for being such a great father to Henry, loved him doubly for the agony she had gone through away from him.

And he seemed to be settling into life on the ranch. He went out to work on the range, taking an interest in every facet of the operation. She dared to hope that he had changed. And she hoped that whoever had tried to blow up the barn had moved on or would soon be caught, because life was better than it had ever been. She loved Jonah deeply, although she suspected they both were still wary of getting hurt.

She turned into the drive and thought about her job. In some ways she loved the work, and Henry would start school this year, so she wouldn't mind so much being gone during the day. Jonah was with him constantly when she was away, too. They still hadn't hired a nanny. Kate knew Jonah was waiting until life was safer and quieter before he hired a stranger to come into their lives to care for Henry.

In some ways, Kate wanted to quit and just be home with their son, but she wanted to be more certain about her relationship with Jonah. She wanted a declaration of love from him, because that statement that he would never trust her again was impossible to forget.

Nights with Jonah were magical and she missed being away from him days. She was falling more in love with him every hour and no longer tried to resist him.

She took a deep breath now, her pulse accelerating because in minutes she would be with him. Yesterday when she had gotten home from work, she had walked into his arms, and they had made love there in the kitchen.

She tingled as she recalled scalding kisses and lovemaking. She was eager to be in his arms again now. She'd made the last turn and was driving toward the house when she saw a car she didn't recognize and wondered if they had company. Kate knew Jonah had given the help time off so he could be alone with her.

She parked, climbed out and hurried forward, to meet Jonah on the porch. "Is someone here?"

"Yep, this someone," he said, smiling at her and picking her up in his arms to carry her inside. She wrapped her arms around his neck and kissed him, forgetting the car or company or anything else except him.

He set her on her feet while he continued to kiss her, and she ran her hands over him, tugging off his T-shirt and tossing it aside. When she did, she looked into his dark eyes and saw desire that stirred hers even more.

Then she was back in his arms, pulling off clothing, and he walked her into the family room and lowered her to the thick rug while he kissed and caressed her.

They loved frantically, as if it were the first time in a long time, and finally lay exhausted in each other's arms. "Welcome home," he said softly, his tongue following the curve of her ear.

"That's an incentive to keep working, so I can come home every day to that kind of welcome."

"If you don't want to keep working, we can arrange something like this every day, even if it isn't an official welcome home."

"Are you trying to bribe me into staying home?"

"Not at all. You do what you want. But I'm glad you're here now."

"I don't know where my clothes are."

"Doesn't matter. You don't need them."

She touched his jaw. "I'm not spending the evening running around the house nude."

"Suits me fine if you do," he said.

"No way. Now let's gather the clothes and go have one of those long, luxurious baths in your great big tub."

"Will do. You go on. I'll bring the clothes."

Smiling, she left, turning at the door to watch him walking around, picking up scattered clothing, oblivious to his own nudity. When her gaze raked over him, her pulse raced again.

She hurried upstairs to start a bath, and it wasn't until dinnertime that she remembered the black car parked by the back gate. "Jonah, whose car is that outside?"

"Actually, it's yours. I bought—"

She screeched and jumped up, dashing outside to look at it. She ran to the shiny, four-door sedan and turned to see that he had followed her out. "You did what I told you not to. This is brand-new."

"Do you like it?"

"I love it!" she exclaimed, running back to throw her arms around him.

He hugged her and laughed. "I didn't know you'd be this enthused. I should have gotten this for you sooner."

"It's wonderful now, Jonah. Thank you!" As they kissed, she forgot about the car once more, and soon he picked her up to carry her inside, kicking the door closed and leaning against it, letting her slide down his length until she stood on her feet while they continued kissing.

Thursday night when she lay in his arms, she asked him, "Will we go get Henry on Saturday?"

"If you want. I don't know that it's one degree safer than it was when he left. Nothing has happened."

"I want him to come back home."

"We can't lie around in bed like we have been or make love all through the house the minute you get home," Jonah said.

"Do you object to him being here?"

"Of course not. I miss him, too."

"Then I want him here," she said.

"In the meantime, darlin', I have you all to myself and I want you naked and I want to love you senseless."

"I think that's what you've got right now. Or have you forgotten what we've been doing the past few hours?"

"Completely. Why don't you show me what I've forgotten?"

"Sure thing, honey," she said in a sultry voice that made him draw a deep breath. She turned to kiss him, winding her arms around his neck and pulling him close against her.

Later, when Kate was asleep, Jonah lay back with one arm folded behind his head while he played with Kate's hair with his other hand. The past few days had been paradise. The more he loved Kate, the more he wanted to love her. And he had heard her declarations of love when she had thought he wasn't awake, or in the throes of passion when she thought he wouldn't hear her.

Yet she hadn't declared that love to him when she knew he *would* hear her. He suspected she was holding back, just as he had to admit he was doing. He knew Kate too well. Right now, nothing was happening to cause any conflicts between them, but when Henry returned, there would be moments when he would want to let Henry do things that Kate considered dangerous. If she didn't get her way, would she walk out of his life again?

He knew he was having a difficult time letting go and trusting her. As much as he loved her—and he had loved her once with all his heart—he couldn't let go of his doubts.

They couldn't resist each other, but at the same time they couldn't trust each other. And that was not the way it should be, he knew. He wanted her badly, but he couldn't change himself.

He knew Kate hadn't changed, either, and she wouldn't. He tugged on his earlobe as he mulled over the dilemma, and then he looked down at Kate sleeping blissfully beside him.

Maybe he was worrying needlessly. He rolled over, pulling her into his arms.

* * *

On Saturday they returned to his parents' place to pick up Henry. During the afternoon, Jonah was with his dad as they sat in the shade of a tree in the backyard and watched the boys playing ball.

"You think it's safe for Henry to go home with you again?"

"I don't know, Dad. Nothing's happened since someone tried to blow up my barn. I've got more alarms installed and now the men patrol the ranch. I keep two dogs up by the house."

"Well, we like having him here, so if anything happens, bring him back for however long you want. He's well-mannered and easy to have around, and you know your mother loves having him here."

"I know she does. Thanks for keeping him this past week. I know he's had a great time."

"I think he has. He likes his cousins."

Jonah saw Kate cross the patio and head toward the kitchen. She wore a yellow sundress and she looked wonderful. He had bought a bracelet for her and wanted to give it to her tonight after they got home and had Henry tucked into bed.

Kate stepped into the kitchen from the patio, her hands full of tumblers. "Here are more glasses the boys had outside," she said to Maggie, who stood frying chicken in a skillet. "What can I do to help you?"

"You can pour water and milk for the kids. We're nearly ready to eat." She got a platter from the cabinet and turned to Kate. "Things are better between you two, and I'm glad."

Kate smiled. "Did Jonah tell you that we're back together?"

Maggie shook her head. "No, he didn't. But it shows in both of you, and I'm so happy for you."

"We haven't told anyone because we don't know our-selves if it will last."

"I think it'll last. He loves you very much."

"He doesn't say so," Kate replied, looking into Mag-gie's friendly brown eyes. "We'll have to see how things work out."

"Well, Jonah is happier than he has been in a long time except when he found out about his son. For all of your sakes, I hope you are back together."

"Thanks, Maggie."

The topic of conversation changed and in minutes lunch was on the table. Shortly after eating, they left to drive back to the ranch.

That night, after Henry had been put to bed, Jonah and Kate went to their room and closed the door. As soon as it was shut, Jonah pulled her into his arms to kiss her.

The man stood without moving, staring at the ranch house in the distance. Even at this late hour, lights still burned in several rooms. Around him, crickets chirped, and the man could hear the occasional rustling of critters in the underbrush. Somewhere an owl hooted, a forlorn cry in the night.

Frustration made the man grumble softly to himself. "Tonight won't be for nothing," he muttered. "I'll go back to the Long Bar in future. Next time he won't find the bomb—he'll never know it's there. It won't be in the barn, but in the house. And tonight, here at the Rivas's place there'll be no failure."

Still muttering under his breath, he moved through the darkness. Gone now were the trucks and the rustling of cattle. It was over, and they would never catch him or any-one connected with him. Penny-ante stuff that was a cover for what he really wanted. The rustling had worked, though, and he was certain the sheriff of Piedras County was still searching for a gang of rustlers, still checking feedlots and cattle sales for livestock bearing the stolen brands.

He moved with stealth across a field, keeping to shadows, knowing he had picked a night when there would be little moonlight. He carried a can with him, the contents sloshing as he walked. All he needed was gasoline and a match, and that ranch house would soon be gone. And the rancher with it. Probably asleep in a drunken stupor, the victim would never know about the fire until the place was in flames all around him.

If firemen came to help, they would be too late. It would all be over by the time they arrived, and they'd struggle to keep the fire contained. There was a wind tonight, wind to fan the flames, and maybe more than the ranch house would burn. If he could have carried another can of gasoline, he would have torched the barn, too, but the house was the main target. Get the house and the rancher in it.

He laughed. Now he would have his revenge. No failure tonight, no one to stop the flames or catch him. He fingered the knife in the scabbard he wore on his hip.

He would slip into the house. This one had an old, faulty alarm and he doubted if the rancher even used it. If the wire to it were cut, no one would come. He had been in the house before when no one was home, dismantling the alarm and then putting it back together because it was ancient and simple. He had looked the place over and even taken some money he'd found. No theft had been reported, though, because no one had known that a stranger had been in the house.

Kirk Rivas tonight. In a few weeks, the Long Bar, and finally Duane Talmadge. Then Ashley Brant. He would take her with him when he was through. He had his plans for the future, and no one would ever suspect him of having anything to do with the crimes. But even if they did, they wouldn't be able to get him.

He had made money off the rustling. Good money that

he could put to use. That was the irony of it. He didn't care about the money.

He slowed as he drew near the house and stood watching it. Was there a girlfriend in the house with Rivas now? He knew the boys no longer lived at home.

The man stood for half an hour, waiting, and didn't see anyone. Finally he moved to the back of the house and pulled out his knife, cutting the cord to the alarm.

In minutes he was inside through an unlocked window. He raced through the downstairs, pouring gasoline as he went, splashing it on drapes and chairs, carpet and stairs, until every last drop was gone. He walked to the open window and looked back.

"Revenge. Finally," he said aloud. He took a match from his pocket, lit it and flipped it away, climbing out the window and running to leap off the porch and land on his feet in the yard.

He heard the boom when the gasoline ignited, saw flames shoot up inside the house as the fire raced along the trail of fuel, bursting into flames as it went until the downstairs windows glowed bright orange.

The man ran across the yard, and as he went, he frowned, listening. He heard a car engine growing louder. He ran on, pushing through a gate and running along a drive.

He was caught in the glare of headlights when a car raced up the lane. It stopped and a man got out, swaying and cursing.

"What the hell?" he yelled. "Fire! My house is on fire!"

It was him! Rivas! And he must think he was talking to one of the cowboys who worked on the ranch for him. Kirk Rivas, drunk, but realizing something was wrong.

The man glanced over his shoulder. Fire could be seen raging throughout the downstairs now. Flames danced at every window.

"My house is on fire!" Rivas yelled again. "Get the

others,'' he bellowed. "Don't just stand there. Do something!"

The man reached for his knife.

Jonah lay holding Kate in his arms, his leg thrown over hers, when the ringing of the phone awakened him. He stretched out his arm and picked it up, speaking softly to try to avoid rousing her.

"Jonah?"

Jonah recognized the voice of Sheriff Dakota Gallen.

Kate stirred and rolled over. Jonah sat on the side of the bed, listening as he swore softly. "Dammit! And you still don't know who or what? There has to be a connection somewhere."

She sat up, a chill running down her spine because the rustlers had struck again. Jonah sounded grim and angry.

And they had just brought Henry home. She thought of the ranch as home now. Home was Henry and Jonah, and Jonah's ranch.

She touched his bare back, running her fingers down it lightly, momentarily forgetting the danger as she caressed his warm, smooth skin.

Then she heard him swear again and knew that whatever had happened, it was bad. She worried about Henry, wondering whether they needed to take him right back to his grandparents' house. She wanted him safe and out of harm's way until the rustlers were caught. Only she suspected Jonah's swearing and anger was not over a bunch of stolen cattle.

In minutes he hung up the phone and twisted around to look at her.

"What's happened?" she asked.

"It's bad, darlin'. Really bad this time."

She realized he didn't even want to tell her, and she sat up, pulling the sheet to her chin. "What about Henry?"

"I'll be with Henry. Don't worry," he assured her.

"Jonah, what happened?"

"Remember the rancher Kirk Rivas?"

"I remember him. He may have had a little too much to drink at our party."

"Yeah, well, someone torched his house tonight."

"No!" she exclaimed, and shivered. "Gabriel Brant and Kirk Rivas have lived here a long time, haven't they? It has to be someone on this ranch that the hate is aimed at, Jonah. You're too new in the neighborhood."

"That isn't all, Kate."

She sat quietly waiting, dreading what he was going to tell her. "Was he hurt in the fire?"

"They found Rivas outside his house, and think he drove up and surprised the arsonist. He was stabbed to death."

"Oh, no!" she cried, remembering the jovial man at their party. "That's horrible, Jonah."

"Damn straight it is. The guy is an arsonist, a bomber and now a murderer. The crimes have gotten bigger and worse each time. Dakota wants me to come by his office tomorrow. I'll get Scott to ride in and stay with Henry while I'm in the sheriff's office, and then we'll all go to lunch. Come join us, okay?"

She bit her lip and stared at Jonah. "Why are you going to the sheriff's office? You don't know anything about what happened tonight, do you?"

"No, I don't, but I think Dakota has some leads he wants to run past me. He was in the Air Force in Special Ops. He knows I was Special Forces. That gives us a tie."

She nodded. "All right, I'll meet you for lunch."

"Great!"

"Jonah, I'm scared for Henry's sake.. Should we take him back to your folks?"

"We'll see. Let me talk to Dakota tomorrow and see what he comes up with, and then we'll decide. Kate, I think you and Henry are safe here. You know no one has a grudge against any of us. It has to be someone else on the ranch being targeted. It would be senseless for the hate to be directed at John Frates, who's dead.''

"Killing Kirk Rivas was senseless. The killer may not be acting rationally. I can't keep from worrying about Henry.''

"Well, don't worry about him. I won't let him out of my sight unless he's with Scott. Clementine is the one I worry about, because she'll be here alone sometimes. I may get one of the guys to stay close to the house. And if you get off work early or come home at some unexpected time, you let me know.''

"I will,'' she said, rubbing her arms, feeling chilled in the warm night.

"Dakota is calling all the ranchers in the area. He's warning every one of us.''

"Why would rustlers resort to bombs and murder?''

"I don't know what the tie is, but I think this is the work of one person and so does Dakota. The placing of the bomb in our barn was done by just one man.''

"How do you know that and how do you know it was a man?''

"A bomb is rarely a woman's weapon. And a gang putting a bomb in a barn? I don't think so. That's someone acting alone. How that ties in with the rustling, I don't know.''

She reached for her robe and slipped into it. "I want to go look at Henry.''

"I'll go with you,'' Jonah said.

She turned and smiled. "Then put on some clothes. You can't go running around naked.''

He grinned and picked up his jeans, stepping into them and fastening them partially. "Now am I presentable enough to go look at a kid who can sleep through a bomb going off?''

"Yes, you are.'' He walked over to put his arm around her and pull her close against his side. She slipped her arm around his waist and held him tightly, glad to have him hold her.

Together they looked in on Henry, who slept with a teddy bear in his arms.

"All's quiet and peaceful here. I want to call Scott and let him know," Jonah murmured.

They returned to the bedroom and he sat on the side of the bed to pick up the phone and call his foreman.

While Jonah talked, Kate slipped out of her robe and scooted across the bed to hug him from behind, pressing against him, feeling the hard, solid plane of his back against her breasts. She rubbed his thighs and kissed his ear while he talked, and he turned around to look at her.

His voice thickened as he spoke. As soon as he replaced the receiver, she tried to scoot away, but he caught her. "You asked for it," he whispered, coming down on top of her to kiss her hard and long, while his hand slid down the length of her.

At ten o'clock the next morning Jonah walked into Sheriff Gallen's office again. Dakota came around the desk, which was still covered with papers. A coffee cup and a half-empty pop bottle were on the cluttered surface, along with a half-eaten sandwich.

Dakota held out his hand to shake Jonah's. "Sit down," he said, moving papers from a chair. "It's been a busy morning."

"Even without seeing you, I'd guess that you were up all night."

"Yes, I was," Dakota said, rubbing his unshaved chin. His uniform was rumpled and stained, his brown hair tangled and his gray eyes filled with concern.

"No one was in Rivas's house?" Jonah asked, stretching out his long legs.

"No, they weren't. His boys are away in summer jobs and the latest girlfriend wasn't home last night. Rivas had been to a bar—we've tracked that down. From what I figure, he came home, surprised the arsonist and was attacked.''

''Now the same old question—any leads?''

''Not much, but we may have a print off Rivas's clothes. We've sent it to the lab. I've been trying to tie all these crimes together. They don't make sense. Rustling is for money and takes several men, at least on the scale it's been done around here.''

''I agree,'' Jonah said.

''The bomb, the fires, the murder—that looks like one man, not a gang.''

''I agree with that, too.''

''I've made a list of the victims in this area. There's Gabe Brant, you and-or John Frates, Kirk Rivas. Rivas and Frates were friends. Brant has lived here forever, but he was younger than those other two so doesn't fit that way. He wasn't a friend of either Frates or Rivas. I've listed every family in three counties—Piedras, Lago and Denville. I don't want to get into Bexar County because that's got the city, where it's impossible to tie people together. But in Piedras, Lago and Denville, there are five people I can come up with who might be disgruntled. None of them seems the killer type.'' He pulled out a manilla envelope. ''I've put all the information together here. Would you like to look at it and see what you come up with?''

Jonah stared at the envelope Dakota was holding out to him as if it were a snake. Jonah thought of Kate and how she would want him to stay out of this. Then he thought of the bomb in his barn and now a murder. He wanted to protect Henry and Kate at all costs. If he took the envelope, he might be able to do something to guard his family.

On the other hand, he might be doing something that would send Kate packing forever.

Yet the safety of his son was paramount and there was no choice about it. Jonah reached for the envelope.

''Want to be a deputy now?'' Dakota asked.

Chapter 13

Once again, Jonah hesitated, because he knew what the cost might be. But he came right back to the same reasoning. He wanted to protect Henry and Kate above all else.

He nodded his head, and Dakota smiled. "Thanks. That means a hell of a lot, because I know about your training. Some of my deputies are green as grass, and the last murder around here was under another sheriff and different deputies. I want to swear you in. Raise your right hand."

Jonah repeated the oath of office solemnly and accepted the copper star that declared he was a deputy. He turned it in his hand and wondered if he had just ruined his future.

"Do you have time to join us for lunch? I brought my foreman and son into town with me," he told Dakota.

"Sorry, no, I can't spare the time. I'll take a rain check. As soon as you've looked that stuff over, if you have any conclusions about it, I'd appreciate if you'd give me a call."

"I will."

"Thanks, Jonah, for serving as a deputy."

"Sure." Jonah left, walking through century-old marble halls with vaulted ceilings and a musty smell in spite of the offices being used daily. He stepped out into the shade of oaks and headed toward his car. Scott and Henry were waiting on one of the benches and they joined him.

"I'll call Kate, because she said she'd meet us for lunch." In the car he slid the envelope beneath the driver's seat.

When he drove up, Kate was standing outside her office. He climbed out of the car and went to meet her, his gaze raking over her and his heart thumping faster. Her hair was fastened up on her head, but tendrils had fallen loose around her face. She wore a white silk blouse and a full red silk skirt that swirled around her legs as she walked. Bracelets jingled on her arms, and earrings dangled from her ears, and he wished he had her alone, heading home or to a hotel.

"You look gorgeous enough to eat," he said when she walked up to him.

She smiled. "Thank you, but you're being ridiculous. Although you look rather gorgeous yourself."

"That I can't relate to," he remarked dryly. "I wish I could get you off to myself for the next hour."

"But you can't, so you'd better stop drooling," she teased.

"Do you have to wear something that sexy to work? Are there any single guys where you work?"

"Yes, there are, and there is nothing about this plain white blouse that is sexy."

"Darlin', are you wrong there! What fills it is what's sexy. And you do fill it nicely."

"Jonah, behave now. You've got Scott and Henry in the car."

"Yes'm," he said, but as he held the door for her, he patted her bottom when she slid past him into the car. She turned to glare at him and he smiled, closing the door and going around to the driver's side.

Conversation centered around Henry over lunch. The three adults listened to him talk about what he had done at his grandparents', and what he wanted to do when he got back to the ranch that afternoon. Finally Jonah drove Kate back to work and got out to escort her into the building.

"You don't need to walk me to the door here at work," she said with amusement. "And I'm going to get you tonight, Jonah Whitewolf, for that pat on the fanny."

"They couldn't see you."

"I'll bet someone looking out the window of my office building could, however."

"So what? Do you care if they know I'm a man in love?"

She turned to look at him. "Are you, Jonah?" she asked, gazing up at him solemnly.

"Yes, Kate," he admitted. "I am in love."

She closed her eyes. "Jonah, you would tell me now, when we're out in public."

He brushed a kiss on her cheek. "There. I've kissed you in front of Henry. That should make him happy. And he knows you've moved in with me."

"Now how does he know that?"

"I told him, and he nodded as if he gave us his approval."

"You better get back to the car. It's too hot for him and Scott, sitting there with the engine off."

"Sure. See you tonight, darlin'. And then I will have you all to myself."

She caught his chin in her hand. "And I'll kiss you all over from head to toe, Jonah Whitewolf," she said in that sultry voice she used upon occasion.

"Kate, dammit—"

She laughed and turned to enter the building, leaving him sweating and tied in knots on the sidewalk behind her. He turned and headed back to the car, glad to devote the next few hours to Henry.

That night, after long hours of loving Kate, Jonah got up and crossed the room, pulling on his jeans. He went to his desk to pick up the envelope Dakota Gallen had given him.

He headed downstairs to his office, switching on a light and sitting at his desk to read. An hour later, he knew the histories of most of the ranching families in Piedras and two neighboring counties.

He had three names on a sheet of paper: Aldo Hill, Martin Talmadge, Wilford Nelson. Three men who were disgruntled with their lives and their families. Aldo Hill was thirty-three, years younger than John Frates or Kirk Rivas but the same age as Gabe Brant.

Martin Talmadge was the brother of a local rancher, Duane Talmadge. He was the same age as Kirk Rivas and the age John Frates would have been had he lived.

Wilford Nelson was that age, as well, and had been involved in various schemes that kept him on the fringe of the law. He could have known Rivas and John Frates. Jonah put a question mark beside Nelson's name.

Jonah read the histories of the three men and crossed Aldo Hill off the list. He just couldn't see any reasonable connection. The man might be unhappy with his lot in life, and grumpy with his neighbors, but a murderer? Jonah didn't think so.

He looked again at Martin Talmadge. The man had grown up with John Frates and Kirk Rivas as close friends. He came from a successful old ranching family. Because of his irresponsible and profligate ways, he had been cut out of his inheritance, which had all gone to his older brother, Duane. From all reports Martin Talmadge hated his brother, left home years ago and had gone to California. When he was young he had done odd jobs while trying to get into the movies. One of his jobs had been a three-year stint with an alarm company where he could have learned how to build and dismantle alarms.

Jonah circled Martin Talmadge's name, figuring he had motivation for at least some of the crimes. But what would the tie to Gabe Brant be? Jonah remembered Brant and his wife at the party. Ashley Brant was a beautiful woman.

He circled Martin Talmadge's name again, crossed off Wilford Nelson and picked up the phone to call Dakota.

A sleepy voice came over the phone. "Sheriff Gallen."

"Sorry to wake you."

"It's okay," he said, sounding more alert. "You must have found something, Jonah."

Jonah was surprised Dakota even recognized his voice that quickly. "You interviewed Gabe Brant. Did you interview his wife, Ashley?"

"No, I didn't. Think I should? Never mind. You wouldn't have asked if you didn't have a reason."

"Maybe the connection there isn't Gabe Brant. Maybe it's Ashley."

"Oh, hell, I should have thought of that and talked to her. I will first thing in the morning and let you know. Which one is it you're looking at?"

"I think you already know. He worked at an alarm company when he was young. Do you know where he is now?"

"I called and his maid said he was out of the country. She wouldn't be any more specific than that. He's done well in California."

"I saw. He's into porn movies."

"I'll talk to Ashley Brant in a few hours. If he's our man, then his brother, Duane, may be in a lot of danger."

"Have you warned him?"

"I've talked to him about it, but he doesn't think he's at risk and he doesn't think his brother is capable of crimes like this. He hasn't seen him in years, though, and he said they wouldn't speak if they did encounter one another. He didn't speak kindly of his brother."

"I'd say you have your man, but I'll keep reading and you go see what Ashley has to say."

"Thanks, Jonah."

They broke the connection, and Jonah straightened the papers in front of him. Before starting to read again, he opened the desk drawer and picked up the badge Dakota had given him. Someday when the case was solved, he would show the badge to Henry, who would think it cool that his father was a deputy. In the meantime, he meant to keep it in the drawer and tell Kate when the time seemed appropriate.

He read again all the information, going over it bit by bit and still coming out with the same conclusion. On paper, a lot of details indicated Martin Talmadge could be the man. And if it *was* him, his brother Duane was in danger.

Finally Jonah switched off the light and went up to bed, moving to the window to look out at the grounds, knowing his men were patrolling the area. He saw one of the dogs moving around below. It was Prince, a shaggy Border collie that was a good watchdog and adored Henry. And that was mutual. Henry adored the animal.

Jonah peeled off his jeans, moved to the bed to look at Kate, and his pulse speeded up. She was on her side, her hair spread on the pillow. Her long legs were stretched out and she had her hands beneath her head. She looked warm, soft and appealing, and he lowered himself carefully to the bed, moving close to her and reaching out to caress her breast, waiting for her to stir so he could make love to her again.

At eight-thirty the next morning, Kate was in the kitchen, lingering over breakfast, when Dakota's call came for Jonah. It was Friday and she didn't need to go into work that day.

Jonah answered in his office. Henry was still asleep upstairs.

"Jonah," Dakota said, sounding wide-awake now, "you were right. Martin Talmadge is a lot older than Ashley Brant, but he tried to date her all through high school and while she was in college."

"Did she ever date him?"

"No. She thought he was creepy."

"That ties him to all three victims."

"Yes, and to an alarm company where he could learn to build alarms. And if he knows how to build them, he knows how to dismantle them. I'm going out to see his brother now. We don't know where Martin Talmadge is, but I've talked to the Orange County sheriff's office and they're looking for him."

"I'd say the brother is in a lot of danger."

"I've tried to make that clear. Just in case, you keep up your guard, okay? You've been hit twice by him and you foiled him that second time. He might return. I'd like to try to get a warrant for his arrest, but at this point, I think the judge would say the evidence is nonexistent. I'm waiting to hear from the lab about the fingerprint. I'll keep you posted, but you keep on alert, okay?"

"I'll be careful."

"You'll be careful about what?" Kate asked from the doorway. "I couldn't keep from hearing you."

"Come in and I'll show you what we've got," he said, making a quick decision to include her in the process.

She crossed the room. She wore cutoffs and a tank top, and he forgot about danger or the task ahead of him.

He pulled two chairs close together and sat down beside her to give her the papers to read. As she studied them, he couldn't resist and pulled her onto his lap.

"Where did you get this? From Sheriff Gallen?"

"Yep. He wanted to see what I thought about it."

"Next thing you know, he'll want you on his staff."

"What do you think about that list?"

"I see you have one name circled several times. Let me read more."

As she did so, he lifted her hair and kissed her nape, trailing his tongue lightly over her skin.

"Jonah, how can I concentrate?"

"Go ahead. I'm not doing much."

She gave him a look and turned back to her reading, and he continued caressing her nape, sliding his hand beneath her shirt to cup her breast.

"Jonah!" Kate caught his wrist and wriggled, pulling his hand from beneath her shirt. "Will you stop that! Henry is still asleep, but he could wake up and come down at any time."

"I'm watching the door."

"Oh, sure you are," she said, then looked into his eyes and turned to kiss him soundly. Finally, she straightened. "You adorable, irresistible man," she whispered. "Now let me read this."

"Yes'm," he said, but continued to play with her hair and rub her back.

"You have this Talmadge man's name circled, Jonah, but what tie does he have with Gabe Brant?"

"He wanted to date Ashley Brant and she would never go out with him."

"Can the sheriff arrest him?"

"Nope. That's just speculation and could be all wrong."

"He worked in a security company so he knows alarms, and he may know bombs."

"Probably, but Dakota will need more than that to go on."

"Mommy!" Henry's call on the intercom was faint.

"He just woke up. I'll go see about him," Kate said, sliding off Jonah's lap and hurrying out of the room. As she went, he looked at her hips and mentally stripped away the cutoffs, wishing he were alone with Kate right now.

Jonah thought about their future. When this problem was settled, did he want to ask Kate to marry him again?

He raked his fingers through his hair. Love and trust should go hand in hand, but they didn't. He could love and still be scared to trust. If he told her he was a deputy, would she walk out again?

He suspected she would, but he hoped this would all be over within hours and he wouldn't have to tell her.

At noon Dakota called him again.

"We didn't get anywhere with the print. They can't identify it."

"Bummer. Sorry," Jonah said, feeling his hopes plummet that this would be quick or simple.

"We've warned Duane Talmadge, and he's beginning to take me seriously. He's worried, because he said his brother does have an uncontrollable temper. I'm going to stake out the Talmadge house and watch it 24–7 for the coming week. These incidents have come closer together, and I think Martin wants to get his revenge."

"What about the rustling?"

"I don't know if it was tied together or not. May have been a gang of rustlers and Martin Talmadge acting on his own, and the two were just coincidental."

"My guess is that they weren't. I think it's him and I think he's the one who rustled my cattle and tried to blow up my barn."

"All that past history of his indicates that he's the one. We're staking out his brother's house, as I said. Want to join us?"

"No, I don't."

"Then you don't have to. I'll keep you posted, and if we're desperate for more help, I'll let you know."

Jonah replaced the receiver and hoped he never got that call from Dakota. And he hoped they caught their man quickly.

The weekend passed, and on Monday Kate went to work

while Jonah spent the day with Henry. That night Jonah and Kate both played games with Henry and finally put him to bed.

Far into the night Jonah lay awake, with Kate sleeping in his arms. Warm and soft, she snuggled against him and wrapped her arm more tightly around him. He stroked her hair from her face and kissed her temple lightly. How he loved her!

When the phone rang, he wriggled away from her and grabbed the receiver, speaking softly.

"Jonah, I wanted to warn you," Dakota said, his voice filled with urgency. "Martin Talmadge is our man. He tried to kill Duane tonight."

"The hell you say! Tried? He failed?"

"Right. Duane is still alive and he's being flown by chopper to Marcus Whiffle Memorial Hospital in San Antonio. Talmadge got away and I'm warning ranchers. We have an APB out for Talmadge and roadblocks set up, but warn your men."

"Thanks, Dakota," Jonah said tersely, already yanking on his jeans. He crossed the room to the closet to get down his pistol, and turned to find Kate sitting up in bed, watching him.

"What are you doing, Jonah?" she asked.

He related the contents of Dakota's phone call. "I need to phone Scott and warn the men, and we have to get this ranch secured." He left the room, rushing downstairs to begin making calls. In minutes lights were on all through the house. Jonah had pulled on a T-shirt and boots.

Kate found him in his office.

"I'm going to meet Scott and we'll assign men patrols and put guards on the house. No one will get in here, Kate."

Pulling her robe together under her chin, she nodded solemnly, looking at the gun tucked into his waistband. "Jonah, why did Dakota give you all that information and why did he just call you? Isn't that information that would only go to lawmen? Do you have any official capacity?"

Jonah's head came up, and when he looked at her, she knew that he did. Her heart dropped. She clenched her fists and stared at him.

"What did you do?" she whispered. "Are you a deputy?"

"Kate, I did it to protect you and Henry. It just gives me official status. If the killer comes on our property, I can arrest him—"

"Jonah, stop!" she cried. "I don't want to hear all the excuses. I already know them. You haven't changed one degree and you never will. You'll always rush into danger. Go on. Just go!" She turned and ran blindly for the stairs. She heard him call her name, but she didn't stop. She didn't want to talk to him.

Jonah followed her into the hall. "Kate, wait a minute!"

She stormed up the stairs without looking back at him.

Jonah clamped his jaw shut. He had to go talk to Scott and the men who worked for him, to let them know about Martin Talmadge being the killer and on the loose. It was urgent to get the ranch secured, and now wasn't the time to argue with Kate.

He knew the hopelessness in that, so he headed for the kitchen and jammed his hat on his head, pulling out his cell phone to call Scott again as he left the house.

Upstairs, Kate shook with fury. She loved Jonah hopelessly, completely, but she wouldn't live with him or subject Henry to a father who was a lawman.

Jonah had accepted being a deputy behind her back, while at the same time he was making love to her and telling her that he could change.

She went to her old room and slammed the door, then took a deep breath. "All right, Jonah Whitewolf, you made your choice this time, just as you did five years ago. I'll make my choice. I'm not going to love you and sit by and become a widow, and watch Henry become fatherless, because you have to save the world!''

She crossed the room to get what she wanted to wear and then headed for the shower. In another half hour she was dressed in jeans and a red T-shirt, and had called her office to leave a message that she would not be in for work today.

Hurriedly, she began flinging clothes into a suitcase—just enough to get through the rest of the week. She could come back and collect all her and Henry's belongings later.

She should have known it would never work for her to live in Jonah's house. How could he agree to become deputized when he professed to love her and knew how she felt about it?

When she finished packing and closed her suitcase, she went to Henry's room to pack for him, knowing he would sleep through her bustling around the room.

At seven o'clock the phone rang, and she picked it up to hear Jonah's voice. ''Kate, I told Clementine to go into town. She won't be coming in today. None of the help will. The men will be outside the house, so it's covered.''

''Fine,'' she answered.

''Kate, I want to talk to you. Will you please just—''

She replaced the receiver. She didn't want to talk to him at all. It was an old and useless argument.

She fed Henry breakfast as she loaded their things into the car. As she was helping him get his boots on, she said, ''Henry, there's a bad man loose in this area, and I think we'll be safer away from the ranch, so we're leaving.''

''Is Daddy going with us?''

''No, he's not, because he has to stay to guard the ranch.''

''Can't we stay? If Daddy guards the ranch, it'll be safe.''

''No, we can't stay. Not today. We might go to Grandma and Grandpa Whitewolf's tonight. All right?''

He brightened at that and nodded. "Then Daddy will come be with us?"

"I don't know what Daddy is going to do," she said stiffly, hurting. "I've packed a bag for you, and you can take some things with you in the car."

She gathered toys Henry liked and fought back tears, because at every turn she was reminded of Jonah. She gave her son a sack to hold items he wanted to take along, and finally she had the car packed.

She buckled Henry into his seat and climbed behind the wheel, driving away without looking back, yet aware of every square foot of ranch she passed because, once she picked up all her belongings, she'd be leaving it forever.

She glanced at the gas gauge and saw the tank was low, so at Mayville, the first small town, she stopped at the only gas station to fill up. She paid at the pump, and was just climbing back into the car when a man yanked open the other door and slid into the car beside her.

He caught her wrist and pointed a gun at her.

"Get in," he snapped.

Chapter 14

Kate panicked, wanting to scream, terrified for Henry, yet she could feel the gun poking in her ribs hard enough to hurt.

"Just drive and you'll be all right, and so will the kid. Get in and drive, Mrs. Whitewolf."

She had carried her purse on the side away from the man. As she climbed into the car, she let go of her bag and let it fall to the ground. She prayed that someone would notice it and contact Jonah, because of the Whitewolf name on her credit card and driver's license.

She turned the ignition, glancing at the man who sat beside her. His pale blue, watery eyes were filled with fury. Splotches of color made his cheeks red. His blond hair was a tangle and he needed a shave. He was dressed in a black, long-sleeved T-shirt that was spattered with stains, and she shuddered to think what they might be from. His rumpled black pants held more stains.

"Where are you going?" she asked, her mind racing.

She had to think of some way to get rid of him and protect Henry.

"Just drive. You're going to get me out of here. If we come to a roadblock, you get us through it if you want the boy to be safe."

She looked back at Henry, whose eyes were enormous. All color had drained from his face. They were still in the small town and she passed people doing ordinary things, yet she was too frightened to try to cross the man. "Can we let my son out? You'd still have one hostage, and that's all you need."

"Just drive!" he snapped, holding up the gun.

Jonah talked to Scott, then turned his pickup and headed back to the house. The place would be under guard, and if he could keep Kate from going into town to work, he could protect her and Henry. He knew she was furious with him about becoming a deputy. He clamped his teeth and clenched the steering wheel, wondering if he had just destroyed all they had found together this past week.

It was dawn now, the first gray light of day chasing away the night. Jonah drove by the garage and saw the door open, her car gone. He frowned and then swore. It was too early for her to leave for work, and she wouldn't have left Henry home alone.

She had taken him and left. Just like that. She had gone exactly as she had before, without letting him explain that all he had done so far was read some information and give Dakota his opinion. Nothing dangerous there, but she wouldn't even listen.

Jonah hurt, and anger pulsed in him with every heartbeat. He'd known she might do exactly this, leave him, but he'd thought maybe she would understand his wanting to protect her and Henry.

He raked his hand through his hair and tugged at his

earlobe. ''Damnation,'' he said, and swung his fist through the air.

He entered the empty house and knew there was no use in calling to her. They were gone and they wouldn't be coming back.

The phone rang, and he strode to the family room to answer it, wishing it was Kate, but hearing a man's voice.

''Mr. Whitewolf?''

''Yes.''

''This is Bud Thompkins at Thompkins Service Station in Mayville. A Kate Whitewolf was just in here, and when she got into her car, she dropped her purse.''

''Thanks for telling me,'' Jonah said, mentally seeing Kate stopping in the station in the nearby town. ''I'll come pick it up. She'll be glad to know you have it.''

''She and the man just drove away. They can't be far down the road.''

Jonah stiffened. ''What man?''

''I didn't see a man with her when she drove into the station, but there was one in the passenger seat when she left. It kinda worried me, because I could have sworn she came in here without him.''

''Thanks,'' Jonah said tersely, his heart thudding. ''Which direction were they headed?'' He gripped the phone so tightly his knuckles were white.

''Toward Stallion Pass.''

As Jonah broke the connection and got his cell phone out of his pocket to call Dakota, he ran outside, racing to his pickup. The minute he heard the sheriff's voice, he broke in.

''Jonah here. I think Talmadge is in the car with Kate and Henry. She stopped for gas in Mayville.'' Jonah related what he had been told and what he guessed as he started the engine and turned the truck to speed away from the ranch. ''I'm going after them, Dakota, but do what you can.''

"Right."

They broke the connection and Jonah tossed aside the phone, pressing the accelerator to the floor and hunching over the wheel. He had to get to Kate and Henry before Talmadge could hurt them.

Kate drove without speaking. The gunman had switched on the radio, scanning the stations to find news bulletins. The broadcasters droned on, but said nothing about Talmadge or his brother. Once, Kate heard a helicopter overhead, but then it was gone. Cars passed her going the other way, and she wondered what she should do if she came to a roadblock.

Her mind raced, trying to figure out how to save Henry. She had to get him out of the car, away from Talmadge. The man had killed Kirk Rivas and had shot his own brother during the night, and she knew he would care nothing about a small child he didn't even know.

She had no weapon in the car and wouldn't be able to use it if she had. Her purse was gone, but that would be of little help, anyway. Soon they would be in Stallion Pass. If she yelled for help, he could easily shoot her, take the car and drive off with Henry, so she didn't dare take that risk.

Yet she knew she had to do something. To let him take her and Henry away with him was the worst possible choice.

"Where do you want to go?"

"Just drive, Mrs. Whitewolf."

"You know who I am," she said in surprise. She glanced at him as he still fiddled with the radio, turning the volume up slightly and changing to another station.

"I know you and your husband, and his inheritance that he didn't deserve."

"Is that why you're taking us with you?" she asked.

"Hell, no. You were just in the wrong place at the wrong

time," he said. "I need to get away from here. I just killed my brother and escaped from the police."

She inhaled deeply, knowing if he was admitting the killing to her in front of Henry, he had no intention of ever letting them go.

"Why? My husband didn't know he was getting the inheritance."

"Doesn't matter. He got it and he didn't deserve it, and I hated John Frates. I hated my brother and he didn't deserve to get the ranch. I was cut out of everything. Frates, Rivas, my brother—none of them earned what they got. It was just given to them. Well, it won't do them any good now, and I'm on my way out of the country. We'll head south, down Mexico way."

"Let my son go. He isn't any part of this and he's only a little boy. He's done nothing to you."

"I'll let him go when you get me across the border."

She knew he was lying, and her desperation grew. She had to think of some way for Henry to escape.

They sped along the highway, Kate driving automatically, her mind searching for possibilities, until she had to slow down at the outskirts of Stallion Pass. It was a weekday morning, the town just beginning to stir, and people were going to work. The main street through town, which was the highway, had little traffic at this hour.

"Just keep driving and keep your windows up," Talmadge snapped. He switched stations again, stopping on another news report.

They passed shops that weren't open yet, the town quiet and peaceful—a huge contrast to the danger in her car. A boy pedaled a bike along the sidewalk. A few pedestrians were out. A tall man was walking a small dachshund on a leash. A cowboy stepped out of a pickup and went into a café.

Kate scanned every inch of each block, looking for help. They passed the square and the courthouse.

In a minute they would be through town, and she feared if they left Stallion Pass, her chances for doing anything to save Henry would diminish. She glanced back at him, to see him still in the same frozen position, round-eyed and pale. He couldn't have seen the gun stuck in her side, but he evidently guessed they were in a lot of danger.

She passed the newspaper office and a barbershop that was open for business. She could see the end of the downtown section of Main Street looming about three blocks away. Three more blocks and she would leave the safety of town and people. She didn't want to keep driving with the killer.

Desperation to save Henry gripped her and she struggled to think. What if she wrecked the car? she wondered. Could Henry escape? She felt she had to take that chance. Anything to try to get her son away from the killer.

As she approached a street corner that was clear of pedestrians, she gripped the wheel tightly. Suddenly she jammed her foot on the accelerator. As the car lurched forward, the man's head jerked up and he swore. She yanked the steering wheel, turned the car and slammed into a lamppost.

With a loud crumpling of metal, they crashed.

"Henry, get out!" she screamed.

The car spun around and Kate grabbed the man's arm, wrestling with him for the gun. Still spinning, her car struck a parked vehicle and finally lurched to a stop.

"Run, Henry. Run!" she screamed as she fought with the man. He struck her and pain exploded in her head, stars dancing in front of her eyes.

Kate doubled her fist and hit him back, yanking off her seat belt to scramble on top of him and fight him for the gun. She clawed at Talmadge's face, jabbing his eyes while she elbowed him in the neck. She knew he had dropped the gun and was struggling to get out of the car, but she kept after him, glancing up just once to see that Henry was gone.

And then the passenger door was yanked open, and Talmadge jerked out.

"You bastard!"

Kate recognized Jonah's voice as she scrambled blindly to get out on the driver's side. Jonah came around the car and caught her in his arms.

"Kate!"

She threw her arms around his neck. "Where's Henry?" she cried.

"He's safe. A cop already has cuffs on the creep, but not before I hit him. Damn him. He hit you!"

"Jonah, where's Henry?" she insisted, wanting to hold her son.

"Henry's safe, darlin'—over there with a policeman. And you're safe. Ah, Kate, I was so damn scared about you two."

"I smashed that new car you bought me."

He stroked her hair away from her face. "You did a great job, Kate."

"Daddy, Mommy!" Henry cried, and left the policeman to run to them.

Jonah caught him up and held him tightly, all three of them hugging. Kate's knees began to shake, and in seconds she was trembling all over. "Jonah, can we get out of here? My legs are like jelly, my head's pounding and I'm feeling dizzy."

"Come on," he said, putting his arm around her and moving through the crowd that had gathered. People stepped aside for them and Jonah got them into his pickup, climbing up beside them. "We need to get away from here, Kate. The police will want to take your statement, but I'd guess the media will want to interview you any second now."

"Jonah, I don't want to talk to any reporters!"

"Don't worry. I'm a deputy, so I can take you with me. Henry, we shouldn't drive with you up here in the front where there are airbags. Would you climb in back, into your seat?"

Henry scrambled to do what he asked. "Mommy, you were awesome!"

Kate grinned and looked at him, and Jonah laughed. "She *was* awesome, Henry," he agreed. "You did a great job to protect Henry and save you both," he told her.

She shook in the aftermath and hugged her arms around herself. "Jonah, I was so scared for Henry."

"I know, darlin', but you did great."

Kate looked at Jonah, who was so calm and collected. "You know, I understand now," she said, feeling dazed and full of regret. "Until this happened, I never understood what you do. But now I know something of how you feel. I wanted to do anything I could to keep Henry safe."

Jonah glanced at her and squeezed her hand. "You did, darlin'. At the end, that creep was trying to get away from you. You beat him up plenty."

"Mommy, he was all bloody when Daddy finally grabbed him."

She couldn't laugh, but Jonah grinned and gave Henry a thumbs-up. "You did great to get out of the car, son. That was fast thinking and quick moving," Jonah said proudly, and Henry grinned back.

"Do they know any more about Talmadge's brother yet?" Kate asked.

"He's going to live," Jonah replied.

"Jonah, he told me why he committed those terrible crimes. He was jealous of what you got, jealous of Kirk Rivas and his own brother. He told me he'd just killed his brother."

"Well, hopefully he's wrong, and Duane Talmadge will survive. That's what Duane told Dakota. That his brother didn't want others having ranches when he had been cut out of his own inheritance. Martin hated his brother. He despised the people he grew up with who went on to own big ranches.''

''I guess Gabe Brant was another one.''

''Nope. It was Ashley Brant he wanted to hurt. He always wanted to date Ashley, and she wouldn't go out with him. Jealousy and revenge and greed... Dakota said he told Duane that he hitched up with a gang of rustlers, to give him a cover of sorts. He made money out of the rustling. They crossed the border with the cattle and sold them out of the country.''

''Do we have to go to the police station?'' she asked.

''Nope. I'm a deputy. I'll take your statement at home.''

''Oh, Jonah, thank goodness! I feel like I might faint at any moment.''

''Faint away if you want to, darlin'. I'm here to take care of you. First we stop by the hospital ER to make certain you and Henry are all right. No arguments about that.''

After their release from the hospital, Henry jabbered all the way to the ranch, while Jonah talked to Dakota Gallen twice by phone, and to Scott Adamson and to Clementine. Kate barely heard what he was saying because her mind was fuzzy, reaction setting in. She was chilled and shaky, and profoundly struck by the realization of why Jonah did what he did to protect and help people. All she had wanted to do was save Henry. She'd had no other thought in mind; that had been her total aim. She realized how harshly she had judged her husband and what a mistake she had made this morning when learning he had become a deputy. He'd done so to protect her and Henry.

She held Jonah's hand and patted it with her other one. ''Can you forgive me?''

''For what?'' he asked.

''For not understanding.''

The caring in his dark eyes was unmistakable. ''Kate, I love you. That's what's important.''

"I love you," she said softly, and leaned over to kiss his cheek. She reached back to squeeze Henry's hand. "Henry, you were so great. You weren't scared and didn't cry, and you did just what I told you. You're like your daddy, Henry."

He grinned and swung his fist in the air. "Mommy, you really got that bad guy. You beat him to jelly."

She could finally smile, and Jonah laughed. "You're right, Henry. She certainly did. Wait until his picture comes out in the paper. You'll see what you did."

"Oh, mercy! I don't remember much except trying to keep him from shooting us and giving Henry time to escape."

"It'll be all over the news. The television reporters were there before we left. They were just more interested in him than in you at that time. That'll change, though, and I'm having some of the guys stand guard at the gate to keep out the media. We'll have peace and quiet."

She squeezed his hand and loosened her seat belt slightly, so she could sit closer to him.

At home Kate showered and changed into a sundress and sandals. She had a bruised cheek and she suspected she would have a black eye.

They watched the news, and though Henry was enjoying the whole situation now, it was still too frightening and too real to Kate. Jonah fielded phone calls from the media and turned down all requests for interviews. He talked to Dakota twice more and carefully took a detailed statement from Kate, which he promised to take to the courthouse Monday morning.

And finally that night, after Henry was asleep in bed, she walked downstairs to the family room with Jonah. He had turned the lights low, put on music, and he brought her a glass of wine and one for himself.

"It's a happy ending, darlin'. Here's to my quick-witted wife."

"Jonah, I love you, and I've been so foolish when—"

He put his fingers on her lips. "Shh, darlin'. It's over. We're together and we're going to be a family. Kate, I don't know what you did with your wedding ring, but I bought you another one." He fished in his pocket and brought out a black velvet box, holding it out to her. "Will you marry me again, darlin'?"

"Jonah!" she cried, opening the box and looking at a dazzling ring, a four-carat emerald-cut diamond resting between graduated baguette diamonds set in platinum. "My word, it's beautiful! And I still have my old one."

"You can make a necklace out of it." Jonah took the ring and put it on her finger. "Will you be my wife?"

"Yes! I love you," she cried, and threw her arms around his neck, to hold him and kiss him.

"I love you, Kate," he said. "Always have and always will." She pulled his head down to kiss him again.

Epilogue

On Saturday, the second week of July, Kate stood on the terrace of the Stallion Pass Country Club. They'd had a small ceremony that morning, and now they were having a wedding party for all their friends to celebrate with them.

She wore a simple white silk dress with a beaded fringe around the hem and across the straight neckline. Spaghetti straps ran over her shoulders, and she had a large white orchid from Jonah pinned to her dress.

He stood with a group of his friends, all of them tall, handsome, rugged men. But only one man stood out in her eyes, and she gazed at her adorable husband, filled with love.

Jonah laughed at something Gabe said, and then Mike Remington turned to him. "You know the Stallion Pass legend?"

"Yeah, about the wild white stallion?" Jonah answered. "And I've heard about the current stallion that a lot of you guys have been passing around."

"I don't want any part of that horse again," Josh Kellogg said.

"Wyatt tamed him," Gabe remarked. "And then got rid of him."

"For one reason or another," Mike said, "I think that horse has been passed among all these guys. All of us are married now, so I think it's your turn, Jonah, to get this animal. So that's my wedding present to you," he added, grinning.

Jonah laughed and the others raised their glasses. "To the white stallion of Stallion Pass," Gabe said. "He's caused me a passel of trouble, but if he brought me true love, he was worth it. Now hopefully, true love and that horse belong to Jonah."

They drank, and Jonah turned to Boone Devlin. "Boone, when are you moving down here with us?"

His friend's blue eyes widened. "I'm not. I've got an appointment in two weeks to go out to the ranch. I'm putting it up for sale."

"There will be a line of eager buyers at your door," Gabe drawled. "I want to know when it goes on the market."

Talk turned to ranching, and Jonah looked around, seeing Kate standing alone on the terrace, watching him. He crossed the room and went outside to her.

"Think we can get away from here now?" he asked, wanting to have her in his arms. "You're gorgeous, Kate. When I look at you, my heart misses beats."

"And you're the most handsome man in the whole state of Texas. Which is really saying something. You Texans are a handsome lot. And yes, I think we can leave. The party is in full swing without us. Let's tell Henry and your folks goodbye. The others won't care."

Jonah took her hand, and they found Henry with his cousins. Jonah hugged and kissed him, and then Kate did.

As they left to find Jonah's parents, she said, "I don't think Henry is going to miss us at all."

"He'll have a wonderful time at my folks' house, you know. There's Mom."

They said goodbye to Jonah's parents and slipped away from the crowd to a car Jonah had waiting. In minutes they were speeding to the airport. They expected to be in New York tonight and on their way to Switzerland tomorrow.

It was after dark when they entered their hotel room, which was the bridal suite, high above the city. "Look at the lights, Jonah," Kate said, moving to the floor-to-ceiling windows.

Switching off the lights in their suite, he crossed the room to stand behind her. He shed his coat and tie, and then leaned down to trail kisses across her nape.

"I have champagne, I can put on music, we can go out if you want, or we can have room service. Or..."

"Or? What's the other choice?" she said, turning to look into his dark eyes as he wrapped his arms around her waist.

"Or we can just kiss the night away."

"I like that choice best, Jonah. How I love you! I want to spend the whole night showing you," she said.

"Ahh, darlin'. Thank heavens you're back in my arms and my life. I love you with all my heart, Kate. I mean it. I always have and I always will."

She slipped her arms around her handsome husband's neck. "You wild, reckless man, I love you! Come here and let me show you," she said, pulling his head down to kiss him passionately.

*   *   *   *   *

*Sara's tantalizing tales of these Texas Knights
continue in Silhouette Desire with*

STANDING OUTSIDE THE FIRE

All his life, Boone Devlin has been a high-flying, no-commitment bachelor who draws women like flies to honey, but never stays with one for long. So what happens when he falls head over heels for the one woman who seems resistant to his charms? Seems like the boot is on the other foot for once....

*Coming in July 2004
only from Silhouette Books.*

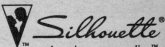

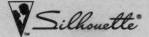

COMING NEXT MONTH

#1303 RETRIBUTION—Ruth Langan
Devil's Cove
Had journalist Adam Morgan uncovered one too many secrets to stay alive? After witnessing a terrorist in action, he'd escaped to Devil's Cove to heal his battered body. He never expected to find solace in the arms of talented artist Sidney Brennan. Then the cold-blooded killer closed in on Adam's location. Could Adam protect Sidney against a madman bent on murder?

#1304 DEADLY EXPOSURE—Linda Turner
Turning Points
A picture is worth a thousand words, but the killer Lily Fitzgerald had unknowingly photographed only used four: *You're going to die.* Lily didn't want to depend on anyone for help—especially not pulse-stopping, green-eyed cop Tony Giovani. But now her only protection from the man who threatened her life was the man who threatened her heart.

#1305 IMMOVABLE OBJECTS—Marie Ferrarella
Family Secrets: The Next Generation
The secrets Elizabeth Caldwell harbored could turn sexy billionaire Cole Williams's hair gray. Although she'd kept her life as a vigilante secret, the skills she'd mastered were exactly the talents Cole needed to find his priceless statue and steal it back from his enemy's hands. When they uncovered its whereabouts, Cole wasn't prepared to let her go, but would learning the truth about her past tear them apart—or bring them closer together?

#1306 DANGEROUS DECEPTION—Kylie Brant
The Tremaine Tradition
Private investigator Tori Corbett was determined to help James Tremaine discover the truth behind his parents' fatal "accident," but working up-close-and-personal with the sexy tycoon was like playing with fire. And now there was evidence linking Tori's own father to the crime....

#1307 A GENTLEMAN AND A SOLDIER—Cindy Dees
Ten years ago, military specialist Mac Conlon broke Dr. Susan Monroe's heart…right before she nearly lost her life to an assassin's bullet. Now the murderer was determined to finish the job, and Mac was the only man she trusted to protect her from danger. Mac just hoped he could remain coolheaded enough in her enticing presence to do what he'd been trained to do: keep them both alive. Because Mac refused to lose Susan a second time.

#1308 THE MAKEOVER MISSION—Mary Buckham
"You look like a queen" sounded heavenly to small-town librarian Jane Richards—until Major Lucas McConneghy blindfolded her and whisked her away to an island kingdom. To safeguard the country's stability, he needed her to pretend to *be* the queen. But even with danger lurking in every palace corridor, Lucas's protection proved to be a greater threat to her heart than the assassin bent on ending the monarchy.

SIMCNM0604